# MY FAVORITE BAD DECISION

## ELIZABETH O'ROARK

# 1

## KIT

### KILIMANJARO INTERNATIONAL AIRPORT

When I reach the gates of hell, there will be one familiar face.

Miller West.

He'll still be indecently handsome even then, no matter how old, no matter how uncomfortable he finds the temperature. He'll have that same snide fucking smile on his face, the one I'd kill to throw a punch at.

"Little Princess Kit," he'll say, as if I'm still his girlfriend's irksome kid sister and not a fully grown adult. "Fancy meeting you here."

It's also what he's just said to me now, at Kilimanjaro International Airport—the last place I'd ever have expected to run into him.

Naturally, he's in a perfectly cut suit and looks like a million bucks, while I look like someone who just flew for nineteen hours—which I did—and barely survived the experience.

At least *I* fit in. He's the only person within two hundred yards who isn't dressed for a safari...or a nineteen-hour flight.

"What the hell are you doing here?" I demand with the

grace and good humor he came to expect from me long *before* he broke my sweet sister's heart.

He looks at the sea of people around us with wide eyes, as if seeing them for the first time. "I'm sorry...do you *own* this airport? Is it private? I was unaware."

He's the same smug asshole he was at twenty-two, when he first entered our house in his dumb Vineyard Vines pullover and khakis, too self-assured for his own good.

I was seventeen at the time, and I hated him on sight. I hated him more than I'd ever hated my worst high school enemies or Maren's loser dad. I hated him as much as Jacob, my former stepfather, or most of my mother's ex-boyfriends, which was a little unfair since I'd yet to witness Miller hit a female or call her a dumb whore at the dinner table.

I couldn't entirely explain the extent of my hatred, even to myself. But it's starting to make sense now. He's as snide as ever, a decade after he left our place in the Hamptons and dumped my sister by text a few hours later. Maren cried for a year straight afterward. I don't know why I'm even speaking to him.

"Forget I asked," I say with an aggravated sigh, turning toward baggage claim. "I'm glad you're here. Stay forever. The weather's lovely, and the dollar goes far. You fit right in wearing that suit, too."

"As opposed to you, Blondie?" he asks, reaching out to gently tug my ponytail. "You don't actually think you're fooling anyone with that faux-casual outfit? Those sneakers alone probably cost a grand."

"Spend a lot of time shopping for women's clothing?" I ask, picking up my pace. "I'm not surprised."

It sounded like more of an insult in my head. I'd meant to imply he was a douche. Instead, I now sound like a transphobe. This is what Miller has always done: brought out my bad side, and somehow made it worse.

He's still unruffled, strolling casually beside me, while I'm walking as fast as I can to get away from him and am incredibly winded. This does not bode well for climbing Kilimanjaro over the coming week. "I have two sisters, if you recall," he says.

"I *wouldn't* recall because I make a point of hearing as little about you as I can." I glance at my watch as if I'm in a hurry and veer toward the bathroom. "Well, it was as lovely as ever to see you, Miller, by which I mean it *wasn't*, but I've got places to be."

"Good luck, Kitten," he says softly. There's a note of regret in his voice—one that makes me want to glance back at him, though I refuse to do so.

Wisdom comes with time. Perhaps he's finally realized that Maren was The One Who Got Away. Sure, since they broke up ages ago, he's dated a variety of women just as glossy and perfect and leggy as my sister, but none of them could have been as wonderful.

So I hope he misses her. I hope he misses her every fucking day for the rest of his natural life, the same way I suspect she's still missing him. And I really hope this is the last time I think about Miller West, because this trip sucks enough on its own.

I enter the bathroom and go straight to the sink, splashing water on my face and studying my weary reflection, newly irritated that my father is making me do this.

The hoops I've jumped through in the vague hope of one day leading Fischer-Harris Media never seem to end—I've worked in the mail room, I've worked as an admin, in ad sales, in marketing—but those made sense: they're all departments I'll one day supervise or pieces of the eventual job I'll take on myself. Climbing a mountain, however, is part of very few job descriptions—certainly not my dad's—and if he actually *needed* this article, Kilimanjaro is a gig every writer at *Wanderlust* wants.

There's also the more than suspicious timing. "So, you're sending me away when you know Blake's about to propose," I accused. "How convenient."

He sneered, of course. He always sneers at the mention of Blake. "And you're so deeply, overwhelmingly in love with him that you'd say yes?" he scoffed.

It annoyed me, the way he made it sound preposterous. I was even more annoyed that he was right. I was *not* deeply, overwhelmingly in love with Blake but more...in love *enough*, which is preferable. *Deeply and overwhelmingly* leaves you broken when it ends. Or willing to look the other way when he shoves you during an argument or drinks too much.

I like Blake, but he sure as fuck won't throw a dish at my head and get away with it the way Jacob did with my mom.

"If you actually care about him," my father continued, "then perhaps you need to let a few things go before you say yes. Anything less isn't especially fair to Blake."

And I could have argued that my dad doesn't give a shit about what's fair to Blake, but I also knew he was right, which is why I didn't fight this harder, why I didn't insist I needed more than three weeks to get ready for a climb people spend a full year preparing for.

Right now, though, I sort of wish I had.

I head down to baggage claim, where a man in a Smythson Explorers tee holds an iPad with my name on it.

Another daughter would be grateful her father had sent her here and had chosen the most luxurious Kilimanjaro outfitter to take her up the mountain.

*This* daughter remains pissed off she was forced to come.

"Hi," I tell him with a small wave. "I'm Kit."

He nods his head. "I'm Joseph. If you'll point out your bag, I will get it for you."

I feel silly—if you're theoretically fit enough to climb Mount Kilimanjaro, you're fit enough to lift your own bag. I'm also several inches taller than this guy, but since I'm not here willingly and have not adequately prepared for this climb, I guess I won't waste my energy arguing.

While we wait, I reach for my phone to tell Maren about the encounter with Miller but think better of it. She's already unhappy in her marriage. If I tell her he's here, she'll spend the entire night peppering me with questions. She'll want to know how he looks, if he's single, if he seems lonely, if he's asked about her. She'll allow herself to hope that Miller has missed her, that seeing me has reminded him of what they had.

Maren is like that—a dreamer—which is how she dreams herself into abysmal relationships like the one she's currently in. She fills in all the hollow spaces with what she *hopes* might appear there in time, ignoring one key fact: few men turn out to be *better* than they seemed when they were trying hard to make you like them.

I'll tell her when I get home. Or maybe I won't even do that. She thinks about him too much as it is. I see it in her face every time she discusses her miserable marriage—that wistful thing, as if she's watching a different life unfold. "The problem is that I married Harvey when I still wanted someone else," she's said more than once. And we all know exactly who she's referring to. A decade after it ended, it's still about Miller.

I point out my camping backpack and small suitcase when they descend onto the carousel. Inside there are multiple clothing changes, a sleeping bag, hiking boots, and the little I'll need above and beyond that to survive the next eight days.

I would argue that what I actually need is a Four Seasons and a pool, but apparently, we are limited to fourteen kilos each on the way up, so that's probably off the table.

Joseph lifts the bag and nods toward the doors. He doesn't appear to be struggling under the weight, but I still hope Miller isn't around to witness this moment of me looking very much like the spoiled Manhattan princess he believes I am.

And to be honest...the spoiled Manhattan princess I *actually* am. I did fly here in business class.

"Have you been to Africa before, Miss Fischer?" Joseph asks as we walk through the doors.

"Once, when I was—" I step outside and a wall of pure heat and humidity slams into me. It's February back home—when I left, it was thirteen degrees. Here, below the equator, it's the height of summer. And feels it. "I was, uh, fifteen when I was here last."

"But have you climbed Kili?" he challenges, as if he already knows the answer. Perhaps because he's assessed the designer outfit and the carefully highlighted blonde hair and decided that I'm not the sort of person who willingly takes on extra adversity but rather the sort who pays people to handle the adversity for her. This is fair. I am exactly that sort of person.

"Not yet," I reply with a half-hearted grin. "Ask me again in a week."

He gives me another beneficent smile, the sort that says he's not optimistic about what he'll discover in a week either, and I have to crush yet another moment of self-doubt. Sure, on Reddit, there are a million posts from people who trained for a year first, people who then said nothing can prepare you for it. But Mount Kilimanjaro isn't fucking Everest. There's no three weeks at base camp, no need to ice climb or cross glaciers by rope or fear avalanches. It's a walk. A long uphill *walk*. And I just ran the New York City marathon three months ago—it's not like I'm a couch potato.

*There are probably worse gigs*, I tell myself, as Joseph opens the door of a black Mercedes Sprinter Van. *Not everyone gets to take a trip like this, all expenses paid, and...*

"You've got to be fucking kidding me," says Miller West as I step inside.

Miller West. Here on *my* bus, full of people planning to climb Kilimanjaro with the mountain's best tour group.

Okay, maybe there *aren't* worse gigs.

My head jerks from him back toward the door, hoping I've

stepped on the wrong bus. I must have. Because there's no way this suit-wearing asshole is actually planning to climb Mount Kilimanjaro, unless he can somehow fuck it for a summer, then text to say it's not working out.

"What are you doing here?" he demands. For once, the snide smile is gone.

I glance toward the excited people already on the bus, laughing and comparing hiking boots, and slip into the seat across from his. "What are *you* doing here? In a *suit*."

"I'm in a suit, since you're so desperate to know, because I came here straight from a meeting in Germany. I'm not planning to climb in it."

There's so much here to respond to. First of all, I was *not* desperate to know. Second of all, I want him to die in a fire.

This has always been my issue with Miller West. Too many goddamned things to say at once.

I roll my eyes. "You expect me to believe that you, of all people, love nature so much that you've signed up for this of your own volition?"

"Everyone loves nature," he says. "And why are *you* here? Does Kilimanjaro potentially have a reputable news source your dad can turn into a gossip rag?"

My nostrils flare. My father did that *once*, but damn if Miller didn't have it locked and loaded for the day we ran into each other.

"It's none of your concern," I reply, turning away from him and pulling out my phone.

"Have you even trained for it?" Miller demands. "Your occasional ski trips and Peloton rides aren't the groundwork you need to ascend to eighteen thousand feet."

*Jesus. My sister dodged such a bullet with this guy.*

"Thank you for mansplaining altitude to me, West, but I think I'll be okay."

"No, you won't," he says, his voice hard. "Go home."

I gape at him. "Are you serious right now? Do you actually believe you can *command* me to leave like you own me? You couldn't even command me when I was seventeen."

His eyes widen ever so slightly, as if he's been caught at something. "I never attempted to command you when you were seventeen," he mumbles. "But if you want to die, by all means, be my guest."

The bus takes off and he starts furiously typing on his phone. I'd tap out a text of my own, except the person I want to complain to is Maren, who'd grow hopeful and dreamy-eyed in response, picturing him confessing his love for her over some fireside chat with me.

> DAD
>
> Why is Miller West telling me to make you come home?

My head jerks up. "You texted my *dad*? Are you fucking crazy? I'm twenty-eight years old. What's he going to do? Ground me?"

Miller's hazel eyes are cold, unrepentant. "I'm hoping someone with a little sense will prevail since you clearly have none, and I assume he's still paying every last one of your ridiculous bills. Maybe you'll listen to the sound of purse strings tightening."

"I work for his company and I'm here on assignment. Not *all of us* are trust fund douches."

I have a trust fund too, but he probably doesn't know that. It works.

I pick up my phone.

> Because he's the same fucking asshole he was ten years ago.

> DAD
>
> You tell him, Kitty Cat.

I sigh. If my father had orchestrated all of this, it couldn't have worked out better than it has: he's forced me to go on this trip with no preparation and has now set it up so I'm *fighting* to go on this trip, refusing to give an inch.

The only reasonable course of action is to pretend Miller's not here and push him off the mountain should the opportunity present itself. Because I'll need character references when it happens, I turn around and introduce myself to the couple sitting behind me, who tell me they're taking this trip as a ten-year-anniversary gift to each other.

"It beats spending money on diamonds," says Daniel, the husband.

"Only one of us actually thought that," replies Deb, his wife, with a tight smile.

Will Blake and I be like this when we hit ten years? Misunderstanding each other, full of silent resentments and failed expectations? I doubt it. Mostly because I don't expect an awful lot. Entering marriage with low expectations seems somewhat wise. My parents now have eight marriages under their belts between the two of them—maybe the number would be smaller if they'd been more realistic. If they'd chosen a partner the way they'd choose a colleague, weighing the risks and benefits, studying their qualifications.

"Which route are you taking?" asks the woman.

I blink rapidly. I'm not *entirely* unprepared for this trip. I know it will take six days up and a day and a half to get down. I know the altitude we'll reach, and what I need to bring.

But I didn't realize there was another way to go up.

"Route?" I ask blankly. "There's more than one?"

Across from me, Miller's jaw drops. "There are eight routes. Do you seriously know this little about it? How could you be so unprepared?"

I give him the finger before I open up the trip email on my

phone. I turn to Deb. "My employer booked the trip. Lemosho? Is that a route?"

Miller blows out a breath and starts texting furiously again. "Yes."

"Which route are *you* doing?" I demand.

"Lemosho," he grunts, facing straightforward with his jaw set hard.

Fuck.

This is a disaster on so many levels. There's the fact that I don't want to spend eight days with him, but there's also the guilt.

Because no matter how awful Miller is, Maren would be happier with him than she is with Harvey.

And I might be the reason she didn't end up with him.

# 2

## MILLER

**M**aren's little sister is a fucking brat.

That's the first thing I thought when I met Kit Fischer—seventeen and too lovely for her own good—at a family dinner I'd never wanted to attend in the first place.

I'd bumped into Maren over a drunken spring break. She was beautiful. I was twenty-two. That's the entire reason we got together. I thought I'd made it clear that I was leaving for law school soon, that I wasn't looking for anything serious, and if asked I'd have said we were just hanging out. Insisting I attend her family dinner didn't feel especially like *hanging out*.

"You *have* to go," my youngest sister had said. Maren was already making a name for herself, but it was the chance to meet *Ulrika*—a model so famous she needed only one name—that really wowed my sister.

Because her dating history was a fixture of gossip columns, I knew Ulrika had used her long legs and blonde hair to run through wealthy men for twenty years straight, producing two lookalike daughters along the way. But I had no idea what I was in for with *one* of those daughters when I agreed to go to her house.

"Would you like something else to drink?" asked Maren as I set my empty wine glass on the linen-covered table.

"Do you always drink that quickly?" asked Kit.

"*Kit*," Maren and her mom hissed, horrified.

She shrugged. "Just wondering if this is a pattern. Alcoholism tends to present early in life."

While Ulrika and Maren both had this sweet, almost child-like innocence about them, the youngest member of the family came off like a bitter war veteran who'd seen some shit and had nothing left to lose.

She made fun of my hair and what I was wearing, and followed this by asking how much my father had to donate to my alma mater to get me in. Henry Fischer—Kit's biological father and Maren's adoptive one—was known for his brutal takedowns. It seemed the apple hadn't fallen far from the tree.

In the kitchen, Ulrika's boyfriend, Roger, clapped a hand on my shoulder. "Don't mind Kit," he said. "She means well."

I raised a brow, and he laughed. "Her mom hasn't always made the best choices with who she's brought around. It takes a while to win Kit's trust. She took a golf club to the guy before me, though he absolutely deserved it."

Ulrika had run through four husbands at that point, and there were rumors about the last one—suspicious bruises, a drinking problem. I'd assumed they were bullshit.

Maybe they weren't.

Maybe Kit's animosity wasn't about me at all. Maybe it was how she protected the people she loved. I could respect that.

"So how much of your family's income comes from the Greek mafia?" she asked when I returned to the table.

I handed her my phone. "Check with my mom. She handles the finances."

She asked if it was true that my father's firm made most of their money representing human traffickers.

"Everyone likes a client who can pay in cash," I replied.

For the first time all night, her mouth twitched, and it was as if I'd won something, though I had no clue what it was or why I cared about winning it.

"Sorry about Kit," Maren said as she walked me to the penthouse's private elevator to the lobby. "That was unusually bad, even for her. I'll make sure it doesn't happen again."

Weirdly, by that point, I no longer wanted Kit's abuse to stop. Because it served a purpose, yes, but also because I'd begun to enjoy it. When she sent that acid tongue of hers in my direction, it was like she was throwing down a toy she wanted me to fight her for.

As I left, I could suddenly picture staying with Maren, becoming part of her family. Returning, week after week, to bat off Kit's abuse.

It would take me way too long to understand what had really changed.

# 3

## KIT

The bus slows as we turn down a tree-lined lane and then stops inside the gates of the resort, where we will spend one last night in luxury before venturing onto the mountain. I climb out, intentionally cutting Miller off to do it, and come to a shocked halt.

Tents. All I see are tents. And sure, they're nice tents, on platforms, but they are still fucking *tents*.

I've come to such a short stop that I'm knocked into from behind by someone, and naturally that person is Miller. He reaches out, grabbing me by the waist to keep me from toppling forward, and for a half second, my back is pressed to his very firm front and his incredibly large hand is tight against my stomach and half around my hip.

I'm a tall girl. It takes a whole lot of man to make me feel dainty by contrast. There's a tiny clench of desire in my core before I can stop it. I'll go to therapy for a decade if necessary in order to forget it ever happened.

"I really hope you're able to walk uphill a little better than you climb off a bus," says Miller, releasing me, "or Kilimanjaro is going to be painful for everyone hiking behind you."

My jaw grinds as I move out of the way. *If that person is you, I will go out of my way to make it painful.*

The white-clad hotel staff exits the largest of the tents and form a line to greet us. Somehow, they seem to already know who each of us is...a nice touch, yes, but I wish I could swap that nicety out for an actual hotel room.

One with a door.

"Miss Fischer?" asks a smiling man. "Come. I will show you to your lodging."

He leads me to one of the tents, opens the flaps, and secures them to the sides before he gestures me in.

Inside, there's a bathroom and a canopy bed shrouded with mosquito netting. It's actually quite nice, if you're someone who doesn't worry about being murdered. I'm from New York, however, so wondering if I'm about to die occupies roughly fifty percent of my waking thoughts.

The bellman shows me how to operate the shower and indicates the way I can secure my tent—a way that will stop no one with opposable thumbs. When he's gone, I go straight to the bed and pull back the covers to discover what will prove a woefully insufficient sleeping situation. At home, I sleep on a temperature-controlled mattress that raises and lowers on command, on sheets my mother orders from France, and this...is very far from that.

I wasn't always this way. With Rob, my ex, I was different, but I was also younger then. With every year, I get a little more inflexible, a little less able to roll with the punches.

> You said it was a five-star hotel. This is not five stars.

DAD

> "Five stars" is relative. I'm sure you'll survive. You and your sister could stand to learn a bit about how the other half lives.

This from the man who will return a gin and tonic that is accompanied by a slice of lime rather than cucumber and who bought a private plane in a fit of pique after a flight he was on didn't have lie-flat seats.

> It's a TENT. I have no DOOR. When I'm murdered in my bed, I will hold you responsible.

DAD

> Once dead, you won't be able to hold anyone responsible. Technically.

With a groan, I flop down on what I pray is a newly laundered blanket to mope.

Yes, I sort of knew what I was in for, but it's hitting me with renewed vigor. Because I've gotten used to a certain lifestyle. I've gotten used to my morning protein shake, my expensive supplements, an ice-cold eucalyptus-scented towel when I finish working out at my bougie gym. I've gotten used to sheet stitching so delicate you can barely feel the seams, and long, hot showers with my rose-scented bodywash followed by a six-step routine for my skin.

And I realized I would have none of those things for a few days but...what if I can no longer exist without them? What if I'm incapable of sleeping without my temperature-controlled mattress and my perfectly seamless sheets? What if I can't stomach the food, if my gut revolts against all the starch? It would be bad enough to be sleepless and shitting my pants in front of *anyone*, but to do so in front of West?

It's a fate worse than death.

I sit up.

I can't do it. I just can't. There are seven other routes, and I have money. There's got to be a way to switch.

Reinvigorated, I leave my tent and cross the grounds, which are bustling with the arrival of a second bus. Couples wander by hand in hand, smiling. I guess *they* knew what they were getting into with the sleeping situation.

I enter the large tent, which has some kind of dining area on one side and employees behind a counter at the other.

"Hi," I say with my most winning smile. "I was wondering if I might be able to change tour groups and go on a different route?"

The two women behind the desk look at each other with raised brows. Their shoulders sag at the same time. "I don't know what is in the water today," says the shorter of the two. "No one ever asks to shift tours this late, ever, and you're the second request in an hour."

My stomach tightens. Did Miller ask to move to the other group because of *me*? How incredibly insulting. *I'm* the only one who is allowed to be mad. And God, it would just figure if I changed to some shittier, longer tour only to discover that West had changed too.

"Someone changed? Do you know who?" I ask.

"A couple just switched to the Machame route," she says. "So if you're on that route, we might have space available on Lemosho."

*Fuck.* I shake my head. "I was hoping to switch *from* the Lemosho route. Is there any way to add a person onto Machame? I'm happy to pay extra."

She smiles, but her eyes are saying *rich fucking westerners will waste money on anything.*

"I'm sorry," she replies. "It just isn't possible. We'd need to move porters from one route to the other, and since the Lemosho route takes two days longer, those porters wouldn't get any rest between journeys."

I'm tempted to suggest that I don't need the porters, that I can carry my own belongings or make do with less, but who am I fooling? I'm standing here with a fresh blow-out, wearing a designer T-shirt I own in five colors because it doesn't irritate my skin...No one is going to believe I will need *less* help than others on this trip. Even *I* don't believe it, and I'm capable of tricking myself into an awful lot.

"Okay," I say, swallowing hard. "Is there, uh, room service? I didn't see a menu."

She shakes her head with another apologetic smile. "It's best that you not eat in your tent—it draws animals."

*Gulp.* I'm not about to argue with that one. Trekking to Mt. Kili with West might be a fate worse than death...but not death by lion attack.

The woman directs me toward the dining hall. I'm chagrined to find Deb and Daniel there as I carry my salad to the table. Daniel laughs, again, at the fact that I didn't even know what route I was on, and then describes how much better Machame is than Lemosho. "So much faster," Deb says. "But not everyone can stomach ascending that quickly."

"It's stomaching the days without a shower that troubles me," I say with a laugh, though I'm not entirely joking. This is going to be *so* hard, and I'm furious at my dad for all of it.

I wonder what Rob would say if he could see me now, mad that Daddy made me go on this expensive once-in-a-lifetime trip, one I didn't have to pay for. I picture him with his wide smile and his sun-warmed skin, raising a brow, amused even as he was about to set me straight.

He'd probably tell me I was turning into a not-nice version of Maren, and I guess he'd be right. I've always been a not-nice version of Maren, and perhaps that's part of what offended me so greatly about Miller breaking up with my sister.

Because she's a hundred times better than me, yet he still decided she wasn't enough.

∼

WHEN I GET BACK to the tent, I send out my last texts since I'm not sure what the internet situation will be going forward.

> You know what would make this trip better? If someone hadn't stolen Umbrellas in Paris from me.

MAREN

> That's MY lipstick. But yes, I have heard a nice red lip helps with mountain climbing. It's why so many people now survive Everest. Too bad you don't have any left.

I text my mother, asking her to let the world know my dad was responsible if I die. She replies by saying she'd likely blame him whether or not it was true, and then asks if I can give her a call because she can't remember the password to her checking account.

When all this is done, I video call Blake, which is how most of our relationship is conducted since he splits his time between Vegas and New York.

I don't mind the distance, and I like the way we're able to withstand it all without the drama and jealousy that plagues my mother's relationships so often. There was always an ache when I was separated from Rob. I prefer this—the absence of an ache.

Blake picks up the phone and tips back in his chair. He's what I would call generically handsome—nice features, nice hair—the face of someone who could be a news anchor. Any time I walk through an airport, I see at least ten men I think might be Blake for a half second.

"There you are," he says. "I was gonna give you a call tonight." Blake is not one to think of things like the difference in time zones. He doesn't mean any harm. He just has never really had to think about anyone but himself.

"I'm eleven hours ahead," I remind him. "I'll be on my climb in eleven hours."

"Oh shit, for real?" he asks. "I assumed you'd be on London time."

Which would still make it the middle of the night if he'd called, but there's no point in quibbling.

"How is it?" he asks.

I stretch out on the bed, arranging the mosquito netting with my foot. "Well, my five-star hotel is a tent, so I'm not optimistic about the luxuriousness of the coming eight days. And you'll never guess who's here...Miller West. He practically lived with us for an entire summer at the Hamptons while he dated my sister—he drove out every single weekend—and then dumped her by text."

Blake laughs. "Another of your mortal enemies, then?"

"Indeed. We've already argued three times and the trip hasn't even started. I don't think I can deal with him for a full week plus."

"Go up with another company," Blake says, and I fight a twinge of irritation. He's somewhat prone to solving problems I didn't ask him to solve, in ways that are not nearly as easy as he tries to make them sound.

"The trip's already paid for. And it's expensive. Like, ten grand. I can't throw ten grand in the trash because I don't like the guy."

Blake shrugs, as if ten grand is meaningless. And I suppose it sort of is, but changing companies would also mean a last-minute scramble to research alternatives and find one with space and probably changing my flight home. It's a whole lot of effort because I don't like one person on my trip. And I'm currently with what's considered the most luxurious of the companies that climb Kili and I'm already complaining. I doubt a cheaper company is going to make me *happier*.

"Look, go to reception and slide a crisp twenty-dollar bill to someone, and you can probably get them to do anything you want."

I wince. He sounds like a dick who thinks he can buy anyone and anything, the kind of person I'd loathe back home. My dad would probably say I shouldn't be marrying someone who is already showing early signs of narcissism, but clearly my dad doesn't have the greatest judgment either—I mean, look where his judgment has left me now. Plus he once chose to marry my mom.

Blake has found a couple of houses he wants us to look at when I get back to NYC. He's wanted us to move in together for a while now, and though I've resisted his push to move to the suburbs, he's probably right: it'll be easier there once we have kids. We discuss a restaurant we both want to try and then I remind him that the sign-up deadline for our next marathon is looming. We'll have to do most of our training separately, but at least we can commiserate after our long runs.

"Oh, shit," he says. "Were you serious about that?"

I sigh. "Blake, we discussed it. We picked out a hotel. I've already registered." I researched that trip for a week and he was endlessly enthusiastic at the time. Now he's acting like this is news.

"Do you know how many flights that'll take?" he asks. "It's in the fucking arctic circle."

I pinch the bridge of my nose. *Yes, I know how many flights it will take. I showed you the flights. I showed you the train ride. And you fucking agreed.* "Right, that's what makes it so cool. Twenty-four hours of sunlight, polar bears. What could be more memorable?"

"Look, if you really need to do something different, let's just do the London marathon instead. Direct flight. In and out."

I want something magical, something exciting, because my regular life is fairly dull. There's nothing wrong with running through London, but it isn't what we discussed. It isn't twenty-four hours of sun and polar bear sightings, with a side trip to a city that has abandoned the concept of time. But a successful marriage means compromise. It's fine that he doesn't want to do it. I just wish he'd fucking said so before I put in the work.

"Okay," I say, grinding my teeth to hold in my disappointment. "I'm not going to have Internet for the next week so can you get all the details?"

He agrees readily...just like he agreed to the Norway marathon back in November, so I'm not holding my breath as we end the call.

It's still early, but there's not much to do so I slide into bed. The sheets are rough and too warm and this is the height of luxury compared to what I'll go through for the next week. What if I can't adjust? What if I'm sleepless every night, prickled by small irritations, my body too soft and pampered to deal with a sleeping pad on the hard ground?

All this just to get a story for my dad, knowing full well he's unlikely even to publish it.

It's the "all this" he's after—the mysterious lesson he hopes I'll learn along the way.

And Miller West is going to be gloating the entire time, watching me learn it.

# 4

---

## KIT

I wake the next day on minimal sleep. I've always been like this: tell me it's important to get a good night's rest and I guarantee you I'll lie awake, staring at the ceiling until dawn.

I slip on shorts and a T-shirt and go to the reception area for coffee, still dumbfounded that I'm here and actually doing this. All so I can get a view I really don't care about, a view I could access by googling the phrase "pictures of Mount Kilimanjaro." In fact, I could get *better* views. There's a fifty percent chance the summit will be fogged over when we arrive and we won't see a freaking thing, anyway.

Dad wants me to do this so I can move on with my life— even if it means moving on with Blake. But this stupid climb is not going to help me get over the past. It's not going to get me over Rob. Nothing is going to do that.

It's early enough that the coffee station is empty...aside from Miller. *Figures.* He hasn't shaved this morning. It's an unfairly attractive look on him. *Everything* is an unfairly attractive look on him. He's half Greek, which means he's always a little tan. The light brown hair and hazel eyes make it stand out even more. It's the dead of winter, and he looks like he just got back from a Mediterranean cruise. It annoyed the hell out of me that summer in Hamptons, the way I'd spend every day doing my best to get a tan, even if I shouldn't have, and Miller would turn up after a week working at his dad's office looking as if he'd been the one on vacation.

Then again, everything about him annoyed me. His loveliness, his smirk, his quick comebacks. His existence.

His gaze drops to the running shorts I slid on to come here. "You're not planning to wear that, right?"

I roll my eyes. "Says the guy who was wearing a suit yesterday."

He blows the steam off his coffee. "You're a little hung up on the suit thing, aren't you?"

I turn away from him to pour myself a cup. "I'm not hung up on anything but steering clear of you."

"It's not too late to back out," he says quietly.

"Don't worry about me," I reply, looking at him over my shoulder. "Worry about yourself."

"I'd *planned* to worry about myself," he grumbles, walking toward the exit, "and now, apparently, I've got to worry about us both."

I add some milk to the coffee and sigh. At home, I have a very complicated system with expresso shots and protein powder. I miss my system. I miss my rules. I don't know why my father seems to think my life must be constantly shaken like a snow globe when his is just as regimented, if not more.

And if he thinks I'm not over Rob, allowing me to stay home and plan my wedding to someone else would *prove* I'm over Rob a hell of a lot more than going without a shower and freezing for a week.

I chug the coffee while I pout, then return to the tent and reluctantly open my suitcase.

On the trip up, I will only carry a daypack with snacks, water, and my camera. Everything else will go into a separate porter bag to be carried for me, while my luggage and a few clean outfits will remain in storage here.

I'm torn between the fear that I've brought too much and the fear that I've brought too little. It would be hard to experience greater variety in weather and temperature than we will endure during this climb, progressing from rainforest to arctic. Rain is guaranteed, as is tropical heat at the start of the climb. Blizzards and dust storms are also entirely possible. It's eighty degrees here while the summit is currently negative twenty-five.

In other words, I need to pack for pretty much everything, yet somehow keep it under fourteen kilos.

I change into hiking pants, boots, and a T-shirt, followed by gaiters around my boots and the bottom of my pants to keep them relatively mud-free. In my daypack, I stash my rain jacket, water bottles, a few protein bars, and some magnesium salts.

I've got every last thing I was told to bring, but I feel wildly unprepared nonetheless.

"How did you sleep, miss?" asks the porter who comes for my bags.

"I'm nervous," I admit.

"Nervous is good," he says. "It's the arrogant ones who fail."

Miller is arrogant. Unbelievably arrogant. This cheers me up a little—the one silver lining to this whole trip would be watching him turn back halfway through.

Outside, our bus to Lemosho Gate awaits, and is already surrounded by a small group of people way more excited about climbing than I am.

There's a family of four: Adam and Stacy Arnault, along with their kids, twenty-something Alex and Maddie. There's me and Miller, obviously—the two solo tents on the expedition—and finally Gerald and Leah, who were on the bus yesterday and who I *assumed* were father and daughter or even grandfather and granddaughter until he grabbed her ass a minute ago.

There are also thirty-two porters. Four porters per person seems like overkill, but a porter has to carry a bag for each of us and whatever he's bringing for himself, plus there are the tents, food, dishes and cooking supplies.

There's also an actual toilet being loaded on top of the bus, which unlocks a new level of anxiety. "Don't worry," says Stacy beside me. "It will be inside a tent."

That doesn't actually help. I don't need Miller standing outside the tent, loudly commenting about how long I've been in there.

I wonder if I can just hold it all week.

"We're going to know each other real well by the end of the trip," says Gerald, clapping me on the shoulder slightly too hard while he strokes his overgrown gray beard. "You'll get used to it, kiddo."

I silence the urge to tell him where he can shove that condescending *kiddo*, but other than Miller, he will definitely be the person I hate most on this trip. In the five minutes we've stood here, he's mentioned his previous expeditions to Kili several times and offered unsolicited advice to all of us. He's even making suggestions to the *porters*, for fuck's sake.

"You're sure you've got your epilepsy meds?" Stacy asks Maddie.

"Yes, Mom," says Maddie, rolling her eyes. "For the fiftieth time."

"You know, epilepsy can be completely cured with a keto diet and mindfulness techniques," offers Leah, Gerald's girlfriend. "It's so much better than polluting your body with medicine."

Everything she's said is absolute bullshit, so I may have

been hasty about who I'll hate most on this trip. I'll give it some time.

Gideon, the lead porter, reaches us with a clipboard and Miller extends his hand. "Miller West," he says. "Nice to meet you."

I roll my eyes. Fucking Miller. Even in Tanzania, he's got to pull out his whole *man of the people* bullshit. He won over every member of my household in seconds when Maren first brought him home. I was the only person who was suspicious. If I'd remained suspicious a little longer, I might have spared her some pain.

I give a tepid wave. "I'm Kit Fischer."

He looks between us. "Ah. New York. You came together?"

Of course he wonders. Because what are the odds that two people from the Upper West Side would both decide to climb Kilimanjaro at the same time and on the same tour?

"No," we say in unison, with equal vehemence.

Gideon's smile flickers, then regains strength. He gestures toward the bus's open door. "Well, come along then. You will be friends by the time the journey is through."

That sounds more like a threat than a promise, under the circumstances.

When everyone is checked in, Gideon stands on the first step of the bus to get our attention.

"Are we ready?" he shouts, his voice a mix of enthusiasm and command. He's pleasant enough, but he's also telling us we'd better get on the goddamn bus and be cheerful about it.

I like this. It means he might tell Miller and Gerald to keep their mouths shut.

After another few minutes, we begin driving down a long dirt road, with people walking on both sides of it—mostly women, carrying baskets, wearing dresses I'd expect to see on Easter Sunday, circa 1980: baby pink, yellow, pastel green. The tall grasses soon turn into twisted trees and palm shrubs, creating an overhang that plunges us into shade, growing increasingly dense. By the time we arrive at Lemosho Gate—buzzing with people and buses—we are fully in the rainforest.

"Look at the monkey!" squeals Stacy, squeezing her son's arm as she points to the roof of the open-air shelter Gideon told us to wait under while our bags are weighed.

"Mom," he says, raising a brow at me over her head and grinning, "the entire roof is crawling with monkeys. You're not planning to do this the whole trip, right?"

I reach into my daypack for my phone and Gerald is immediately by my side with more unsolicited advice.

"Keep your candy closed up, babe," he warns, nodding at the monkeys running along the tree branches and shelter roof. "They'll steal it."

"I didn't bring candy," I reply icily.

*And don't call me babe.*

"Oooh, rookie mistake," he says with a wink. "Don't worry. Maybe I can help you out."

Miller steps up beside me and places his hand on my shoulder in a way that feels a bit proprietary. "I'm sure she'll be fine," he says. As much as I want to slap that hand away, I do not because Gerald has noted the gesture too and is moving across the shelter in Maddie's direction.

"Ugh. Now he's off to hit on the twenty-two-year-old."

"Her father's here," Miller says, letting his hand fall. "I doubt he'll get far."

"Speaking of fathers," I say, stepping away to face him, "how is it that you even had my dad's contact information?"

Aside from the fact that Miller long ago became my family's mortal enemy, he's also sort of...fallen off the grid in New York society. I figured he'd eventually join West, Keyes and Greenberg, the powerhouse law firm his grandfather founded, but he hasn't, and aside from appearances at the occasional wedding, he's otherwise disappeared.

Miller raises one perfect eyebrow. "Are you under the impression that just because I'm not attending the weekly black-tie Manhattan fundraiser, I can't still access a number if I need one?"

"Well, I guess I should have known, since you were connected enough to find out I was coming here in the first place."

His nostrils flare. "What's that supposed to mean?"

I release an exasperated huff. "There's no way you just *happened* to be climbing Mt. Kilimanjaro the same week I was, on the same tour, *and* the same route. Someone must have told you, and you did it for reasons that are still unclear but probably involve making my trip worse."

He laughs. "Your arrogance never ceases to amaze me, Kitten. Do you actually believe *you*—a woman I barely knew a decade ago—matters enough to me, bad or good, that I'd fly seven thousand miles and climb for a week?"

I suppose he has a point. "Don't call me Kitten. And I guess it's pretty easy for me to imagine you having a lot of free time on your hands and also being infinitely petty. I've got ample proof of the latter, after all."

"Breaking up with your sister doesn't make me petty," he retorts, turning away. "And if anyone is stalking anyone here, it's *you* stalking me."

He's gone before I can form a reply—not that I'd have one. Because while it's obviously an insane suggestion—not only do I not want to be on this trip, but I clearly had nothing to do with booking it—it also feels oddly as if I've been caught at something, though I'm not entirely sure what.

Gideon soon calls our group to the gate, which is an actual wooden arch, tall enough to drive a truck beneath.

The porters, assembled with all the bags on the ground in front of them, begin to sing something for us in Swahili. The only words I can identify are "*Kilimanjaro*" and "*hakuna matata,*" so I assume we're not meant to sing along.

Gerald is clapping as if this is a hoe-down and Leah is doing a cringeworthy dance which I imagine she thinks is "African style." I want to look at Miller, to see if he's wincing too, but I refuse. No camaraderie will exist between us for the next eight days, if I have anything to say about it.

When the song finishes, Gideon leads us to the sign marking the distances to each camp until we hit the peak. How many thousands or millions of people have read this sign, have experienced this same swirl of hope and dread in their stomachs? I don't want to feel as if I'm part of something...but I'm part of something anyway.

We set off along the trail, which is muddy and surrounded on all sides by trees that are dense and green—the flora's more like something you'd see in Hawaii or Costa Rica than a mountain that will be covered in snow when we reach its peak. Despite the shade, I'm soon sweating. I fix my ponytail, trying to keep my hat from slipping around. My jog bra is clinging to me, beneath my layers. I strip down to my tank, wishing I was less acutely aware of Miller somewhere behind me, possibly watching and judging. I still can't believe he accused me of stalking, even if I accused him first.

The porters begin passing us, carrying bags on their backs and many balancing an additional bag on their heads. Joseph lopes along beside me for a few minutes, pointing out things I'd likely have missed: sweetly curling little orange flowers called elephant trunks that apparently only grow on Kili, a tree whose bark is used as medicine and is good for congestion.

Joseph tears off a piece and tells me it can be eaten. It tastes a bit like eucalyptus.

"I wouldn't start randomly putting plants in your mouth," warns Gerald. "Stick to real medicine."

"Twenty-five percent of the world's medicines come from

the rainforest," I tell him. "So your *real medicine* very likely began here."

"Keep telling yourself that, kiddo," he says. "I'll try not to laugh when you wind up carried out of here on a stretcher."

If he keeps calling me kiddo, *he* will need the stretcher.

He continues on and Stacy moves up beside me. "That guy is already on my nerves and we're an hour into the trip," she says, nodding toward Gerald. "And his girlfriend is nearly as bad."

I grin. "So you're not going to try to cure Maddie's epilepsy with mindfulness techniques?"

She laughs. "You heard that, huh? No, I think we'll just stick with her meds, thanks."

"The meds control it pretty well?" I ask. "No break-through seizures?"

I don't want to ruin the Arnaults' trip, but epilepsy is impacted by altitude—new onset seizures are not uncommon in places like Colorado, when people arrive without accli-mating—and I'm wondering how much research they did before they set out.

"She hasn't had a seizure since we switched meds a year ago." Stacy glances at me. "Are you a doctor?"

I swallow. "No, just kind of a hobby."

*Medicine is a hobby? Who says that?* But I've got no idea what I should have said in its place. The truth will just lead to more questions about things I don't want to discuss. Sometimes it feels as if the harder I try to bury the past, the more the world conspires to dig it right back up.

Overhead, a branch shakes as two monkeys leap from one tree to the next, and I attempt to take a picture as I walk—only to tumble over a big stone in the middle of the trail.

Stacy asks if I'm okay. Miller just raises a brow, as if I've stumbled on purpose, for attention.

Unfortunately, my accident means he's now ahead of me,

and I can't seem to stop watching. It was always like that with him, though, that athletic grace of his movements, his sheer size...he never asked me to watch, he simply caught my gaze and refused to relinquish it. He'd be engrossed in a conversation with no awareness of himself at all, the way his calf would flex as he leaned forward, a tendon popping in his forearm as he reached for a glass, his biceps clenching as he lifted a surfboard.

I'll never know if it was my abuse that sent him careening off into the horizon, but I sensed blame from my family when he left the beach house so suddenly. One minute, everything was fine. The next, he was throwing his backpack into the trunk of his Audi and making excuses that sounded patently false even before Maren got the "*it's not working out*" text later that night.

As insane as it is to think a seventeen-year-old could run a man off...there are parts of that last afternoon in the cottage that sort of make me think I did.

We take a quick break, which is when I discover I'm the only person here who brought healthy snacks. The sugar-free protein bar is a dry ball in my mouth while everyone around me is eating potato chips and candy. I'd told myself that climbing Kilimanjaro was no excuse to fill myself up with garbage, that a week of climbing and healthy eating would be just the thing before that engagement party I already know my mom is planning for me and Blake—now, I'm wishing I hadn't been quite so ambitious.

The climb continues and gets progressively worse. As we ascend, the trees grow less dense, the air thinner, and I'm finding that my ability to run twenty-six miles slowly isn't as helpful a skill as I might have hoped. "*Pole, pole!*" the porters shout. It apparently means "slowly, slowly," but if I'm already struggling at a relatively low altitude, what's it going to be like when it's theoretically time to summit in seven days?

And the harder it gets, the more my temper begins to fray. Over Gerald's advice to the porters, over Miller's friendliness to everyone but me, and over Leah's singing most of all. She's one of those women who has a passable voice but thinks she's Adele and wants all the attention she can get. For the first part of the climb, Maddie and Stacy both gave it to her, telling her how beautiful her voice is. Two hours in, they've stopped saying it, but she's still going strong.

I've got the start of a headache and can't stomach another of her especially dramatic versions of the songs from *Hamilton* and *Wicked*. Our shoulders sag when the now familiar intro to "Popular" exits her mouth.

"Leah, no one wants to hear you sing," Gerald says, reminding me of the subtle disdain Maren gets all the time from her husband. The way he'll say, "*Maren is under the impression she could run a business*," with that little note in his voice, the one that says, *hey, everyone, let's all laugh at what a naive idiot she is but not too hard because she's so pathetic*. Or the way he'll tell and retell the story about how Maren thought Cuba was the same size as the Bahamas, always hoping someone won't have heard it and will marvel at her stupidity...except Maren isn't stupid. At all. Harvey is just looking for weaknesses and exploiting them, crafting an image of her that will allow everyone to share his contempt.

"I want to hear Leah sing," I say loudly.

"Then I guess your taste is as bad as hers," Gerald replies.

"I've definitely got better taste than her in *one* area," I snap, looking him over, my nose curling in disgust. Behind me, the Arnaults explode in laughter while Gerald gives me a narrow-eyed glare and storms off ahead of us.

"Well, that didn't take long," Miller says, falling into step alongside me. "Day one and you've already got an enemy."

"Correction," I reply, "I already had an enemy, *Miller*."

His teeth sink into his lush lower lip. I despise him, but

*goddamn,* that's a nice lower lip. "Why do you hate me so much, Kitten?"

I adjust my daypack. "For starters, because you're the kind of man who calls a grown female *Kitten.*"

His mouth curves. "You love it, but that's fair. Why else?"

"Because you dumped my sister by *text...*days before her birthday, no less."

He glances down at me. "Your sister appears to have recovered, unless that big wedding at St. Patrick's was a ruse."

"She's recovered and then some," I lie, because I'm not about to tell him she's unhappy, "but that doesn't change the fact that you did it."

My words just seem to bounce off him—he's not the least bit guilty about anything he's done. "Let's be clear about what, precisely, I did," he says, with a brow raised. "I—at that point a twenty-two-year-old kid who was about to move across the country—told a girl I'd only been dating for a few months that I was worried we wanted different things, after being incredibly clear all summer that I didn't want a relationship. Obviously, I should be tarred and feathered on the town square, but remind me which piece of this was so incredibly evil?"

For a moment, before common sense prevails, I'm worried he might be correct. How many dating mistakes have I made since Rob? A million. How many times have I entered a relationship knowing at the outset that something felt wrong?

But no, I'm not letting him off the hook that easily.

"I think you're significantly underselling your part," I reply. I stumble over a root and his hand shoots out to steady me. I pretend as if I haven't noticed because I'm trying to make a point. "If you weren't serious, you shouldn't have done all the shit you did. You shouldn't have sent her flowers after you met. You shouldn't have flown her down to the Bahamas for that party. You shouldn't have allowed our mothers to get involved."

He winces. At last, a few of my words have sunk under that

hard shell. "You're right. I've apologized to her, I've apologized to your father, and now I'm apologizing to you. I was young and stupid, and I hurt your sister, who's one of the kindest people I've ever known, but you and I are about to spend a week together. It might help matters if we tried to get through it without open hostility."

"I'm already trying," I reply, dropping back. "It's just that difficult."

He shakes his head, aghast at my pettiness, and that's just fine. I don't want to come out of this trip feeling like his friend. And I definitely don't want to emerge caring about him again.

We arrive at the camp a few hours later. Joseph leads me to the tent he's already set up for me, in which he has placed my bag and sleeping pad. Thanking him, I climb inside, spread out my sleeping bag, and shed all my sweaty clothes.

This is day one of an eight-day trip, and I'm already desperate for a shower. I make do by cleaning myself with a wet wipe, followed by a towel, then I change into dry clothes and lie on my sleeping bag.

Other than the stumbling and the resulting cut on my knee, it wasn't as bad as I'd anticipated today...but we are at a lower altitude than Denver, the air is still warm, and I haven't had to spend a full night sleeping on the ground.

Which means I haven't actually *experienced* any of the bad parts yet.

If I was a better girlfriend, I'd try to phone Blake while I still can, but I'm tired and a little annoyed by how cavalier he was about ruining the Norway plans, so I lie down until they call us to dinner, then reluctantly stumble to the dining tent.

Inside, the table is laden with food—kebabs and stew and rice, plus pitchers of coffee and cocoa and water. I slide into the space next to Alex and reach for the water at the same moment Miller does.

"I'd say ladies first," Miller says, taking the pitcher, "but I don't see any at the moment."

"I'd say that I'm surprised at your shitty manners," I reply, "except I'm not."

Alex chuckles beside me. "I guess you two know each other."

"Intimately," replies Miller, pouring water into my cup.

"Your vocabulary is just as poor as it ever was, Miller. *Intimately* implies something entirely different." I turn to Alex. "He dated my sister."

"I take it that ended badly?" Alex asks.

"She'd tell you it was a huge waste of a summer," I reply.

Miller raises a brow. "She would never say that," he replies, "because Kit's sister is a far nicer version of her. It's hard to believe they share a parent."

*Wow, Miller. Shots fired. I guess I started it and I know it's true, but still...*

Stacy winces at the tension and turns toward me. "What do you do for a living, Kit? You look just like this model back in the states, and Maddie and I have been trying to figure out if you're her."

I give Miller a furtive glance. I don't especially want everyone to know whose kid I am, or that it's my mom or my sister she's referring to. "Nothing that glamorous," I reply. "I'm, uh, in marketing. What about you?"

Miller raises a brow, his mouth quirking upward. I swear to God, if he outs me, he's a dead man.

Leah is a "healer" which sounds a little too vague to be a real profession, and Gerald claims to be a CEO, but doesn't say who he's a CEO for, which means it's probably his own one-man company.

Adam claps a hand on Alex's back. "We have a family business. Cabinetry. And I'm trying to get Maddie on board too."

Alex and Maddie exchange a look, and Alex gives her the

tiniest shake of his head. I wonder what the story is there. One of them definitely does not want to be part of the family business.

"What about you, Miller?" asks Maddie.

He shrugs. "I designed this app. It helps you locate available health care in any city. We're trying to get it into less developed countries, where that can be difficult."

I begrudgingly acknowledge, to myself, that this is really cool. I wouldn't fawn over it, of course, but Maddie and Leah are doing enough of that anyway. I'm sure Miller's paid handsomely, but you'd think he was suddenly Nelson Mandela. Only one they're horny for.

The conversation moves on to the shows they've all downloaded to watch each night of the trip. When I admit that I didn't download anything, Gerald—once again—claims it's a "rookie mistake."

"You keep using that expression," Miller says. "Except we're all rookies, so it doesn't make much sense."

"We aren't all rookies," Gerald replies with a condescending sneer. "This is my fifth time making this climb."

"Climbing it five times doesn't make a lot of sense either," says Miller. "There are a lot of other places to see."

I'm not sure if he said it to defend me or simply because he doesn't like Gerald. I don't think anyone likes Gerald, other than Leah, and even she appears annoyed at times.

Adam and Stacy say they downloaded *Downton Abbey*. Maddie and Alex have mostly downloaded blooper reels and some dude on YouTube they like. Miller has downloaded *30 Rock*, a show I love.

If we didn't have the shared past we do, he'd probably be my favorite person on this trip.

# 5

## KIT
### DAY 2: MTI MKUBA TO SHIRA ONE

**9200 feet to 11,500 feet**

J oseph wakes me at six with a gentle tapping on my tent poles. "Good morning, Miss Kit. Would you like some coffee?"

I thank him and groggily reach for my headlamp. I fell asleep last night about twenty minutes into reading *The Future of Publishing*, woke a few hours later, and proceeded to remain awake for most of the night. It also feels as if elves took tiny hammers to every bone in my body while I slept, and I'm not sure who in the Smythson Explorers marketing department thought it was acceptable to describe the sleeping pad as "luxurious," but I'm fairly certain I can sue.

I religiously apply sunscreen, pull on clothes, and head to the dining tent. The table is laid out with a platter of eggs and some kind of fried bread that looks a bit like French toast. Miller, disgustingly well-rested and handsome, is the only one here.

I slide onto the bench across from him unwillingly and

pour myself a cup of coffee. "Why did you say that yesterday?" I blurt. "That I was stalking you?"

I'm trying to be casual, but I don't think I've succeeded. There isn't enough oxygen in this tent suddenly. My chest constricts.

"Because I told your dad two months ago that I was going on this climb, and here you are," Miller says.

I blink. That's impossible. My father seemed as surprised as I was to discover Miller was on the trip. More to the point, my dad wouldn't talk to Miller in the first place. "When the hell did you talk to my father? He *hates* you."

He gives me a smug smile. "*Au contraire*, squirt. Your father adores me. We have lunch once a month at Il Buco."

Il Buco is my dad's favorite restaurant. If Miller's fucking with me right now, he's doing a really good job of it.

"Why the hell did my dad go from hating you to having lunch with you every month?" I demand, scooping eggs onto my plate. "After the way you treated Maren, he should be on the dark web finding someone to put you down, not asking you to lunch."

There's the tiniest pulse of a muscle in his jaw. I wouldn't even notice it if I hadn't been watching so closely, but there's something in his face that tells me he doesn't want me to know *why* my dad forgave him.

"That was a long time ago, Kitten," he says, regaining his equilibrium. "Most people don't hold a grudge for over a decade. You, apparently, are the exception."

"Do not call me *Kitten*," I hiss as the Arnaults enter.

I'm glad they've arrived. I need a little time to process the fact that my father—the most loyal, intelligent man I know—has behaved in a way I can only deem intensely disloyal and really fucking stupid. I can't believe he's been lunching with our family's enemy and never said a word.

"I need a new tentmate," Alex says, taking the seat beside mine, nodding toward his sister. "This one snores."

"I don't snore," Maddie argues. "Mom, tell him to stop saying that."

"Alex, stop saying that," his mother commands. "She just has allergies."

"Great," he says, handing me the platter of sausages, "since it's just allergies, you sleep with her."

"Oh God no," Stacy says with a grin. "Those allergies would keep me up all night."

I pour myself a second cup of coffee. When Alex asks if I'd like the sugar, I shake my head. "I'm trying to keep this trip healthy."

"You sure?" Miller asks. "You could use some sweetening up. And you've barely eaten. Finish your food."

It's unfortunate that he's being so abrasive and bossy publicly. No one's ever going to believe his death was an accident now. Very deliberately, I throw my napkin atop my plate. He's not going to say 'finish your food' like I'm a toddler and watch me obey.

Instead, I'm going to refuse to eat just to show him who's boss.

Which is very adult.

After breakfast, we each fill our water bottles and grab our daypacks for the six-hour climb ahead. As miserable as the sleeping situation was, I guarantee I could nap for a couple of hours right now if only the porters would leave me behind.

Alas. They will not.

We set out through the rainforest, with Miller just ahead of me, speaking Swahili to his porter and Joseph. It's irritating, the way he charms them. Hopefully they don't take it too seriously because he will definitely make them all fall in love with him and then dump them by text. I have a mental image of all these lovely porters staring at their phones, waiting for him to change his mind. Possibly followed by a little light stalking of him on social media the way Maren did and perhaps still does.

Rob, my ex-boyfriend, charmed people, too. We'd met during the single year we'd overlapped at the University of Virginia: my first year of medical school, his final year of his master's program. It was a year when I shouldn't have had a spare minute to think about dating, but I couldn't resist him. He was handsome, sure, but it was quiet strength I liked most. He was friendly to everyone, but he was also the person you'd look to if shit went downhill. If he was a character in a movie, he'd be the general, the captain—the leader who'd inspire you to go out swinging.

Miller's a lot like that too. How strange that the guy I loathe and one I loved have so much overlap.

I talk to Stacy and Maddie for the first hour of the walk. Twice a year, the Arnaults take a family vacation—usually somewhere sunny and warm. As they describe past family trips, I fight a burst of envy. Not at the trips themselves—I've been to most of the places I'd like to see. I envy their cohesion. My parents split when I was small and though they still get along—my mother's current husband is now best friends with my dad—we never had that traditional family feel. For the most part, when my mother was traveling, she dumped us with my dad, and my father would attempt to take us on a trip and wind up working the whole time while we sat in the kids' club. One of the things that appealed to me about Blake, right from the start, is how much he wanted to be a hands-on father. Of course, Blake says a lot of things he doesn't entirely mean, but I'm hoping that wasn't one of them.

Stacy is telling me about a disastrous cruise they went on when Gerald charges past us. "Chat a little less," he says, "and walk a little faster."

"Is it wrong that I'm praying he falls?" Stacy asks.

I laugh. "Not as wrong as me actively planning to make it happen."

After several hours, we emerge from the rainforest onto the beginning of the Shira Plateau, a distinct dividing line between the rainforest and the drier, more barren moorlands, where Gideon announces we will be taking a break.

I climb onto a boulder and stretch my arms overhead, looking over the grassy plains and the dense treetops below.

There is so much *land*, so much *green*. That this is just a tiny piece of a single country, surrounded by other countries, is a realization that hits me anew.

I'm an ant, one of a million ants, and my contributions will mean very little, if anything. For me, that's a relief.

For a long time I've felt as if I needed to have a very big life —that I needed to have the best clothes and go to the best parties and get a better seat at Fashion Week than other people; that I needed to have a job like my father's, one that has everyone stopping by our table at Le Cirque to pay homage even though I *loathe* the way people stop by our table.

Standing here, I can almost believe it doesn't matter— that whether I've got the best seat at Fashion Week or never attend again won't make a difference to anyone in a hundred years and probably makes little difference to anyone now. My father is powerful and important, but in fifty years, he'll be a footnote at best. And if it doesn't matter...who do I decide to become? Because I doubt I'd remain on the path I'm taking now.

I sit on the boulder, laughing to myself as I recognize these thoughts. Am I about to grow as a person? I really hope not. I don't want my father to be right about the need for this trip.

"We're in fucking Africa, man," says Alex, climbing up beside me. "It's wild, you know?"

I smile. "Yeah. It's pretty wild. It's so...vast."

It's a stupid thing to say, but Alex won't judge me, mostly because he's not an asshole like Miller. But it's actually pretty cool that I'm doing this. I'm excited to see the terrain in the days ahead and I can almost picture eventually forgiving my dad.

Alex pulls out a bag of gummy worms and shakes some into my lap. "I know you said you're not doing sugar, but come on."

"It was not my best plan," I reply as I throw a few in my mouth.

I glance over my shoulder to make sure we can't be overheard. "So, which of you two doesn't want to go into the cabinetry business with your dad?" I ask, nodding back toward his sister.

He laughs and sighs at once. "Neither of us. Maddie just got into a masters program for social work and I want to get my real estate license, and we're in a standoff about who tells him we're jumping ship first."

Legs appear on the boulder beside mine. Muscular, olive-toned legs. I follow them up to Miller's scowling face.

"Are you drinking enough?" he demands.

"Miller, I'm twenty-eight, not twelve. You fret over me more than my mother does."

"That's setting the bar pretty low," he grunts in response. "You probably learned to crawl because she kept forgetting to feed you."

"Shows how much you know," I reply. "I probably learned to crawl because she was refusing to give me anything but skim milk."

Alex waits until Miller's walked away before he raises a brow. "So the two of you really never dated?"

My laughter is equal parts shocked and amused. "*What*? No. He dated my *sister*."

He glances back toward Miller. "Not necessarily a deal breaker for a lot of guys."

"Well, it's one for me," I say firmly. "Especially when the guy in question is *him*."

It's only later, as we set out again, that I remember the most relevant point wasn't that Miller dated Maren. It's that I'm about to marry someone else.

I'd sort of forgotten.

My father would say it's a bad sign, the way I forget about Blake for long periods of time and don't really need to talk to him, but my dad's also on his third marriage. It's not as if he can claim he's got the recipe for success. And it's not as if I haven't thought this through.

It took me a while to start dating after Rob, and it took me a long while to meet anyone I could picture staying with. And I really tried. I dated rich men, and I dated poor men. I dated men who barely spoke and men who wouldn't let me get a word in edgewise. I dated men who couldn't accept that I *wasn't* dumb, and men who were hell-bent on proving to me that I *was*.

I dated men who were saving themselves for marriage and on one especially memorable occasion, I went out with a guy who asked to use my bathroom and then walked out nude...at the start of the date.

And at last, there was Blake. We went to the same parties and knew the same people. He had a real job and waited until a reasonable point in our relationship to walk out of the bathroom naked. He had interests beyond drinking and football...he ran marathons, he'd just taken up jujitsu. He understood the demands of my job.

I know it's not perfect. He isn't Rob. But I don't need perfect, and I'm not sure I can handle another Rob because I doubt I'd survive losing one.

Blake is sort of the perfect compromise.

*This is perhaps the one area of your life where you shouldn't compromise, Kitty Cat*, my father says in my head.

"Shut up, Dad," I say aloud.

If he's befriended Miller, he's got no right to judge me for anything.

THE SECOND HALF of the climb is harder now that we've ascended two thousand feet. Gerald, who went straight to the front of the group, shouts at us to keep up, earning him annoyed looks from Gideon and the porters, who continue counseling us to "*pole, pole.*"

My quads ache. I need to pee but don't want to call attention to it lest Miller notice. Leah is behind me, telling Maddie's mom that pasteurized cow's milk has killed more people than the bubonic plague.

It's no longer cool that I'm doing this. I don't care about the terrain. I'm definitely not going to grow as a person, nor will I ever forgive my father.

"I'd like to get there before next winter," bellows Gerald at the lot of us.

I hope Gideon pushes him off a cliff. None of us will say a word.

After a few more hours, we reach Shira Camp One, where we will stay for the night. We are now in the moorlands, not the rainforest. It's dry and entirely unprotected from the wind, and a fine dust has settled over the tents, the latrine and even Gerald, who despite his whining about our speed, looks suspiciously exhausted.

I climb inside my dust-coated tent and divest myself of my filthy outer layer, then remove my sweat-soaked T-shirt and bra and panties. I wipe myself down with one of my precious wipes, dry myself off, and climb into the woolen base layer I'll sleep in later. Already, it's getting chilly, so by the time the sun is down, I won't be willing to strip out of this stuff again.

Though it's still light and dinner's coming, I pull my sleeping bag out and slide inside it, relishing being dry and warm and inert...things I'd barely notice, much less appreciate, at home.

We only hiked for six hours. It seems as if I shouldn't be as exhausted as I am.

It's probably the altitude, the stress, the shitty night's sleep... but what if it isn't? What if I can't hack it on this trip and Miller's got to carry me all the way back down the mountain?

As much as I despise him, as much as I resent the way he's treating me like a child...there's a despicable piece of me that's slightly relieved he's here.

I don't know the porters. Who's to say they won't leave me for dead if I break an ankle five days into the trip? But even though I hate Miller and he hates me, I know he wouldn't. No, he'd dump his backpack and climb down with me on his back if necessary. He'd probably bitch at me the entire way, but he wouldn't stop until I was safe.

I guess he'd have made a really good husband for Maren. I went out of my way to run him off, and I succeeded. Maybe I wouldn't have, if I'd known how much *worse* Maren would end up doing.

These thoughts fade as I sink into one of those deep, sudden afternoon sleeps, the delicious kind you wake from without a clue where you are or what month it is.

It's Miller I dream about. He's back in our cottage in the Hamptons and he's brought me a popsicle just because I love them.

*"Why did he bring you one but not me?"* Maren asks.

I insist it didn't mean anything, but it's a lie. It does mean something. It feels like a diamond ring, a bouquet of roses. And I *want* it to mean something, even if I shouldn't.

"Kit," says Miller. "Kit."

My eyes fly open. It's dusk, and Miller, who's apparently been outside my tent saying my name, is warning me that I need to answer or he's coming in.

*What a weird thing to dream. Nothing like that ever happened.*

"You'd better be clothed," he says.

"What?" I ask, just as the zipper slides up and his head peeks in, a mountain of dust blowing in with it.

He frowns, relief and irritation stirring in his eyes. "Jesus," he says. "Answer when I call your name next time. You scared the piss out of me. It's dinner. You slept right through the bell."

I'm so tired, and I'm not especially hungry. Both of these are signs of oxygen depletion, but I'm too exhausted to care.

"I'm gonna skip it," I mumble, rolling over, tucking myself into fetal position as I bury my face in my pillow.

The pillow is snatched out from under me. My cheekbone smashes into the sleeping pad.

"Hey!" I shout.

"Get the fuck up or I destroy it."

My jaw falls open. "You wouldn't."

His eyes are flat and calm and definitely *not* those of a man who's bluffing. "Won't I?"

"Fuck you, Miller," I growl, flinging the sleeping bag off me and reaching for my pants.

"Fuck you, Kit," he replies, removing his head from my tent...but not returning my pillow. When I stumble outside, he's waiting with narrowed eyes. He hands the pillow back, and I've got half a mind to climb inside my tent and make him fight me for it—there's a strange charge in my stomach at the idea—except he *would* fight me for it and now that I'm out, I'm actually a little hungry. I throw the pillow inside and stalk toward the dining tent.

"You can't just start blowing off meals," he says. He is beside me effortlessly, though I'm walking as fast as I can.

"I know," I growl. "I just didn't sleep well last night."

"Because you realized this was a terrible fucking idea?"

"Because I was trying to figure out how to make your death look like an accident and couldn't remember which local plants were poisonous," I reply. His mouth twitches. I'm fighting a twitch of my own.

And then I realize this moment has occurred just as we've reached the entrance to the dining tent, where six pairs of eyes have witnessed the exchange, this half second of accidental truce, and I feel as if I've been caught at something.

As if it's suspicious somehow that Miller and I are here together, arriving late, almost smiling at each other. I flush and take the nearest seat that isn't beside Gerald. Miller follows, taking the seat across from mine.

"We must check you," says Gideon, holding a pulse oximeter in the air.

"It's to test your oxygen levels," says Gerald. "It—"

"She knows what it is," growls Miller, and our gazes meet again.

He knows far more about what I've been up to the past few years than I do him. And I wonder what else, exactly, he knows.

I really hope it's not everything.

# 6

## KIT

### DAY 3: SHIRA 1 TO SHIRA 2

**11,500 feet to 12,800 feet**

It's still dark when Joseph wakes me with his gentle morning greeting. My eyes open and for a half second, I just stare at the tent's ceiling, wallowing in misery.

After my hard nap yesterday afternoon, I found myself unable to sleep. It was nearly two when I finally unearthed the handy stash of sleeping pills I'd brought, but the four hours of sleep I managed was not nearly enough.

Though it's freezing, I force myself to strip off the base layer inside the toasty sleeping bag since I'll get warm as the day goes on. I slide on the hiking pants and a T-shirt, grabbing my jacket before I exit the tent.

"You're not wearing enough clothes," Miller grunts, walking up beside me. "We're ascending and then doing an acclimatization day hike farther up from there. You'll need a base layer."

I roll my eyes. It's six o'clock in the fucking morning and he's already bossing me around. "When I need a man to comment on my wardrobe choices, I'll time travel back to the eighteen hundreds when it was socially acceptable behavior."

"While you're time traveling, you also might want to revisit the start of this trip and tell Alex you've got a boyfriend," Miller adds. "Or maybe you just like the attention."

My jaw falls open. Once again, there are too many things to say.

One, how does he even know I *have* a boyfriend?

Two, I don't like the attention, and how dare he suggest it?

Three, he sounds kinda jealous.

"He's just being friendly, weirdo," I reply. "I'm sure it's a foreign concept to you."

"Pull your head out of your ass, Kit," he replies just before we reach the tent. "He's not being *friendly*."

There's eggs and coffee and fried bread and sausages once more. I'm not really in the mood for it again so I only have the coffee, ignoring Miller when he hisses at me to eat.

After breakfast we set out, crossing the Shira Plateau, which is relatively flat. Aside from the peaks in the distance, the only vegetation is brush and these weird, twisty trees with what appears to be hundred-pound pine cones at the top. I still manage to trip several times, however.

Maddie walks beside me, explaining how deeply she did not want to come on this trip. "We normally do a winter trip to the Caribbean," she grouses. "I wish we'd just stuck to that."

I wish they had too. She hasn't seemed to struggle much with the altitude yet and her oxygen level was good this morning, but we'll hit thirteen thousand feet during today's acclimatization hike and tomorrow's will take us to fifteen thousand feet. If she has a seizure while we climb the Barranco Wall on day five, she could plummet to her death before anyone realizes it's happening.

*You're not a fucking doctor, Kit. Keep your concerns to yourself.*

"Where do you like to go?" I ask.

"We went to Anguilla last year," she says. "It was amazing. Have you been?"

I nod. "Yeah. I was just there last spring, actually."

I went with Blake. It wasn't a terrible trip, but it wasn't my favorite. He was laughing at stupid shit on his phone—dogs knocking over babies or people throwing cold water on a sleeping sibling—and he kept demanding I put down my book to watch.

Eventually I told him I had a headache just so I could go back to the room and read in peace, and there was a part of me that thought, *Should I be doing this? Should I be with someone who's this different?*

But...I've watched my mother and Maren fall madly in love before. Year after year I saw them come waltzing into the house after a first or second or third date with someone who was, ostensibly, perfect. Men who were endlessly charming and loved Matisse or happened to have been at the same party a decade prior in some far-flung place, and it all seemed so... meant to be. Like something from a movie.

And then I watched each of those relationships implode, because it's not real, all that seeming soul-mate-ry. Being at the same party as someone twenty years prior means nothing. Lots of people love Matisse. And lots of men will *say* they love Matisse or your favorite band, place, movie, or activity. They'll say whatever it takes, and you'll discover a couple months later that he actually was confusing Matisse with Monet, that he only knows *one* song by your favorite band, that he thinks your favorite city is overrated.

If you're a romantic, like my mom and Maren and even my father when he's in the throes of lust—typically with someone he'll stop wanting six months later—you can convince yourself of anything.

So why not just pick the guy you can still stand at the six-month or one-year point, when all the illusions have faded away? Why demand that he like Matisse, enjoy reading, or want to ride a bike? He won't be doing any of that shit with you even-tually anyway.

Blake and I get along. We agree on the things that matter. But I don't need him to remember my birthday, which is good because he probably won't. I don't need him to act as if I hung the moon because he'll eventually notice I didn't hang it correctly.

Maren and my mother drown every time a relationship falls apart. I've drowned myself in advance, so at least it won't come as a shock.

Gerald points out a road as we cross over it. "That's for medical evacuations," he says, looking at me. "Just so you know what road you'll be returning down."

"I hope karma comes for him," says Maddie.

"I'm open to helping karma along if you are," I reply like the sociopath I am.

We reach Shira Two around noon. It's shrouded in mist, but more protected from the winds than Shira Camp One was, so there's no dust. From the cook's tent, I smell something deli-cious, and I no longer care what they're serving me. I was wrong when I said I'd be willing to starve all week just to avoid Miller catching me leaving the bathroom.

I'm beginning to suspect I said a lot of things simply because I had the luxury to say them.

We're served kebabs and a stew I'd politely decline if there were any other option. My sports bra and T-shirt—both damp with sweat—cling like a cold, wet rag in the chilly air.

Yet another thing I'd like to take back...the way I mouthed off to Miller about not needing his input. Because now I can't change without proving him right.

"At two," Gideon announces, standing at the head of the table, "we will hike up to acclimate. Then return to sleep here."

*Hike high, sleep low.* This concept felt a lot more acceptable to me back when I was hearing it stated on YouTube. Now that I'm here, I've got to say I'm not a fan.

I get inside my tent and, giving up the last shred of my pride, strip out of my wet clothes and don a base layer. I'm sound asleep when the porters call to us an hour later to do our extra hike. I'd give almost anything to avoid going, except that would just make tomorrow more difficult in the thinner air. And it's not as if Miller would let me get away with it anyhow.

I pull my clothes on and go out to join the group.

"Well, here's the sleepy little straggler," announces Gerald as I approach. "If we get caught in the rain, it's on you."

"You just got here thirty seconds ago yourself, Gerald," says Alex.

"I'm moving a lot faster than she is, however," Gerald replies, turning toward me. "I mean, I heard you and Miller on the bus. Did you even train? Because it's not fair to the rest of us if you didn't."

I open my mouth, ready to tell him to fuck off when Miller steps up beside me.

"She's a quarter of a century younger than you," he growls, straightening to his full, towering height. It's subtly done, but there's no mistaking the quiet show of force, one that says *you can stop or I'll make you stop.* "That's all the training she needs."

Of course, it's partly his fault that Gerald is now getting on me about this—*he's* the one who's been pointing out my failings publicly. But he also defended me and did it in a far less ruinous way than I would have.

I'm beginning to see why my dad forgave Miller. His ridiculous charms are even starting to work on me.

We begin to climb, boulder after boulder, and the mist hangs so heavy that it's like walking through a fine shower. We keep going until we finally reach a flat plain of rocks. Below us, the tents look orderly and colorful while, up close, they're chaotic and messy.

Much like life, then: pristine from a distance and messy and imperfect up close.

I wonder if that's why Maren has idealized that summer she dated Miller—because it's seen from afar. Because she's forgotten all the insecurity she felt—all the moments of wondering why he didn't call and worrying that he didn't like her as much as she liked him. I remember them, but I guarantee she does not.

"I'm starting to wonder what we're even going to see when we get to the top," says Stacy, walking along beside me. It's been a constant topic of conversation: what the weather will be like when we summit because we are two and a half days into this trip and haven't seen Kilimanjaro once. It's a lot of effort for something that is entirely dependent on chance.

I smile. "I guess I should say it's about the journey, not the destination, or something like that, huh?"

"Well, honestly, it's sort of true. Now that Alex is out of the house and Maddie's away at college...getting them for a full week like this, all to ourselves, is a rarity. Of course"—she glances over her shoulder to make sure we're not overheard—"between Alex's obsession with you and Maddie's crush on your friend, I'm not sure we've really got all that much of their attention here either."

I guess that means Miller was right. And Maddie's apparent crush doesn't thrill me either. It's a small pulse of irritation dead in the center of my chest. I'm tempted to warn her about Miller, but I don't know why. Yes, he screwed my sister over, but that was ten years ago. A third of his life. I've changed a great deal since then, so I guess he could have too.

So if I don't need to warn Maddie off, why the hell do I still want to do it?

On the way back, it begins to rain. We all quickly open our bags and drag out jackets before continuing on through the slippery mud. What was already not fun is now freaking miserable—our daypacks are waterlogged, the air is impossibly thin, and we've got to wipe rain out of our eyes every two seconds just so we can see the next steps in front of us.

Naturally, Gerald is glaring at me, as if my thirty-second delay made the difference.

The porters are still warning us to go "*pole, pole*" during the slick, muddy descent, but I'm hell-bent on not being last today. *I refuse to give Gerald more ammunition and I*—

My feet slip. I flail wildly, trying to stop my fall, but there's nothing to hold onto and I land hard, flat on my back. For a moment I lie there, too stunned to be embarrassed, my head throbbing.

"Ouch," I whisper. Then: "Oh God."

My hair. My fucking hair. No shower for another five days and the ground is slush beneath me. I'm going to be caked in mud for the rest of the trip.

Miller drops to his knees beside me, heedless of the mud he's getting on himself too.

"Are you okay?" he demands, his brow furrowed. He almost gives the impression of someone who's intensely worried.

I raise a brow. "Don't pretend you care."

He smiles. "Maybe that wasn't care. Maybe I was hoping I could finally say *I told you so*."

I laugh quietly. "Go ahead then."

"I plan to say it repeatedly once I'm actually sure you're okay," he says. "But that was a hard hit. Can you stand?"

I nod and sit up. I'm about to reach around to assess the damage to my hair when he stops me. "Leave it alone," he says gently. "There's hot water at the camp. You can wash it there."

For someone who hasn't talked to me in over ten years and couldn't possibly know anything about me...he seems to know exactly what I'm thinking a whole lot of the time.

He grabs my arms and effortlessly hoists me up just as Gerald comes charging back up the hill.

"Well, *that's* a shock," Gerald begins. "Look who's holding us up again."

Miller rounds on him and takes a single, threatening step forward. "Gerald, get back down the hill and keep your fucking mouth shut."

"You can't threaten me," says Gerald.

"I just did," Miller replies, "and I assure you I can back it up."

After a moment of tense silence, Gerald stalks off down the hill and Adam slaps Miller on the back. "I was sort of hoping you'd hit him, but that worked too."

Miller glances at me. Discomfort is etched in his features, as if he thinks he went too far.

I guess he sort of did. What I don't understand is...why.

# 7

## MILLER

Three days of continual frustration and resentment.

Three straight days of worrying about her—about her level of fitness or the way Alex keeps hitting on her—along with the knowledge that we've got five more days of this.

That's why it happened, why I lost it. Not that Gerald didn't deserve it—he's been a dick to her ever since she set him straight the first day—but I don't normally disintegrate the way I just did.

I can come up with other excuses too—that we're all exhausted, that the altitude is getting to me—but I'm not sure that quite covers it either. There's a reason beneath all of that, one I don't want to consider, so I just continue on to camp, staying close behind her just in case she starts to slip again.

It really was a hard fall. I wish to God she hadn't come.

The rain has died off by the time we reach Shira Two. Everyone is heading for their tents, desperate to get out of wet clothes and lie down, aside from Kit, who is heading to the big jug of hot water they place near each bathroom, just as I knew she would. I fight a grin.

Those Fischer girls always were vain as hell about their hair.

I follow her to the jug while the porters bustle around us, getting ready for dinner.

"I've got you, squirt," I say, taking the bottle out of her hand and filling it with the fresh hot water. "Take off your hat and tip your head back."

Shockingly, she does as she's told without argument. I pour the water over her hair, working the mud out with my fingers, then fill the bottle again and tug at her ponytail holder, wrapping it around my wrist for safekeeping. This time I pour more slowly, running my hand all the way to her scalp, checking for...

"You've got a bump."

She stiffens. "I think it's fine."

One more thing to worry about. One more thing to lie in my tent, awake, considering.

I go back to pouring the water. It makes sense that she's vain about her hair. It feels like silk in my fingers, still gold even when it's soaking wet, and there's a mountain of it. I've never seen more beautiful hair in my life, but that's always how it was with Kit—some girls had one amazing feature, one amazing quality, but she possessed all of them. The loveliest hair, the poutiest lips, the bluest eyes, the best laugh, the smartest comebacks. Her mother and Maren were both famed for their looks, but she somehow made them look plain when she entered the room.

"I think I've got it," I say, handing her the water bottle. "Alex will be back to slobbering over you any minute now."

She raises a brow. Is she about to point out that I sound jealous? It would be fair. I do.

"This might come as a shock to you, Miller, but I am not actually in the market for someone's twenty-four-year-old son."

*Why are you encouraging him then? Why are you laughing at*

*his dumb jokes and eating his gummy bears and letting him sit beside you at meals?*

My jaw grinds with the effort to hold the words in. She isn't actually encouraging him. She's just being Kit—oblivious to the fact that she is the shiniest of objects, blinding everyone who passes by. She thinks her sharp words ward people off, but I've seen how they function in the real world—I've been victim to them myself—and all they are is something jagged you find yourself caught upon, leaving you to dangle like prey while she continues blinding you.

Or maybe it's just that I've seen her with her family—that I've seen how deeply she cares, how good she is to all of them—so I know it's an act. A role she assumed in order to keep them safe.

"Then you might want to let him know," I reply.

She sighs. "Look, I have no issue with that, but it needs to come up organically. I can't just shout, '*I have a boyfriend*' in the middle of dinner, apropos of nothing."

"It seems to me that people usually miss their significant other or have enough history with them that a mention or two comes up."

She frowns at me. "I'm just a private person."

But she looks unhappy as she walks off. Given how often her father mentions that he doesn't think Kit loves the guy, I may have hit a nerve.

I hope I did.

Ninety minutes later, when we enter the dining tent, Kit's hair is still damp. I wish she was wearing a hat—it's already cold and will get a lot worse overnight.

Our oxygen levels are checked.

"Mine is, once again, the best," announces Gerald when we're done.

"You just climbed here two months ago," Gideon reminds him wearily. "You're still acclimated."

"And actually, we were all at ninety-four or ninety-five yesterday, and we still are," adds Kit, "while you've dropped two points. I wouldn't get too excited."

Gerald pouts while Alex takes over the conversation, telling some dumb story about his athletic prowess that probably isn't even true. It's only Kit's attention he's seeking, and she's too busy picking things out of tonight's stew to notice.

"How come your boyfriend didn't come?" I cut in, and her head jerks up, her brow furrowing as if she doesn't understand the question.

"*Blake?*" she asks.

"Do you have more than one boyfriend?"

She shakes her head as if clearing it. "No, but...why would he..." She stops herself. "This was a last-minute trip for me. He wouldn't have been able to leave work that fast."

"I didn't realize you had a boyfriend," Stacy says, sounding a little disappointed. Alex is probably going to cry himself to sleep. "Is it new?"

Kit glances down the table, a hint of pink in her cheeks. "No, not at all. We're, uh, actually getting engaged sometime this spring."

A strange pit forms in my stomach. "Engaged," I repeat flatly.

She laughs. "I guess my dad hasn't told you *everything*. My mom's had the wedding half-planned since we met."

Granted, until this week I hadn't spoken to Kit in ten years, but I know for a fucking fact she's not in love with Blake Hall. I mean, we're on the third day of this trip and she hasn't willingly mentioned him once.

I also know she *couldn't* be in love with Blake Hall, because he doesn't deserve for her to be in love with him.

Outside, the group stands for a moment, watching the sun set. We still can't see Kili, but the clouds floating toward Meru —Tanzania's second-highest mountain—look like an ocean, and everyone wants to grab a picture. I secretly get a photo of Kit to share with her dad if I ever forgive him for sending her here in the first place, which is unlikely.

In my tent, I get into my sleeping bag and continue to worry. I wanted to warn her about sleeping with wet hair and ask about that bump on her head, but I didn't. She thinks I'm still treating her like a child when I give her these warnings but that's not what my concern is about at all. I'm not sure what it is, but it isn't that.

*Let it go.* I've told myself this a million times since this trip began. It hasn't helped my anxiety to date, so I'm not sure why I'm still saying it.

I watch a couple of shows and then close my eyes, but sleep doesn't come. Because anything could happen to her. She could fall harder than she did today; she could get altitude sickness. It's colder tonight than it's been since the trip began—there's already ice forming inside my tent. I should have told her to wear a hat, even if it annoyed her.

I lie awake for a full hour, listening to the sounds outside, wondering if the footsteps I hear belong to someone sneaking her way. She's an incredibly attractive female sleeping alone in a tent—one she can't secure. All she has to do is fix her ponytail and at least two of the men on this expedition are watching her like she's a show they've paid good money for.

I like the porters and I like the other guys well enough, aside from Gerald, but I don't trust any of them where she is concerned.

I can't deal with four more nights of this bullshit.

I really can't.

# 8

## KIT

### DAY 4: SHIRA 2 TO BARRANCO

**12,800 feet to 13,600 feet**

I lie awake, thinking about a conversation I had with Maren not long before I left. Harvey was traveling and she'd said she was relieved. "At least now I don't have to pretend he's someone else in bed," she'd said.

I was surprised by that. She was *more* surprised that I didn't do it too.

"So when you're with Blake, it's always him?" she asked. "You *never* pretend he's another guy?"

I blinked, uncertain. "Okay, sure. But not some *real* guy. He's, you know, faceless."

"*Faceless?*" she gasped.

The faceless thing—my absolute go-to fantasy—had seemed so innocuous before she asked that question. Suddenly, there was this tug of discomfort in my chest, as if it was a bad thing. Or perhaps something I just shouldn't discuss with her.

I was intentionally vague when I answered. I told her it was at the beach house, minus all the titillating detail: me, sitting on a kitchen counter arguing with someone; him, stalking across the room, stepping between my legs.

He doesn't ask permission; he doesn't even seem to *like* me, but as he rips my bikini top off—I realize...he *really* likes me.

Maren said her favorite fantasy was at the beach house too, but then that's probably because that was the last place she ever saw Miller.

And with her, it's *always* about Miller.

Which I guess I sort of understand.

IT'S PITCH BLACK—THE middle of the night—when I wake to the sound of my tent being unzipped. *Fuck. Fuck, fuck, fuck.* My heart hammers. I open my mouth to scream, but nothing comes out.

The intruder's headlamp shines down on me as a bag is thrown inside.

"Move over, Fischer." Miller grunts, squeezing in beside me and throwing a sleeping pad down.

"What the fuck are you doing?" I demand.

"My tent collapsed," he says, irritated by the question. "I think it was the weight of the ice. Move the fuck over."

He slings a sleeping bag and pillow half on top of me, and commences to zip us both in.

"*What?*"

"I'm not sure how I can make this more clear to you," he replies. "We've all got ice inside our tents and for some reason, mine collapsed under its weight."

I glance up...there is, indeed, some ice hanging from the ceiling of my tent. But that doesn't mean he gets to come into mine. "Go somewhere else. Go sleep with the porters."

The look on his face is positively surly. He has circles under his eyes. "Are you really under the impression that the porters are sleeping in luxurious multi-person tents with room for an additional person? Move over or I'll just lie on top of you."

"Yeah, I bet you'd love that," I grumble as I slowly, reluctantly, acknowledge that I am probably the only person on this trip with space for another human in their tent, and that if Miller goes to the porters, they'll give him their tent and sleep outside because that's the sort of tour this is—the kind where the customer better not come down at the end with a single complaint or someone's out of a job.

I slide over only a little, to show how unwilling I am to be a part of this. Except we're practically on top of each other as he spreads out. *Shit.* I move over to the far edge of the tent instead.

"I don't think you took into account how likely you are to be stabbed in your sleep with me as a tentmate."

"If your performance on our hikes is at all indicative, I don't think you're *coordinated* enough to stab me to death."

He's so annoying. I don't know why I want to laugh. "If you snore, you're out."

"I am *definitely* going to snore, and I'd like to see how you manage to kick me out when I'm twice your weight."

I don't know why it hits me in such a weird way, the fact that he's twice my weight. He basically said it as a threat, and it somehow triggers all the worst things. A not unpleasant clench in my stomach, at the base of my spine. I squeeze my eyes shut, hoping I can forget it was there.

The two of us sleeping this close was not on my Kilimanjaro bingo card.

"I'll probably be up for the rest of the night, now," I grouse.

"Take a sleeping pill. I know you brought some."

I check the time. "It's too late for that. I'll be groggy."

"Then congratulations, you've already gotten enough sleep, but I have not, so shut the fuck up."

His breathing grows even seconds later and progresses to light snores within minutes. I can't believe he got the last word.

I can't believe he just told me to shut the fuck up after he *invaded* my tent, which I'm pretty sure is a felony.

I mostly wish I'd gotten the last word.

"*You* shut the fuck up," I say quietly.

I'm glad he doesn't wake. It wasn't my best work.

WHEN MY EYES OPEN, Miller's sleeping face is the first thing I see. He doesn't look entirely evil in dawn's early light. He looks...stern but kind. Long lashes brush his high cheekbones, and three days' worth of unshaved jaw surround his soft mouth.

*Of course Maren fell in love with you.*

The words float through my head before I can call them back and I sit up abruptly. "Rise and shine, weirdo. And get the fuck out of my tent."

"There's my little ray of sunshine," he replies. "You're just as charming at six AM as you are by candlelight. I can see why your father thought he could set us up by sending you on this trip."

I make some noise that combines a snort, a laugh, and a gasp. "You think my dad sent me here to *set us up*? You slept with my *sister*."

"That was a lifetime ago. I don't remember it, so I doubt she does."

"I doubt she does either, though it has little to do with the passage of time. And my dad couldn't *possibly* have wanted that. He also couldn't have known your precise itinerary, and more importantly, I'm on the cusp of getting engaged."

"Your father hates Blake."

It's still bizarre to me that he and my father are friends. And more bizarre that they've been discussing me. "My father hates everyone. Including you, most likely...he just hasn't gotten around to making it clear. And if he was going to try to push me on someone, you'd be the last person he'd choose."

He rolls toward me. "You could do a lot worse."

"I'm not certain that that's true."

He pushes up, resting his head on his hand. "A serial killer?"

"Some serial killers actually have a loving family life and serial kill on the side."

He grins. "Fine. The kind of person who creates puns with the word *serial*. Like they refer to themselves as a *cereal killer*, while eating a bowl of cereal."

My mouth twitches. "Now you're being ridiculous. Obviously, someone like that is worse."

"Progress, then," he says, reaching out to tug on my ponytail. "We've found the one type of human worse than me."

*Ugh.* I hate how charming he is. I hate how easily he's winning me over. "Cool, now get the fuck out of my tent."

"I think you mean, get the fuck out of *our* tent, Kitten," he corrects.

"No, I absolutely did not mean *our* tent because it is not ours. I've got to get dressed, and you've got to go tell them to fix *your* tent."

"You're already wearing your base layer," he says. "You'll survive me being in here while you pull on pants and a jacket. And I don't think the tent can be fixed. One of the poles snapped."

"Then they can find you an extra one," I reply.

He sits up and starts pulling stuff out of his bag. Reluctantly, I acknowledge that he is not going to leave anytime soon, so I'll need to go ahead and slide on the rest of my clothes. I'm freezing the minute my torso is exposed to the air.

"You saw how much shit they have to carry, right?" Miller asks, tugging on a sweatshirt. "You really think they brought an extra tent up here, just in case? They'd basically need to employ another person just to carry it."

"Then they can go back down and get one," I argue.

His mouth curves, like an indulgent parent who's about to put his foot down—probably because I'm acting like a spoiled little princess who doesn't care about the toll my requests will take on others. "Kit, I would like you to think for a moment before you persist with this."

I hate when he's right. If I have a fit, if I *insist*, then one of these guys is actually *going* to climb the twenty-four kilometers down to the gate and then climb the thirty-four kilometers up to the next camp.

"It's still my tent," I mumble, sliding my feet into my boots and grabbing my toothbrush.

"Sure, Kitten," he says with a laugh.

I unzip the tent.

"I'm definitely coordinated enough to stab you," I add as I climb out. "And don't call me Kitten."

TODAY WE WILL CLIMB up to Lava Tower, at fifteen thousand feet, to acclimate before descending to sleep at a lower elevation. According to Gerald, this is the day when we are all "in for it." He announces this over breakfast as if the highlight of the trip won't be the views or the challenge but watching one of us collapse from pulmonary edema.

Over breakfast, I force down some eggs and watch everyone get their oxygen tested. Maddie remains at ninety-six. I let this calm my nerves, though it really says nothing about how she'll do later on.

We set out shortly thereafter. For the first time since we began at Lemosho Gate, the sun is out. Or, more accurately, for the first time since we began, we are above the clouds and trees that kept us cast in shadow. I was freezing when I woke but I'm soon sweating, taking step after step after step.

We've crossed from the alpine zone to the desert zone and there's almost no vegetation as we ascend. Instead, there are boulders and these weird small rocks stacked one atop the other. Maddie's ponytail is cheerfully swinging in front of me as someone says they're probably memorials or burial sites. I push down another nervous burst of tension.

Miller is my shadow today. When clouds blow in and I'm freezing, he hands me some of his chocolate, which somehow helps. When we cross through slippery patches created by runoff from above, he appears by my side to make sure I don't fall.

I'm annoyed that I like this, that I'm touched, that I can't seem to stay angry at him, though I really wanted to. I'm annoyed that I'm forgetting why I'm supposed to dislike him and that it feels as if I'm the unfair one, and perhaps always have been.

When he first came to our house, with his khakis and his Vineyard Vines pullover and his dimply smile...I hated him without being able to put my finger on *why*.

I was unbearably rude to him every time we were in the same place, and he would just grin. Eventually, he started giving me crap in turn, prompting me to say something worse, and he would smile even wider when I did it, as if he appreciated this side of me.

No one had *ever* appreciated that side of me.

He asked me where I wanted to go to school, and I responded with, "Probably someplace where my grandfather didn't build a library."

"That should be fairly easy since your grandfathers were poor as fuck," he replied.

He asked what my favorite subject was.

"Better-looking men my sister could be dating," I said.

"I'm just glad it's not math or science," he replied, knowing good and well those were my favorite subjects. "Women don't belong in those fields."

He goaded me and I hated it. No, actually, I hated how much I loved it, until the day when I somehow went too far. When he was teasing me about popsicles and we started talking about Maren's friend hitting on me, and suddenly he was walking out of the room, walking out of the house, telling Maren he had to get back to the city for reasons that were obviously fabricated, breaking up with her by text that night.

My mother demanded to know what I'd done as my sister cried herself to sleep. I insisted I hadn't said a word, but of course I had. It hadn't seemed any worse than a million things I'd said previously, yet a part of me wondered if it had been my fault, if I'd somehow pushed him too far.

It's taken a decade, but I can finally admit something to myself: one of the reasons I have hated Miller for so long isn't because he broke up with my sister. It's that I felt guilty about my possible role in it.

I wobble as I plant a single boot on a rock in the middle of a stream. His hand shoots out to the small of my back.

*God, he'd have been so much better for Maren than Harvey is.*

He'd encourage her painting. He'd be the sort of husband who'd brag about his brilliant, talented wife, who'd seek out some amazing artists' vacation in Italy just to make her happy. For their anniversary, he'd get her into the Uffizi or the Louvre after hours instead of just giving her a random necklace he didn't even choose himself. He'd care about her enough to remember her favorite flowers or that Indian food gives her heartburn. Harvey doesn't.

"I'm sorry," I tell him as I reach dry land at last and we are told to take a quick break.

He raises a brow. "For which of your many transgressions are you apologizing?"

I give him a halfhearted smile while flipping him off. "I knew I'd regret initiating this conversation."

"I was just so surprised that you even knew how to say the words,'" he replies, grinning as he leans against the boulder beside me. "Did the porters teach them to you?"

I flip him off again, muffling a laugh. "Never mind."

"But seriously," he says, sipping on his water bottle, "you've actually been significantly more pleasant today than you normally are, so what are you apologizing for?"

The sight of him drinking makes me thirsty. If it's possible to have a really sensual throat, Miller has one.

"I'm sorry I've been such a bitch to you for so long," I reply.

He hitches a shoulder. "It made sense. You've always defended Maren to the death. I broke up with her and I know she was really upset."

"She wasn't *that* upset," I argue, though it's a lie. "Don't flatter yourself."

He laughs. "You're impossible, you know that?"

My family would certainly agree. "I believe I've heard that before, yes. Anyway, I'm sorry that I was such a brat and I'm realizing as this trip progresses that it wasn't entirely about you breaking up with Maren. It was because you did it right after we had that conversation in the Hamptons, and I felt responsible."

A muscle ticks along his jawline. "You weren't responsible."

"But would it have happened if I hadn't been such a bitch to you all the time?"

There's chatter from the group of people coming up behind us, but he meets my eye for one long moment before we start walking again. "It wasn't your fault, Kit. I promise you."

*Then why did it happen, Miller?* There's something he's not telling me here, and my mouth opens to demand the answer, to tell him that Maren *was* devastated...except Maren wouldn't want him to know, and the truth is she wasn't the only one who was devastated when he left.

She was just the only one who was allowed to be.

By the time we reach our next stopping point, the weather has changed. The wind is blowing hard, and the clouds have found us again. We're also on a flat, exposed area, shielded from none of it. I sit at the table the porters have set up for us and pour myself cocoa, quietly grateful that Miller is sitting close, blocking some of the wind.

If I'm this miserable when it's forty degrees, how the hell am I going to deal with it being twenty below at the summit?

"I sure hope it doesn't get any colder than this," I say to Miller, with a grin.

"Always seventy and sunny," he replies, his mouth twitching. "Isn't that what they say about Kili?"

"Did you two plan at all? Kilimanjaro is *never* seventy degrees," scolds Gerald, incapable of reading the room. He looks toward Gideon, who's been listening in with quiet amusement. "You really need to vet your clientele a little better."

"Yes," says Gideon, sighing, "we really should."

After another two hours of climbing—increasingly rocky, with almost no vegetation— we cross a small bridge and arrive at Lava Tower. At 15,000 feet, we are now higher than any point in the United States aside from Denali—and I can tell. The last steps up here were slow, plodding, and miserable. I have the start of a headache. I take a quick glance at Maddie, but she seems fine.

"You okay?" Miller asks, his gaze sweeping over my face.

I force a smile, assessing him as well. "You?"

"I can feel it, but I'm good," he says. I hope he's telling me the truth. Even a big, fit guy like Miller can suffer from the altitude, and it's mostly an issue you can't exercise away.

He smiles. "I'm really fine, Kit. I promise."

The porters have set up a tent for us to stay in while we

acclimate and have lunch. Unfortunately, they've made another stew. It's good to have something hot, and it's amazing that they can even get up here and cook this, but God, I'd kill for a steak taco right now.

"We're thinking about going back through Dubai," says Leah. "Have any of you been? I don't think it's safe."

"It's one of the safest cities in the world," I reply. "Safer than any city in the US."

"When were *you* there?" Miller asks.

I don't love his tone. Why the fuck does he care that I went to Dubai? "My mom was there for, uh, work," I reply, frowning at him because I'd rather not open this can of worms in front of everyone else. "She ran into an issue, entirely her own fault, and needed some help getting out of the country."

Miller frowns. "When was this? She's been with Roger since you were a teenager. Shouldn't she have asked *him*?"

I shrug. "I was in college. It wasn't a big deal."

"You were in *college* and she made you leave for Dubai to get her out of trouble instead of asking her fucking *spouse*?" he demands.

I huff, exhausted by his illogical peevishness and these continual questions he knows I can't answer completely with an audience. "She didn't want Roger to know."

He's still unhappy. "You realize that doesn't actually sound better, right?"

I ignore him. I've grown accustomed to my mother falling apart at the slightest sign of trouble and demanding that I fix it. Miller seems to think it's a bad thing, but I look at it as skill development. I know now how to get someone out of a foreign country when their documentation is stolen. Surely that has broad applicability.

We remain at Lava Tower for well over an hour, adjusting to the lack of oxygen, and then head down to camp. Halfway into the trip, the skies open and the rain starts to fall. We scramble to don rain jackets and ponchos but they barely seem to help. The entire trek back down, I am drenched and miserable, pulling my ball cap low over my eyes just to see a foot in front of me.

And even from a distance, as we approach camp, I can tell that there's one less tent up for our group than there was yesterday.

*Goddammit.* That means Miller and I will continue to share for the rest of the trip, and I *really* want to be alone right now. I want to dive into that tent, strip head to toe, dry myself off, wipe every nook and cranny with a wet wipe, and dress at my leisure.

We unzip the tent and dive in simultaneously, leaving only our lower legs outside so our muddy soles don't come in with us. I swing around to remove my boots, and he does the same. "I don't suppose I can convince you to stand outside while I change," I say.

He raises a brow and laughs. "No," he says, climbing fully inside.

I sigh heavily. *Four more freaking days of this.* "Look, I need to get out of all this shit, and one naked person in a tent plus another naked person equals two naked people in my tent, and when one of those people is you, that equation does not appeal."

"*Our* tent," he replies. "And you'll live. If we both face in opposite directions, neither of us will be the wiser."

I groan, turning away from him and stripping off the first of several layers. "This is definitely the sort of situation that leads to a landslide or earthquake knocking the tent over and ends with me being seen naked."

"If the worst part of a landslide or earthquake is that I accidentally see you naked," he replies, tossing his jacket and pants into the back of the tent, "you must have really gone downhill over the past ten years."

I laugh. I guess he has a point.

I peel my soaking wet socks off and sigh in relief. This is followed by the base layer and bra and panties. "Every single thing I wore today is trashed," I announce, running a towel over my skin.

"You brought extras, right?"

I hear movement behind me and check to make sure he's not looking...and *he's* not looking, but I am, and he's one hundred percent naked, sitting on his knees while he looks through his bag.

For a moment I simply stare. He has...the most perfect broad shoulders leading down to his sculpted back to a narrow waist, and the most perfect ass I've ever seen in my life. Jesus Christ.

I turn away quickly and continue drying off. I'm breathing too hard. It's probably the altitude.

"Were you just looking?" he accuses, laughing.

"You *wish* you were interesting enough for me to look," I reply in the snottiest voice I can manage.

"I didn't know you had a tattoo," he replies.

"*You* looked," I gasp, holding my sweater against my bare chest as I turn to glance back at him over my shoulder. He is still deliciously naked. My God, that ass.

"So did you," he replies. "You *still* are. I can tell by how much closer your voice is."

I turn around quickly. "Yes, but mine was an accident."

"That accident lasted an awfully long time," he replies.

Argh. *It did.*

I pull on dry socks. "I was so bored by the view that my mind wandered."

He simply laughs, as if he knows I'm full of shit.

Which, obviously, I am.

We crawl into our sleeping bags once we're both fully clothed. The rain continues to lash the tent but inside we're warm and dry and I...actually don't mind that he's here.

He opens his phone. "Did you bring anything to do?"

I release a miserable sigh as I reach toward my bag again. "I brought a book." Forcing myself to get through *The Future of Publishing* while on this trip seemed like a great idea when I left home, just like only bringing healthy snacks did.

What I didn't realize was that the hiking, the altitude, the weather, and the sleeping conditions would conspire to rob me of all my self-restraint. My protein bars and boring book now feel like the worst sort of punishment, a nice flogging at the end of an unrewarding day.

"Wow," he says. "There's no way you want to read that."

"I was trying to be responsible. I'm joining the finance team a week after I get back."

"This seems to be a theme with you." He sets his phone between us. "Come here. I downloaded some shows."

"You don't have to share. I was the idiot who didn't plan ahead."

"Contrary to what you seem to believe about me," he says, "I don't mind sharing." For a brief second our gazes catch, and he laughs. "Somehow that came out dirtier than I intended. I just meant that I don't mind having you watch on my phone."

Reluctantly, a smile forces its way out of me and I shuffle my sleeping bag close to his so that we can watch *30 Rock* together.

"This is actually my favorite show," I admit.

He glances at me again. "Somehow that doesn't surprise me."

"Why? Because the main character is sort of mean and cynical?"

"No, Kitten," he says with a soft smile, "because it's my favorite show too."

~

TWO HOURS LATER, the dinner bell rings, and we pull on the rest of our clothes and head to the dining tent.

Dinner is the liveliest time of the day, all of us giddy with relief at making it through the climb, and too exhausted to be as guarded as we might be under normal circumstances.

The topics vary from what lies ahead to weirdly personal stories about life back home. Already, I know things about these people I don't know about my colleagues, and things I probably *shouldn't* know as well: that Leah once slept with a cousin—they were both drunk and it was dark; that Miller's sister once convinced a guy to leave the priesthood and then dumped him; that Stacy once hit a pedestrian with her car. I've told them that Charlie—my darling but utterly douchey stepbrother—once dated a girl and her mom simultaneously.

Tonight, Stacy tells us a story about Maddie wanting to be a singer when she was little and how they couldn't bring themselves to tell her she was tone deaf.

Maddie rolls her eyes. "Thanks for sharing that with everyone, Mom. And I think I wanted to be an actress."

"I know a girl who went to Hollywood to become an actress," Leah says cheerfully, "but she wound up as a sex worker. Then she got HIV. I have no idea what she's doing now."

She laughs at this and no one else does. "Uh, what did you want to when you were little, Kit?" Stacy asks, filling in the awkward silence.

My smile wavers. I didn't want to be a singer or an actress. I wanted to do something that simply involved intellect and perseverance, not luck, which means I've got no excuse.

Since my earliest memories, I've wanted to be a doctor, but if I tell them that, someone would say, *"Why didn't you just go to medical school?"*, at which point I'd have to reply, *"I did."* That's a whole painful conversation I don't care to have.

"A singer," I tell them.

Miller raises a brow. I guess he knows it was a lie. I really hope he doesn't ask why I told it.

When we return to the tent, we strip out of our jackets and pants and hang them on a makeshift clothesline Miller managed to string through the tent.

"You sure you don't need to fully undress again?" Miller asks as I crawl into my sleeping bag.

"I'm sure." I frown at him, gnawing at my lower lip. "Hey, when you get back, can you not mention...any of this?"

He folds his pillow in half and turns toward me, raising a brow and failing to suppress his grin. "You mean the fact that you were so desperate to see me naked?"

"Right, mostly that," I reply drily. "Blake isn't some crazy jealous guy, but...there's no way this would sound good."

"Ah, yes, *Blake*. When's this supposed engagement taking place, exactly?"

I narrow my eyes. "Stop saying his name like it's a punchline. You don't even know him."

"I *do* know him actually," he says. "He was a year behind me at Andover."

I guess I should have realized this, and I'm a little embarrassed that I didn't put it together sooner. "So you're saying the dislike in your voice is about your peripheral impressions of a high school junior, fifteen years ago? That seems fair."

He flips on his back and stares at the tent ceiling. "I don't dislike Blake. He's a decent guy, and he played college lacrosse, as I recall, so he'd provide your future offspring the coordination you appear to lack."

I fight a smile as I give him the finger. "You definitely have a *tone* when you say his name."

"I just don't know that I like him for you, and neither does your dad. He says you're settling."

I roll my eyes. "Yes, let's definitely take advice about my choices from a guy now ending his third marriage."

Miller runs a hand through his hair, laughing, but the sound isn't especially happy. "Wow. I thought you'd object to what was said, not the qualifications of the person who said it. You know, we're four days into this trip and you haven't *willingly* mentioned Blake once."

"Am I supposed to? Am I supposed to be like, 'Hey, Miller, let me tell you about my hot boyfriend while we hike'?"

"No. Also he's not that hot. But it's sort of human nature to discuss the person you love when they're not around. To mention a trip you've gone on, or something funny he said."

I frown. I *have* mentioned trips I've gone on with Blake. I had a whole conversation with Maddie about Anguilla. I just didn't mention Blake because he wasn't the interesting part... but saying that aloud probably won't help my case.

"I don't lead an especially exciting life," I tell him. "That's the problem—not Blake. I have nothing to discuss."

"Didn't you just attend Paris Fashion Week with the editor of *Elite*?" he asks. "Wasn't that you posing in St Barth's last year with a bunch of Oscar winners?"

I want to say that posing for a photo isn't necessarily exciting, but the point would remain that yes, on the surface I lead an incredibly exciting life.

So why isn't it exciting to me?

"Your life is pretty fucking good compared to most people's, Kit. If you were crazy about the guy, he'd be a part of that."

The lantern we've hung from the ceiling sways as a gust of wind shakes the tent. I stare at it, forming an answer. "Look, there's a time factor here. I want kids, and Maren has had issues, so I might too. And it's not as if falling madly in love with someone leads to a better outcome. My parents are a fine example of this."

He rolls toward me, no longer smiling at all. There's a worried furrow between his brows. "It's more than some mathematical equation in which your odds of success are calculated,

Kit. I mean, haven't you ever been so crazy about someone that the rest of the world seemed to pale by contrast?"

I have, and that's sort of the problem. I've been so crazy about someone that the world paled by contrast, and it continued to pale. I'm sick of hoping I'll find that again. "Yes, but that's over, and I'm tired of the hunt."

His face is gentle as he reaches up to turn off the light. "I wouldn't give up so soon, Kit."

"PLEASE TELL me you finished early and you're flying out right now," Rob said when I called him.

I was in my second year of med school, slogging my way through finals. The month we were about to spend driving through Switzerland was the only spot of brightness in my world that week. "No, babe. That's not how med school works. But I've got three exams down and one to go."

Behind him, the noise was deafening. He was there on a guys' trip, but the playful screaming I heard was female. It soured my mood just a bit. Not because I was worried Rob would hook up with one of them but simply because...if it was no longer a guys-only trip, it was harder not to be a part of it. "It's loud there."

He sighed. "Yeah, the party's in full swing. I can't wait until you get here."

I'd never heard him heave a dispirited sigh like that, though I think he came pretty close the first time he met my mother. And he was at Chamonix, skiing with his best friends—he should have been ecstatic.

"What's going on?" I asked. "I thought you'd be having the time of your life."

"I don't know. I'm just tired. I got a couple decent runs in this morning and I've been sandbagging ever since."

There was a tussle on his end and yelling, and then a new voice came onto the line. "Your boyfriend is full of shit," said his childhood best friend Sam. "This kid has been skiing like a maniac since the slopes opened."

Rob took the phone back. "Okay, he may have a point. But anyway, I can't wait to see you."

"You need a drink, motherfucker!" Sam shouted.

"Just make sure you get your rest before Saturday," I warned. "I've got plans for you."

We hadn't seen each other since spring break—I was pretty sure we'd spend half of Switzerland locked in a hotel room, and I was okay with that. "Let me go around the corner," he said. "I want to hear greater detail about these *plans*."

I laughed. "I'm not having phone sex with you one room away from all your dumb friends, and I'm about to walk into a study session. Go have your drinks."

"Fine. I'll let you study, but only because you're all mine for the next month."

It was three years ago but I can still remember the thrill of hearing him say "*all mine*." I can still remember wanting someone so completely and having four weeks with him stretch ahead of me like a soft bed after a long day.

As my eyes fall closed, I realize that what's been missing these past few years isn't excitement.

It's hope.

# 9

## KIT

### DAY 5: BARRANCO TO KARANGA

**12,800 feet to 13,600 feet**

I t's no longer raining when the porter wakes us in the morning.

I thank him, though I want to groan aloud, while Miller turns on the lamp.

Once again, the inside of the tent has iced over, but the tent isn't bowing at all. At the risk of sounding suspicious, I'm not sure why my tent is withstanding the weight of the ice so effortlessly while Miller's buckled.

Whatever. I sort of liked feeling him there beside me in the darkness, heavy and solid. It was oddly comforting, though I'll never, ever say that aloud.

"Rise and shine, Kitten," he says.

*Ugh. That nickname.*

"Give me a sec," I reply. "I'm trying to figure out what symptoms I should feign to be carried back down the mountain."

He laughs. "Imagine all the shit Gerald will talk if you do that."

I throw my covers off. "Thank you for that motivational speech. Let's go kick the Barranco Wall's ass."

We pull on multiple layers over the woolens we slept in, repack our gear, and go to the dining tent. The energy today is nervous and I see why: now that the rain is gone we've got a clear view of the wall, and from here, it looks as if we'll be scaling a cliff.

"One of you is definitely not making it," Gerald says, nodding at me. "The wall is hard as hell." He's generally full of shit, but I've heard about the wall prior to the trip, so I'm worried that, just this once, he might be right.

I sip my coffee and scoop some eggs I probably won't eat—the altitude and nerves have taken a hit on my appetite.

"More, Kit," Miller says quietly, sliding the fried bread my way.

"I was planning just to eat all the snacks you're carrying up," I reply.

"Yeah, that's what I'm worried about," he says, but his grin —that shy dimple blinking to life—says that he'd probably let me.

"Please be careful today," Stacy begs of her kids.

"It's not even supposed to be that bad, Mom," says Alex. He grins at me, but it's definitely been different between us since he learned I've got a boyfriend. Or perhaps it's different because no one seems to believe Miller's tent actually broke.

"There's a portion of it called the kissing wall," Stacy replies. "You know why? Because the trail is so narrow that you have to kiss the wall not to go over the side."

My stomach drops, and the face I seek is Miller's. I never wanted his to be the face in the crowd for me, the point of refer-ence, the thing that reassured me, but it is and up here, he's all I've got.

"*It'll be fine*," he mouths, his gaze holding mine. *I'm not going to let you get hurt* is what that gaze says, and I believe him.

This is how Miller and Blake are different: Miller says very little and means every word, while Blake tends to say things he doesn't believe in the least. He'll announce that every meal is the best meal ever, that your favorite comedian, movie, or sport is the same as his. Tell him your dream destination is Botswana, or Bolivia, or Bhutan, and he'll tell you he's dying to visit.

It's not lying so much as it is agreeability and exuberance, but it makes it a little hard to believe him when we're alone. When he tells me how much he loves me, but he's also watching the game. When he tells me how beautiful I am, except he's just trying to get me in bed or isn't even looking at me as he says it.

If Miller said those things, they'd hit different. He'd look you in the eye as he said them. The words would sink so deep they'd engrain themselves into your very bones.

My stomach flips over at the thought in a way that's pleasant and unpleasant at the same time. I don't even want someone to like me that much because I don't want to like anyone that much in return.

But God, a part of me wishes I did.

We return to the tent for our daypacks and set out. Gerald, as always, is loping off ahead. Leah no longer bothers trying to keep up with him—not that I blame her. I'd have made an effort *not* to keep up with him in her shoes.

Today, Miller stays close to my side. I'm not sure if it's because he actually wants to be there or because he's worried about me climbing the wall, but I no longer mind. I like the porters, and I like the Arnaults, and I don't mind Leah when she's not singing or providing fake health advice, but Miller is my favorite person to talk to.

There's a certain degree of comfort when he's near. It's as if, even should things go wrong, they'd still *feel* okay if he was close. It should probably bother me more, but this all ends in three days. Blake wouldn't begrudge me taking comfort in a friend's presence, even if that friend is a really hot and presumably single male.

"Why did you decide to do this trip?" I ask as we progress ever closer to the wall. The air is cool and the rock-littered ground is relatively flat, but I'm already breaking a sweat in the bright sun.

He hitches a shoulder. "I have this thing. The six-month rule. Every six months, I've got to do something really hard—something I'm not even sure I *can* do."

I laugh. "That sounds...unnecessary."

He smiles down at me, but it quickly flickers out. "Our lives are too easy. Humans evolved by constantly being on the lookout for trouble...When your life is as relatively danger-free as ours, you start finding shit to worry about where there's none."

I take a sip of my water. "What do you mean?"

"Someone's walking behind me for a block, and I start preparing for a fight," he says, adjusting his ball cap to block out the sun. "Something goes wrong with a project and I begin picturing how the whole thing could fall apart, or a flight's delayed and I worry that it's going to be canceled."

That just sounds smart. It's worrying ahead that prepares you when things go to hell. "What's wrong with that?"

"What's wrong," he says, "is that modern life consists entirely of those small, meaningless moments. You're supposed to be able to shut it off. You're supposed to have times when you don't *have* to be vigilant. Except when all the meaningless bullshit constitutes a danger, it means you're never *out* of danger. You'll see what I mean when you get home. For a brief period of time, none of that stuff will bother you."

I want to argue that what he's saying doesn't apply to me, except maybe it does? I'm *always* worried about stupid shit at home, and I worried the whole way here—about the wine stain on my T-shirt, that my luggage wouldn't lock, that some foreign government would try to take my sleeping pills away from me.

Even my concerns about that luxurious tent seem ridiculous now. There were armed guards patrolling that gated camp. We were pretty darn safe.

"So what's your next six-month thing?" I ask as he steers me around a small boulder.

"I'm attempting to summit Everest in June," he says. "I thought the acclimatization here would be helpful."

My chest squeezes. "Everest...are you serious? Isn't that, like, technical stuff? Ice climbing?"

He nods, guiding me around a rock I definitely would've tumbled over if he hadn't. "I've done a fair amount. I think I've got the skills but a lot of it is a crapshoot, with the weather. And that's sort of the point: it's the danger inherent in truly not knowing whether you can pull something off."

My breath stills at the image of him up there, attempting something that has killed so many people.

"You do all these trips alone?" I ask. "Like...you didn't want to do this with a girlfriend or whatever?"

He grins, biting his lip. The dimple appears. "Is that your way of asking if I'm single?"

My eyes roll. "You wish. My sister is happily married now. You blew that one incredibly thoroughly."

He blinks, as if it wasn't the answer he'd expected. Maybe he just suspects it's a lie, which it is.

"A trip like this," he replies after a minute, "or Everest...it's the kind of shit most of my friends don't want to do. Most of the women I've dated wouldn't be into it either, but it's also a big commitment. You don't ask a woman to plan something six months out unless you're positive you'll still be with her six months out, and I never am."

"That," I say, pointing at him, "is exactly why I'm relieved not to be single anymore."

"You were tired of men not inviting you to Everest?"

I laugh. "No. I'm tired of guys my age wanting to sleep with a buffet of women until they hit fifty and beyond. You all turn into Gerald eventually."

I hop from one rock to the next and his arm snakes out to keep me steady. "I'm not turning into Gerald, and I don't want a buffet of women. I just want to find one I can't wait to get home to."

There's something about the low purr in his voice, the steadiness of that hand on my arm, that makes a muscle clench tight in my stomach. Being the girl Miller West wants to come home to would be pretty magical. Being eager for someone to come home to you would be pretty magical too.

And for all the things I have with Blake...I don't have that.

We are nearly to the wall now. It looks only slightly less vertical up close than it did from afar—the rocks appear carved to do maximum damage, smooth and angular, with virtually no vegetation or handholds to cling to if it all goes wrong. "I'll be right behind you, Kit," Miller says. "Don't worry."

I shake my head. "Actually," I whisper, "can you stay behind Maddie instead?"

He raises a brow. "Her dad and her brother can look out for her."

"Epilepsy can be impacted by altitude. We're ascending pretty significantly today...I haven't wanted to alarm them, but I'm scared about what could happen here and they're not expecting her to have a seizure."

He gazes at me. "That's what you've been so worried about. That's why you're memorizing everyone's oxygen levels."

I shrug. "Can you just watch out for her? I'll be fine. I mean, aside from being born without coordination."

"Sure, Kitten," he says gently.

The rock scrambling isn't as terrible as I'd thought it might be, but the big daypack sure doesn't help. Miller stays behind

Maddie, mostly, but does come up behind me at one point to give me a small lift onto a boulder.

I thank him, pretending I don't still feel his palm against my ass as I continue on.

There's not a lot of conversation as we climb since we're all single file and focused. I occasionally check back on him. He nods at me and says, "You're doing great."

Is there a parallel universe in which I could go with him to Everest? One in which it wouldn't upset everyone in my world, and Maren and Blake wouldn't consider it a betrayal? I'd only be there as a friend—ensuring the altitude wasn't getting to him and that he wasn't making stupid choices—but no matter how married Maren is, even a friendship with Miller would be a slap in the face to her—the worst sort of disloyalty.

We pass the kissing wall, which isn't as terrifying as it sounded, and, at last, we're done with the most intimidating part of the trip aside from the push to the summit. Everyone cheers. Leah and Gerald sloppily French kiss—my stomach revolts. The Arnaults hug each other.

I wish I could hug Miller, but that would be weird. He lopes an arm around my shoulders and gives me a quick squeeze instead, as if I'm his kid sister.

It isn't quite enough.

WE GET to Karanga Camp by lunch, an early day for us. The views are astonishing but it's too cold and windy to enjoy them. We change into dry clothes—this time, since it's not raining, Miller gives me some privacy, though he claims he's doing it so I *"don't get too titillated."*

We spend the afternoon in our sleeping bags, watching 30 Rock on his phone. And the whole time I'm wishing we could turn it off and just talk. I want to know why he left the Hamptons the way he did. I want to know why he never could see himself getting serious with my sister and whether there was ever anyone he did get serious with. These are questions I probably shouldn't ask.

"Why didn't you join your dad's firm?" I demand, reaching over to pause the show. He quirks a brow at me in surprise. "I mean, why suffer through it and then not use the degree? I'm assuming law school isn't the cakewalk everyone makes it out to be."

He laughs quietly. "I wasn't aware people were calling it a cakewalk."

I grin. "Maybe not. But your dad built them a stadium so you wouldn't have to go to class."

"Exactly. With the money he made defending human traffickers." He shrugs. "I went to law school for the wrong reasons, and I left in the middle of my second year to start the company."

I curl up with my head on my pillow. I never realized he'd left law school. "What reason? A love of money?"

He grins. "No, I still love money. But there's this expression —rags to rags in three generations. You know, some dirt-poor ancestor worked himself to the bone, but a few generations later his descendants are so accustomed to being given everything that they think they don't have to work and do ridiculous shit instead. I never wanted to be a lawyer, but I also didn't want to be that kid. I didn't want to aimlessly float through my twenties."

I laugh. "I'm not sure I'd consider the creation of some incredible and, I assume, highly profitable, app to be 'ridiculous shit'."

He lies down and faces me. "Careful, Kitten. That almost sounded like a compliment."

"True. And I haven't looked at the app yet. I bet it's terrible."

He laughs again. "There's the Kit I remember. I was just sort of waiting until I had an alternative, and then we got this child custody case at my dad's firm when I was working there for the summer. The mom had taken her kids to the mountains and one of them got stung by a bee and reacted but had no idea where to find a doctor. I just thought how fucking terrifying that would be. I couldn't believe there wasn't some easy way to find the information."

His face has come alive, talking about it; his eyes are brighter.

*What opposite paths we've taken.* He broke away from what he knew to find something that would make him happy, regardless of the risks.

And I gave up the thing that was already making me happy for no reason at all.

DINNER IS stew and kebabs again. The altitude is killing my appetite, as is four straight days of eating the same shit.

"You ate almost nothing," Miller says as we climb into the tent.

"I'm saving room for Chipotle or McDonald's at the next camp."

He grins and reaches toward his bag. "Guess what I brought?" he asks, swinging a box of Raisinets over my head.

I groan. "My favorite. How did you know?"

He glances away. "It was only ten years ago. I haven't forgotten everything."

"Are you going to share?" I ask.

"You'll have to work for it," he says, pushing the words out through his lips in a way that is undeniably sexual.

I blink in surprise and he laughs. "No, I'm not asking you to prostitute yourself. Just answer a question."

I frown, suddenly wary. There are questions he could ask

that I definitely don't want to answer. There are questions, in fact, that I *won't* answer, even when I pose them to myself. "What?"

"The guy you were so crazy about, before Blake. What happened?"

I grow still for a moment, then flop down on top of my sleeping bag. "Are you hoping I'll say I broke up with him by text?"

He shakes his head. "I don't think it ended like that or you wouldn't be this messed up over it."

No, I guess I wouldn't.

"He died," I reply. "And I really don't want to discuss it. You can keep your Raisinets."

He places them on my sleeping bag. "No," he says softly. "You've earned them."

# 10

## KIT

### DAY 6: KARANGA TO KOSOVO

**13,600 feet to 16,000 feet**

"Good morning," says Joseph, tapping on our tent in the darkness.

"Good morning," replies Miller politely.

"Fuck," I whisper, surly as ever.

I slept incredibly poorly last night. My heart was hammering—I'm not sure if it was the altitude or just sheer nerves because today is basically *the day*. We'll spend the morning climbing—passing Barufu Camp, where the bulk of the people on this route stay—and continuing on to Kosovo, ninety minutes closer to the summit.

We're supposed to sleep for a few hours after dinner at Kosovo—I'll undoubtedly be too nervous—and then begin the summit at midnight. Which means I'll be climbing for roughly twelve hours up and several hours down before I get a decent night's rest again.

Miller turns on the lamp. "You okay?" he asks, surveying my face, that pretty mouth of his in a worried pout, a furrow between his brows.

"Just great," I reply with a forced smile.

He sighs. "I didn't sleep either."

I press my face to my hands. "How the fuck are we going to climb all day, then climb for another six or seven hours at midnight?"

He elbows me. "Because Gerald will run his mouth if we don't."

I lift my head with the start of a smile. "What happens to all the people who don't have a Gerald on their trip, I wonder?"

He grins. "Gerald would say they all go down in stretchers."

I laugh and push out of my sleeping bag. "You're a much better tentmate than I am," I admit, pulling on my fleece. "You've got a better attitude."

He begins sliding his pants on. "That's the first flattering thing you've ever said in all the years we've known each other."

"I'm not sure it was flattering," I reply. "I bitch a lot. I've set the bar pretty low."

He tugs on a lock of my hair. "I sort of enjoy your bitching, Kitten."

I narrow my eyes. "You know how I feel about that nickname."

"You've earned it. You claw, claw, claw, but it's more cute than it is irritating."

I'm fighting a smile as I walk out of the tent, and God, I really shouldn't be. The affection I feel for him isn't nearly as sisterly as it's supposed to be.

"TODAY IS GOING to be so much harder than you realize," Gerald says over breakfast. "The hardest day we'll have."

Adam's eyes roll. "You've said that the past two days."

"Every trip there's someone coming down in a stretcher," he

says, with a pointed look at me. "I guarantee one of you won't make it."

"Gerald," says Miller, stabbing his meat with his fork, "direct just one more comment like that at Kit and *you'll* be the one going down on a stretcher."

The tent goes absolutely silent, eyes wide. Alex quietly laughs, and his mother gives him a stern look. I guess most people would say Miller shouldn't be resorting to threats, that we should be operating like a team.

Blake would have ignored it, but I like Miller's way better.

"If you knew who I was, you wouldn't be making threats like that," Gerald says, picking up his fork.

"You don't know who I am either," Miller says with an amused smile. "Or who Kit is. If you did, you'd realize you should have kept your fucking mouth shut."

Gerald doesn't say another word. He storms out of the tent right after breakfast, announcing he's walking ahead because we're all too fucking slow.

"Good riddance," mutters Adam.

"Don't let the door hit you on the way out," adds Alex.

We are united in our hatred of Gerald, which makes me love these people even more than I already did. It's so weird that in two days we'll be saying goodbye and I likely won't see them again.

Even Miller—we're in the same place once a year at most. I swallow a lump in my throat at the thought. The next time I see him after Tanzania, we won't be the way we are here. I'll be engaged or possibly married. He'll be with someone else, most likely. It will be awkward at best, or incredibly sad.

I think it's probably going to be incredibly sad.

Our journey to Kosovo begins with a long, flat walk, and then we are climbing up and up and up. It takes a few hours before Barafu Camp comes into sight below us. We'll be having lunch there, but I'm getting emotional about that too.

"Are you okay?" asks Miller.

It's funny, the way he senses when my emotional temperature changes. Maren and my mother never had a clue. They'd talk about how stoic I was, but I think it's that I had to seem okay with them because they never were. They're both fragile. My distress would distress them, so I kept it to myself.

I force a smile. "It's just hitting me how close we are to being done."

His shoulders sag as if that bothers him too. "Yeah, I—"

At that exact moment, a cry echoes from the other side of the ridge. We glance at each other and start hustling toward the top. A wide-eyed porter runs to meet us and says something urgent in Swahili to Gideon, who winces and then turns to us. "Gerald has fallen. They think the leg is broken. I must go check on him. The other porters will stay with you."

"Kit went to medical school," Miller announces. "Take her with you. She should look at it."

My jaw falls. "How did you—"

*My father.* I suspected my father had told him. This confirms it.

"I only got through two years," I reply. "That in no way makes me trained for this."

"Kit," Miller says, his jaw set hard, "that may be true, but it still leaves you better equipped than the rest of us to deal with it. Give me your daypack, pull your head out of your ass, and go take a look at the injury."

Narrowing my eyes, I hand him the bag and jog down the hill after Joseph. Gerald is flat on his back off the side of the trail and moaning.

His leg is clearly broken, and it's a compound fracture at that. There's absolutely no way he is walking up the mountain or back down it, and I am not equipped for this. At all. These guys probably have medic training and have dealt with more of this shit than I have by far.

I glance up, hoping one of them will take charge, but they all look worried and slightly queasy.

"Send someone on to the next camp," I tell Gideon. "I bet there's a doctor there."

He nods. "They ran there first to ask. Can you help him, though?"

I sigh. *No. Not really.* I can at least stabilize it until they get him out of here, I suppose, but nothing more.

"See if you can find me a board, or a stick, but as straight a stick as you can get. And something to wrap it with." I return to Gerald. As much as I've loathed him from start to finish on this trip, I pity him now. "They're running to the camp to see if there's a doctor there, and they might have some pain meds for you."

"How the hell am I gonna get back down?" he demands, his face screwed up in agony.

"They must be prepared for things like this. I'm sure they have some kind of stretcher, and they'll carry you back. You're gonna be fine."

"I assume it's broken?" Miller asks behind me.

I nod, rising. I have the most inexplicable urge to rest my head against his chest. Why would I want him to comfort me when *he's* the one who put me in this position in the first place? His arm reaches out, as if he wants the same thing, before it falls loosely to his side instead.

I work on making Gerald comfortable until the porters return with a flat board and gauze. I wrap the leg as tight as possible without cutting off the circulation. There's not much else to be done.

Leah is biting her lip and looking from Gerald to the summit. We're eight hours away. She wants to keep going.

"What should I do, babe?" she asks. "They've already carried all of our stuff up."

"We paid them to carry it up, and they're paid to carry it down too," he says. *Selfish prick.*

She hesitates and then shrugs. "I'm gonna go ahead and finish. I'll see you in two days."

Gerald's jaw falls open. "Are you serious? I *paid* for you to come on this trip."

"Right, and we're nearly to the top," she replies with a blithe shrug, "so I want to finish."

I stand up, planning to remove myself from this argument, just as two people reach us with a medical kit in hand.

"We're both doctors," says the woman. "What's going on?"

"His leg is broken," I tell them. "It looks like a compound fracture. I did my best to set it and then wrap it, but take a look to make sure it's okay."

I expect Gerald to mouth off about how I probably fucked it up, but he says nothing as the woman kneels down beside me, undoing a little bit of the gauze to look for herself.

"Are you a doctor?" she asks. "Or a nurse?"

I shake my head. "I got through two years of medical school. That's it."

Her head tilts. "You made it through the rough part and left?"

I give a small shrug and look away. "It wasn't for me." I wonder if that sounds as false to her ears as it does to mine. There's pity in her eyes, so...probably.

"Could we stop discussing Kit and focus on my fucking leg?" shouts Gerald.

The woman ignores him. "You did a good job," she says to me. "I don't think I could've wrapped it that well."

I'm already backing away. I want no part of this conversation. "Anyone could have done it."

"No," she says behind me. "Not anyone."

THE PORTERS HAVE SET up a dining tent at Barafu Camp. Stacy wants to know why I never brought up medical school before. I send an accusatory glance in Miller's direction before I answer, since he's the one who told them. "It just wasn't for me."

"But you're so good at it!" she cries while I struggle to force down a peanut butter and banana sandwich. "And you've been talking about medical stuff through the whole trip. Are you *sure* you don't want to go back?"

Before I can answer, the doctor who assisted Gerald pops her head into the tent and gestures me out.

"You did really well up there," she says. "Why did you actually leave medical school after you made it through the worst part? And don't try to tell me it wasn't for you. I saw the look on your face when you said it."

"I made a mistake," I admit. "I didn't catch something I should have."

She frowns at me, but it's a gentle frown, a sad frown.

"We *all* make mistakes," she says, zipping her jacket up higher against the icy breeze. "You realize that, right? Every doctor who has ever existed has made a terrible, tragic mistake. We just have to tell ourselves that on the balance, we've helped more people than we've harmed."

"I hurt someone I loved, though," I reply, my voice nearly a whisper. "It kind of fucked me up. It's just...too much responsibility."

She traces a line through the dust with the toe of her boot. "The responsibility is the hard part, but it doesn't mean you just walk away from it. Every gift comes with a price, and that's the price of yours. Just think about it. And if you want to talk it through, give me a call." She slips a piece of paper in my hand with her name and number and walks away.

I re-enter the tent, where everyone has clearly been listening but pretends to be consumed with their food. I won't be able to eat with the ugly past now churned up inside me, and I don't want to sit here faking it. I turn on my heel and walk to the outskirts of camp, where I slide behind a rock as I start to cry.

The last time I ever spoke to Rob I was just leaving the library. It was incredibly late in France, and he was so drunk that he was slurring. I was amused but also slightly annoyed because I could *still* hear girls there, and I was about to take one of the most important tests of my life—which he seemed to have forgotten about entirely.

I laughed and told him to sleep it off. He argued that he hadn't had that much to drink. I assumed he was tired or hadn't kept count—I'd seen him with his friends before and he reverted to Frat Boy Rob when they were around, keeping up with them shot for shot.

"Go to bed, babe," I said. "Take some ibuprofen and call me tomorrow."

"I love you so much," he slurred. I told him I loved him too, but I said it the way a parent would to a hysterical toddler, as if I was humoring him.

God, I hate that I said it that way.

The call from his mother came in the middle of the night. When she told me he'd died, I thought it was a mistake.

"I just spoke to him," I argued, but already I was picturing him: reckless on a dangerous slope, unable to stop as he careened toward a tree.

"They think he had—" she began, but she was crying so hard she couldn't continue. Rob's dad took the phone from her.

"Kit," he said, his voice rough and broken, "they think he had a cerebral hemorrhage. It's an altitude thing."

And that's when all his symptoms hit me, the symptoms I'd dismissed: his fatigue, his headache, the slurring. If I'd just thought for one fucking second, if I'd actually listened to him instead of laughing about the slurring, I'd have told him to get to a hospital, and he'd have been fine.

Miller takes a seat beside me on the freezing ground and wraps an arm around me. I lean into his chest willingly, though I don't deserve to be comforted.

"What happened when you were in medical school?" he asks.

I've never admitted aloud that it was my fault. Rob's parents heard from his friends about his symptoms. I'm sure it occurred to them that I should have put it together, but I never admitted it and they never brought it up.

"The guy who died?" I whisper. "The one I mentioned yesterday? His name was Rob. He was skiing at Chamonix and had a cerebral hemorrhage. He was slurring, so I assumed he was drunk. I could have saved him if I'd given it a moment's thought."

"Oh Kit," he says, his voice low and pained. "Anyone could have made that mistake."

My shoulders shake, and he pulls me closer. "No, a good doctor wouldn't have. I knew enough. I should have thought of it."

"You were only two years into your training," he says. "Experienced doctors miss stuff. You heard the woman today."

I take a shaky breath, trying to get ahold of myself. "He had so much ahead of him and because of me, he didn't get it."

Miller presses his lips to my head. "No, not because of you. Because you both had a really bad break."

"He missed out on so much, though," I whisper. "He was going to climb all seven summits. He didn't get to a single one."

Miller tugs me closer. "He got to leave the world knowing he was loved by you. I promise that meant more to him than any summit ever could."

It doesn't remove my guilt, but he isn't entirely wrong...I think what we had *did* mean more to Rob than those summits he wanted to conquer, in the same way that he meant more to me than med school...and we were lucky to find it. Not everyone does.

I know I need to dry my eyes and pull my shit together. But I like being exactly where I am right now—sitting in the dirt, freezing cold, pressed up against the only person I've ever told this to.

Somehow, I knew he'd make it better, and I was right.

WE REACH our final camp before the summit a little while later. Like Barafu, it's a barren desert where the wind blows hard, and you don't really want to be anywhere but inside a warm sleeping bag.

We're fed an early dinner, everyone gets their oxygen checked, and then they brief us about what will happen next. "Sleep," says Gideon. "We will wake you at eleven to get ready, eat a small meal, and leave by midnight."

I swallow. Around me, the faces are serious. Thousands of people manage this each year, but...that doesn't mean it will be easy. We're going to be climbing in absolute darkness for six or more hours, on little sleep, in freezing weather. And then we'll still have to climb back down.

What if I just can't do it? I know I've got Miller there, and the porters, but I also don't want to be the person who fucks up someone else's trip.

"See you in a few hours," I say, squeezing Maddie's hand. She's okay so far. I really hope it stays that way.

"She'll be fine," Miller says as we walk back to the tent.

"You don't know that," I whisper.

"You're right," he says as we climb inside. "But if the altitude hasn't gotten to her so far, I'd say the odds are good that tonight will be no different. I also spoke to Gideon. He's got oxygen canisters if it's an issue. We'll keep an eye on her."

I reach for my brush, swallowing hard so he won't see how touched I am. "Thank you."

I start trying to work the day's knots out of my hair and he holds out his hand.

"Here," he says. "It'll be easier for me."

I raise a brow. No man has ever brushed my hair in my life, aside from hairdressers.

"I have sisters, remember?" he asks.

I hand him the brush and turn away. "Charlie has never brushed my hair once."

"Well, obviously," he says, working out a knot with his fingers. "Brushing your *own* sisters' hair would be gross."

I laugh and then quiet. It's surprisingly soothing, having his hands in my hair. I wonder if this is how dogs feel about being petted. If he kept brushing my hair the way he is, I could fall asleep sitting up.

"The Rob thing," he says. "Is that why your dad actually wanted you to do this? Was it some push to help you get over it?"

I shake my head the little I can with the brush pulling my hair. "No, not exactly. I think it's about the ashes."

He stops brushing. "Ashes?"

I glance over my shoulder at him and take the brush away as I turn his direction. "Rob's mother gave me a little cup full of his ashes. She said I should leave them in a place that he loved or a place that he would've loved. It's almost as if she was asking me not to fuck it up this time."

"Kit," he groans. "I'm sure that's not what she meant. So I guess you must still have them, then?"

I run my fingers through a tangled section of hair. "I've brought them everywhere. I've carried them with me since he died."

His eyes widen. "Jesus. You're saying that you've carried that little cup with you everywhere for *four* years?"

"Well, you make it sound weird when you say it like that."

He looks so incredibly sad, and worried. "Kit..."

I laugh miserably, pulling my hair back as I slide into my sleeping bag. "Yes, I know. It *is* weird. And my dad thinks it's not fair to Blake to be carrying them with me still when I'm considering marrying someone else. Not that he cares at all about Blake, but he probably has a point."

"So you're going to place them at the summit?" he asks, shucking off his coat before zipping the sleeping bag up around him.

I stiffen. "I don't know."

He rolls toward me. There's a slight clench in his jaw, one I don't entirely understand. I'd think he'd prefer to *not* be in the vicinity while I dump human remains.

"You're still not ready? After all this time?"

The breeze outside rocks the tent. "I don't think that I am."

"Will you ever be?"

It's strange...I've thought about Rob a lot less than I normally do on this trip, perhaps because there's been so much else to think about. But that doesn't mean it will last once I get home. "I don't know," I reply. "There are times when it seems like it's getting better, and times when it isn't."

"What's going on when things are better?" he asks.

*You're there.*

I blink, surprised at the thought. A thought I shouldn't have had.

"I don't know," I say again.

My inability to provide a clear answer bugs the shit out of my dad.

I've got no idea why it seems to bother Miller even more.

# 11

## KIT

DAY 7: KOSOVO TO THE SUMMIT

### 16,000 feet to 18,000 feet

It's pitch black, and it feels as if I've just shut my eyes when Joseph wakes us. I turn on my headlamp and roll toward Miller, who's running his hand over his jaw, groggy and beautiful. Such an odd juxtaposition of childlike sleepiness and a very, very adult full beard.

Rob was lovely, but even he wasn't lovely the way Miller is. I think I could stare at him forever and never tire of the sight.

"You fucking hate that beard, don't you?" I ask.

He grins. "It itches. I'd kill Gerald for a good razor right now."

"You'd kill Gerald even if there was no razor as a reward."

He laughs. "True. It might be for the best that he left the trip when he did."

We pull on a billion layers, then chug down some coffee and sandwiches in the dining tent, the chatter nervous, heavy with both excitement and dread.

"Hey," I say to Maddie, "if you start feeling weird up there, say something, okay? Gideon has oxygen."

She smiles and nods. "I will. I promise. But I feel good."

Miller and I return to the tent to shove hand and toe warmers into our gloves and boots, then grab our backpacks. We're told to fill our bottles with hot water rather than cold because cold water will freeze. It doesn't inspire confidence.

While we wait for the rest of the group, stomping our feet to stay warm, Miller points out forgotten constellations that people don't discuss—Tarandus the Reindeer, The Electrical Machine—trying to keep my mind off what's ahead.

I elbow him. "For a guy who only got into college because his grandfather built the library, you sure retained a lot."

He laughs as the Arnaults approach. "He only donated money for the bookstore, you know. So I did have to attend a class or two."

"I know," I reply. "I just like to throw shit at you to see what will stick."

He gives me a lopsided smile. "I've always enjoyed watching you try."

"We are ready?" Gideon asks.

The seven of us glance at each other and nod. "We're ready."

We turn on our headlamps and begin walking. There are a million stars in the sky, but they don't offer us much light—all I can see is Alex in front of me and occasionally a hint of Gideon ahead of him.

The path is so narrow that we have to walk in single file for hours. Alex has headphones in. I'm listening to the wind whipping through my clothes. Miller, apparently, is listening to *me*.

"You okay?" he asks from behind, placing his gloved hand on my hip. "You're sounding winded."

I can feel that glove through four layers of clothing. "Yeah, I'm okay."

I'm not sure if that's true, however. I'm exhausted, and the air is so thin that it's hard to breathe. I'm getting a little lightheaded and loopy, thinking crazy things. Occasionally I hallucinate a little or remember things from long ago as if they've just happened.

Miller, walking into the kitchen to discover me sitting on the counter, eating a popsicle. He was so lovely, even then. Was that really ten years ago? It hardly seems possible.

There's a path cleared through the ice and we trek, stumbling and dazed, upward. It's dark for most of the journey, and the air seems to get a little thinner with each step.

I glance back toward Maddie, and she gives me a thumbs-up. I glance at Miller next. I'm worried about him though he's given me no reason for it. Are his eyes unfocused? It's hard to tell in the darkness.

"Are you okay?" I shout to him.

He nods, but it's not as reassuring as it should be. Because what if he isn't okay? He's just the type to claim he's fine when he's not. If something happened to Miller...I'd be just as destroyed as I was with Rob.

How is that possible? How can I possibly care about him nearly as much as I do a man I was madly in love with for two full years? How can I possibly care about him as much as a man I loved and *more* than the one I'm planning to marry?

"I'm not thinking clearly," I mumble to myself, shaking my head. Nothing makes sense right now. If I allowed myself to, I'd burst into tears and probably cry the rest of the way up, but I have no idea why.

I'm staring at the few feet ahead of me—the snowbanks on either side, a ring of light on Alex's back—but what I'm really seeing is that last day in the cottage at the Hamptons with Miller.

I'd started the morning down at the beach with him and Maren and some of their friends, but I could tell Maren and Miller no longer wanted me there. I was a brat, but not the type of brat who'd outstay her welcome.

I'd gone back to the house to pout and was sitting on the kitchen counter with a cherry popsicle when he walked in to fill the cooler. "Is that why you left the beach? So you could sit up here and eat popsicles in peace?"

I wanted to mouth off, but my head was blank and my mouth was dry. He was in nothing but swim trunks, and I'd never seen anything in my life hotter than Miller's back flexing as he turned to open the refrigerator door.

"You guys didn't want me there," I replied. It was probably the least abrasive thing I'd ever said to him. I just didn't have the capacity for antagonism in that moment.

He stiffened and turned toward me. "That's not true."

I sucked on the popsicle as I pulled it out of my mouth. "Yes, it is. You should realize by now it takes more than that to hurt my feelings."

His gaze dropped to my mouth and the popsicle, and he winced and turned back to the refrigerator. "That wasn't about you. It was about that kid Mare knows from Columbia who keeps hitting on you."

"Why does it matter?" I'd asked.

He stood, nostrils flaring as the popsicle slid back between my lips. "Because he's five years older than you."

"But why does it *matter*, Miller?" I'd asked.

For a single second we just looked at each other, and then he shut the refrigerator door, grabbed the cooler, and walked off.

I thought he'd just gone back to the beach. It turned out that he'd left us entirely.

I hated how upset Maren was, but I was sad too and couldn't say it aloud.

Sad, and also...guilty. *Why* was I so guilty? Did I really believe some dumb argument in the kitchen had driven Miller off? Of course not. I'd said far worse things to him early on.

No, I just let myself believe that's what it was because the truth—oh God—

The truth was that I'd never wanted him gone for her sake. I wanted him gone because I couldn't stand not having him for myself.

I stumble as I realize it fully for the first time. Yes, I'd suspected pieces of this, but I'd pushed them down, further and further, whenever they threatened to make themselves known.

I was crazy about him from the moment he walked into my mother's dining room and I went on the attack, the way I always did with my mother's awful boyfriends, but for entirely different reasons.

I swallow hard, plowing forward in the darkness, but suddenly the steps take more effort. I'm not the savior I thought I was. I'm a selfish asshole who wanted what my sweet sister had so much that I chose to drive him away.

Gideon shouts at us to take a break. I look at the little I can find of Miller's face beneath the balaclava he's wearing, and he looks at me. Ten years Maren has spent quietly wanting this man, and I've been wanting him too. And I'd really like to go back to repressing this information, but I'm not sure I can.

He reaches into his bag and breaks off a piece of chocolate, then pulls down my balaclava and places it between my lips.

It's hotter and more intimate than a single moment I've ever spent with Blake. He pulls my balaclava back up and I grin. "'Ank you," I say, chewing. "I can offer you a grain-free, sugar-free protein bar in exchange."

"We're not trading, Kitten," he says, but his smile is slight. "I brought it all for you."

Those words could mean nothing, but they hit me hard. Blake and I trade. If one of us gets something, the other gives something. Miller is different. Miller doesn't want to take a thing from me. He just wants to provide. He wants to comfort me when I'm sad, feed me chocolate to make me smile, share his phone so that I'm entertained, stay by my side so I don't fall.

He'd have been the perfect husband for Maren, and I didn't want her to have him. Now, neither of us gets him.

And what a goddamn shame that is, because men like Miller are a once in a lifetime.

Just after five, the sky finally begins to lighten. At first it's black with just a streak of orange along the horizon and then slowly those rays spread, and I discover we are surrounded by ice: a glacier on one side, ice-encrusted trees sweeping below us to the other, and frozen peaks directly ahead.

This would be an amazing place to leave the ashes. I *should* leave them here. I have no idea why I can't do it.

"Wow," I whisper, and Miller grins at me over his shoulder, reaching out for just a moment to grab my gloved hand and give it a squeeze. My heart squeezes right along with the motion. There is no one alive that I would rather be sharing this experience with than him. I take a deep breath of icy air and for a single moment I imagine going through life by Miller's side. Going through life with someone I trust implicitly, someone I don't want to be away from.

After another hour, the summit comes into view, marked by a wooden sign:

*CONGRATULATIONS!*
*YOU ARE NOW AT*
*UHURU PEAK, TANZANIA*
*AFRICA'S HIGHEST POINT*
*WORLD'S HIGHEST FREE-STANDING*
    *MOUNTAIN*

We can't quite get up there since another group is taking pictures, but we're cheering as if we've made it. I turn to Miller and he pulls me against him, his rough beard scratching my cheek as he presses a kiss there. His breath is warm against my ear; his body is solid and reassuring against mine. It's possibly the best hug I've ever received. I could die happily, just like this.

"Selfie," he says, pulling out his phone, "to mark the trip where you stopped hating me."

I brush away tears that I can't even explain to myself. "I'll probably start hating you again once we reach a normal altitude."

He laughs and presses one last kiss to my cheek. "I sort of hope not, Kitten."

When he's done, I rip off one of my gloves and throw it in the snow, then reach into the pocket of my pants for my phone. "Stand over there and I'll get a picture of you," I direct him.

His answering grin is almost bashful, the sweetest thing I've ever seen in my life. I wish I could capture it inside me and hold it forever. I get the phone set up and fix the exposure to capture the light. He smiles, I click, and it's absolutely perfect— a photo I'll never show my sister and will probably never show anyone because I suspect it says too much about me that I took it and will also say too much about me that I *kept* it.

I reach for my glove...just as a gust of wind whips it hurtling over the side of the glacier.

My stomach drops to my feet. "Fuck."

Miller startles and looks in the direction of the glove, as if he is going to jump off the cliff after it.

"It's gone," I tell him. *Fuck.* It's 20 below right now and I am going to be without a glove for at least the next two hours. We've got to trek up to the summit, and then it'll be another hour and a half before the air starts to warm. The odds of me coming out of this without frostbite are zero.

Miller looks at my hand and then rips his own glove off, handing it to me. "Just wear this."

"I'm not taking your glove," I tell him. "I'm the idiot who left mine in the snow. It was stupid."

"I'm not letting you get frostbite," he says firmly.

"I'm not wearing your glove."

"Fine, then we'll both get frostbite," he says, shoving the glove in his backpack.

"Are you fucking kidding me?" I ask, staring at him. "You're being ridiculous."

"I never claimed not to be."

He is so infuriating and so sweet. I guess I could suggest that we alternate wearing it, but no, this is *crazy*. I am not wearing his glove. We are at a standoff.

"Here," he says, reaching out his bare hand to encompass mine. "Ninety-eight-point-six degrees. It's perfect."

"The outside of *your* hand won't be ninety-eight point six," I argue. He grunts at me and shoves our joint hands in his large pocket.

When we reach the summit at last, we do so with our hands linked inside his big, warm pocket.

I can't imagine reaching it any other way.

# 12

## KIT

DAY 7: UHURU PEAK TO MWEKA CAMP

### 18,000 feet to 10,000 feet

The descent happens lightning fast. It took us six hours to reach the summit, but a little over an hour to get back to last night's camp. The gravel skids under our feet—if Gerald were here, I'm sure he'd offer us a dire warning about this. We use climbing poles as we skitter and slide down the hill. It's more like skiing than it is hiking, and it's also more terrifying than anything we've had to do over the past six days.

Miller, as usual, doubts my ability to manage this and remains inches from my side. Now, however, I wouldn't want him to be anywhere else.

Everyone's moving at such varied paces that he decides when the two of us will take a break and pulls me off toward a boulder. It's only as I sit down that I realize my thighs are shaking from the exertion. I never dreamed going down would be this taxing.

He hands me half of a chocolate bar. "You looking forward to getting home?" he asks.

I blink at him. I thought I'd be looking forward to it. I thought I'd be desperate for it. Weirdly, I'm not.

"I'm looking forward to a shower and a real bed and food that isn't stew," I reply. "But the rest of it..." I shrug.

He elbows me. "You've got your supermodel mother's looks and your billionaire father's fortune to spend, and the best you can do is shrug?"

I hitch a shoulder as I pull my balaclava off. Despite the cold, I'm now sweating. "My life is a Tuesday."

His head tilts. "Huh?"

"Thursday, you're excited for the weekend, right?" I ask. "You're making plans. And then you get to the weekend. Friday and Saturday are great. Sunday night is depressing; Monday's just drudgery. You don't want to get out of bed. Tuesday also sucks, but you know that if you keep moving forward, it could get better. My life used to be a Thursday or even a Friday. And now it's a Tuesday. I don't hate my life. I'm just moving through it, waiting to get to a Thursday that never seems to arrive."

His tongue slides over his lip. "So what's Thursday, then? A wedding to this boyfriend you ostensibly love?"

I frown at him, ignoring the dig. "I don't know. I don't know if marriage will make my life Thursday again. Or kids. Or moving up in the company. None of those things necessarily feel like the answer, but if they're not, what is? Do I just stay in bed and hope life will move forward *for* me?"

He's quiet. Maybe he just agrees with my plan, though it seems unlikely. When does Miller agree with anything I'm doing?

"I like Mondays," he says after a moment, partly unzipping his jacket. "I like Tuesdays too. You know why? Because I make my own schedule. I don't have to go into a job I hate, so all the days are good ones. When I worked summers for my dad, doing that grind, I was miserable."

I groan. "I thought you might take my analogy a little more

metaphorically than you did. I'm not talking about the *literal* workweek."

"I know. And I'm not either. I'm saying that maybe the reason you can't escape from Tuesday is because you're on the wrong track, because you're living a life where Tuesdays suck. And you keep trying to make this one set of plans—marrying the idiot and taking over a company you're not all that interested in—work. What if it isn't where you're stuck in this life, but that you're not in the right life at all?"

My eyes fall closed. "I wouldn't have the first clue what to do with my life instead."

His exhale ruffles my hair. "Maybe instead of planning a wedding, you should be trying to figure that out."

I say nothing, but it's been hitting me more and more on this trip—how much I miss the way I felt with Rob. I'd thought I was ready to go through life without it and now, looking over at Miller's concerned face...I'm not quite so sure.

EVENTUALLY, we reach Kosovo. The porters cheer for us as tears roll down my face.

It seemed like we were climbing to the summit forever, as if it would never end, and now it has...and I wish I had more time. Not a month. Not even a week. Just a handful more of these simultaneously peaceful-yet-anxious, boring-yet-thrilling days with him.

I laugh as I brush tears away, and Miller wraps an arm around me. "It's okay, Kit," he says, plucking the water bottle from my hand. "Get out of your clothes while I refill these."

I dive into the tent and strip, then quickly wipe myself down and put on a fresh base layer. If I never have to wear another sweaty jog bra for the rest of my life, it will still be too soon.

Miller taps on the pole just as I'm sliding into my sleeping bag and I shout that he can come in.

"I assume you won't be offering me a similar amount of privacy?" he asks, grinning.

"What tipped you off?"

"Well, the fact that you're already in your sleeping bag was the first clue."

I laugh and roll toward the outside of the tent. "I already got an eyeful the last time," I reply, closing my eyes. "I'm covered."

The clothing he's removed lands just behind my ear. "You sure?" he asks, his voice a low growl, and I clench at the sound.

In a parallel universe, one in which I'm not nearly engaged, one in which he isn't the love of my sister's life, I'd roll over and take a nice long look.

And then I'd pull him down on top of me and it wouldn't matter in the least that neither of us had showered in seven days. I'd welcome every dirty inch of him.

*Repeatedly.*

"Positive," I reply, but my voice is wispy, threadbare.

I am not positive. At all.

When I hear him climb into his sleeping bag, I roll in his direction and tear up again. It's just exhaustion making me so emotional, but it's still embarrassing.

"You did it, Kitten," he says, squeezing my hand. "I'm so proud of you."

I smile. "I'm glad you were with me for it."

"Me too."

When we wake two hours later, we are still holding hands.

WE'RE the first ones in the dining tent. Miller smiles when the plate of stew is placed in front of me. "Tell me the first food you are going to eat when we get back," he says.

I groan. "You know what I want? And it won't make much sense given how cold it is, but I want an ice cream sundae. No, scratch that—a brownie sundae with ice cream and hot fudge and nuts and whipped cream. And a cherry. Multiple cherries."

"You've come a long way from the girl who didn't want to have any sugar in her coffee."

"Right now, I would like to pour sugar packets in my open mouth," I respond. "What about you?"

He closes his eyes. "A steak," he says, running his tongue over his lower lip as if he is already tasting it. I picture that tongue in ways I should not and banish the image. "A steak, covered in melting butter, with a baked potato. No, a *loaded* baked potato, dripping in cheese and bacon."

"Okay, that sounds good. What's after that?"

His eyes sweep over my face. "After that, I think I would want something very different."

My breath stops right in the center of my throat. If I didn't know better, I'd say that he was referring to sex, and if I really, *really* didn't know better, I'd say that he was referring to sex with me.

I shouldn't allow my head to go in that direction, but it's been a long day, and I am excruciatingly relaxed, so I allow myself to picture it—the way he would kiss, and the way his beard would be rough against my skin. The way his hands would roam, beginning at my waist and sliding lower, tightening around my hips as he pulled me against him.

And when that happened, I would reach for his belt and then his zipper, and when his jeans fell to the floor, I'd let my palm slide against him, rock hard, eager for friction.

That's when he would take charge, kicking off the jeans entirely and lifting me. Carrying me to the bed, landing above me, every bit as eager for what comes next as I am.

Stacy walks into the dining tent. "I don't know what y'all were thinking about, but it sure isn't this stew."

My gaze meets Miller's. His eyes are burning.

"Ice cream," I whisper at the same moment that he says, "Steak."

I suspect he was lying too.

WE RETURN to our tent to pack up our bags for the second to last time. I want a bed and a closet and regular food, yes, but I'm already sad at leaving this behind.

He dumps his daypack out on his sleeping bag and so do I —we'll need entirely different things for this warmer climb down to the final camp than we did heading to the summit. "So, are you going to call your dad tomorrow and admit you were wrong about everything?"

"Of course not," I reply, tightly rolling up my filthy clothes and shoving them to the bottom of my bag. "He's already way too confident about his dumb ideas. I'm not encouraging him."

"Not all his ideas are dumb," Miller says. "Like having you stalk me here."

I roll my eyes. "You don't actually believe that, right? There are eight routes and a million tour companies. He couldn't possibly have known what route you were climbing or with whom."

He shakes his head, pausing in his own packing to meet my gaze. "No, I don't think he had you stalk me. I think he heard me talk about it and thought it might be just the thing to make you see the light."

I groan, preparing to be annoyed. "And what light is that?"

"Kit, you say that your life is a Tuesday. Well, let me point out what your life consists of: first, a guy you never even *mention,* and you know why? Because he doesn't factor into anything. You don't need him, and you might care about him, but I don't think you love him."

"I told you I'm just a private person."

"Bullshit," Miller says, throwing a candy bar from his daypack onto my sleeping bag. Even when he's arguing with me, he's trying to take care of me. "And you know what else? I know the guy, and he's not good enough for you. Not even close. You deserve someone who has your back."

"I don't *need* anyone to have my back. I've got my own back."

"Yeah," Miller says, "but you shouldn't have to. And you belong with someone who wants to have it for you."

I swallow hard. Miller's had my back this week. He's wanted to have it, too, even when he pretended he didn't. And I loved that he was there, but if he's going to wind up with any of the Fischer girls, it won't be me.

"The other thing you haven't mentioned all week is your job," he continues, rolling up his sleeping bag.

"That doesn't mean anything. Lots of people didn't discuss work."

"Do you know what Leah does?" he demands. "What Stacy and Adam and Alex and Maddie do? Yes, because they've all mentioned it. Over the course of seven days, you haven't mentioned Fischer-Harris *once*. You know what you *have* discussed? Maddie's epilepsy meds. Adam's creaky knees. That growth on Gideon's neck. You memorized everyone's oxygenation and spent an entire afternoon pondering how repeated exposure to altitude might impact the porters' longevity."

I frown at him. He's not wrong. I spend a lot of time, day to day, thinking about health. It fascinates me in a way that publishing does not. But not everything you're interested in has to be a career. "I already told you. I don't want the responsibility."

He cinches the bag his porter will carry. "What that doctor said was right. The fact that you take it seriously means you're one of the few people who's really ready for the responsibility it entails."

"So you want me to give up a cushy job with tons of money so I can go back to school for five years and take on way more stress for way less money?"

"No," he says, motioning me off my sleeping bag, which he begins rolling up for me. "I want you to be *full*. I want every one of your days to feel like a Thursday rather than a Tuesday. And it seems to me that the track you chose back before you were a little broken by life is probably the one that will make you the happiest."

I shake my head. "I'd be thirty-four when I was done."

"You'll be thirty-four either way," he says. "Do you want to be thirty-four at a job you hate or at a job you love?"

He may, once again, have a point.

We get our stuff packed and begin hiking again, descending five thousand feet to Mweka Camp for our last night out in the wild.

I talk to Maddie on the way down about her MSW program. She responds in whispers, which is kind of sad because it isn't something she should have to keep a secret.

But I guess we've both got things we don't want to discuss aloud, because when she asks what the plans are for my engagement, my stomach sinks.

Miller was right earlier. I've barely thought about Blake over the past few days, which is telling in and of itself. What I've thought about, to the exclusion of all else, is Miller. And even if he's off-limits, I now know I'm still capable of wanting someone so much that my bones ache with desire. Marrying Blake isn't fair to anyone, isn't fair to Blake *especially*, because if another Miller comes along a decade from now...I can't swear I'd let him walk away.

"I think maybe I'm going to end it," I tell Maddie. "I don't have a lot of time. I know my mom's planning something for late March that sounds like an engagement party, and I'm just not ready. I sort of suspect I'll never be ready."

"My brother will be thrilled," she says, "but I'm guessing he's not who you're interested in." She glances back at Miller, twenty feet behind us.

"I'm not interested in anyone," I insist, but it sounds exactly like the lie it is.

Blake was the perfect middle ground between everything I wanted and everything I didn't want. I was willing to compromise because it didn't feel like I had a choice. I was willing to run the London marathon rather than something more far-flung. I was willing to move to the suburbs though I dreaded the commute. No one forced me to live this life full of Tuesdays. I chose it for myself. And Blake is the biggest Tuesday of all.

*Haven't you ever been so crazy about someone that the rest of the world seemed to pale by contrast?* Miller had asked me that night in the tent.

The answer was *yes, once.*

And now the answer is *yes, twice.*

Miller shines so bright for me now that I can barely see anyone but him.

WE REACH Mweka Camp at dusk. We are filthy and exhausted, but it's our last night and the air is so warm and oxygen-rich that I've got more energy than I've had in days.

We eat our final dinner together—surprising no one, it's a mysterious stew full of unidentifiable ingredients—talking about the first thing we'll do when we get to the hotel ("shower" is everyone's answer aside from Maddie, who wants to go on social media).

After dinner, we pull our chairs out and sit under a canopy of stars because this is it, our last night, and it's warm enough to stand the chill. We talk about what we'll eat when we get home. Our favorite memories of the trip. What a dick

Gerald was. The hardest moments of trying to reach the summit this morning, though it now feels like a million years ago.

And then Leah asks who brought booze and several nervous hands are raised, since none of us were *supposed* to have brought alcohol onto the mountain. Stacy expresses dismay that Alex and Maddie both brought flasks before admitting that she and Adam did as well.

"Let's play Never Have I Ever," suggests Leah.

"I don't think I wanna play that with my *parents*," Maddie says.

"I don't think I want to play with my kids," says Stacy with a laugh, but she and Adam finally decide they'll be the ones to turn in.

Kindly, they leave us their flask.

"Never have I ever given a blow job," says Maddie.

Everyone drinks, indicating they *have* given a blow job, aside from Miller.

"What?" Maddie gasps at her brother.

He shrugs. "I'm open to experimenting."

"Never have I ever cheated on someone," I say.

Once again, Miller is the only one who doesn't drink, and I'm a little surprised by that—not that I necessarily thought he was a cheater, but I guess that the speed with which he dumped Maren always led me to believe that he thought women were expendable once upon a time.

"Never have I ever received or given anal sex," says Leah, keeping it classy as always. She then drinks and all of the rest of us drink as well. When my flask lowers, Miller is watching me, and he appears unhappy with my answer, which is ridiculous. He drank too.

"Never have I ever dumped someone by text," I say, annoyed that he was judging me.

Miller frowns at me and drinks. Everyone else drinks as

well, so I guess that it wasn't quite as unusual and terrible as I'd thought it was at the time.

"Never have I ever been with two people at once," says Maddie.

Leah drinks. Alex drinks and then, with a shrug, Miller drinks, and a fiery pulse of irritation flares in my chest, though I have no idea why.

"Never have I ever wanted somebody that I was not supposed to want," Miller says, his gaze holding mine.

I hesitate. I am *not* going to drink. But there's a challenge in his eyes, daring me to tell the truth for once. And the truth is that I have never, in my entire life, wanted someone quite this much. That just his gaze on me now is enough to make my every muscle tighten, to send a rush of heat between my legs. He could make me come in two seconds flat if I let him try tonight. He wouldn't even have to remove the base layer. He could probably just roll on top of me and kiss my neck and I'd go off like a nuclear explosion.

I pick up my flask and take a sip. He picks up his, too, and drinks, holding my eye the entire time.

The game ends relatively quickly because we run out of things everyone has done, aside from Leah, who's apparently done everything and everyone, and wants to add Miller to that list, judging by the way she kept eye-fucking him during the game.

"Hey, thanks for helping Gerald," she says as we walk to the bathroom. It's a weird thing to bring up, several days after the fact.

I shrug. "I didn't do much."

"We aren't really a couple," she says. "He offered to pay for the trip if I came with him. It was just kind of, you know, a trade."

I am tempted to point out that this is essentially prostitution, but I don't care enough to bother.

"Well, now you get the trip and a tent to yourself without putting up with him," I reply.

"Yeah," she says, looking at the ground and scuffing her foot. "That's sort of why I stopped you. I just thought that since you and Miller are always bickering and it seemed like you guys were a little pissed at each other tonight, we could switch? I don't mind sharing a tent with him if that works better for you."

Holy shit. This girl's "boyfriend" just got carried down the side of a mountain, and she's already looking to fuck someone else. If I were a better person, I wouldn't fault her for it, but I am not a better person and therefore, I do. "We're good," I reply somewhat coolly. "Thanks anyway."

It comes out sounding an awful lot like "*Nice try.*"

She gives me a small, tight smile. "Well, maybe I should check with him."

"Knock yourself out," I snap, walking into the bathroom. It's just an expression obviously, but I am literally hoping she somehow gets knocked out before she gets a chance to ask. Because she's a pretty girl and he's apparently somewhat single...so why wouldn't he go for it?

I return to the tent, pull off everything but my base layer, and slide into the sleeping bag. This time tomorrow I'll have a shower and a soft bed and cell service. I'd thought those things would matter more than they do.

"Is it safe to come in?" Miller asks from outside.

"Suddenly, you care about that," I reply acidly.

He unzips the tent, and I brace myself to watch him packing up his gear, explaining the situation. Instead, he removes his boots and his pants and then his jacket until he is stripped down to his base layer. And then he removes his shirt entirely.

*Damn.*

"What are we watching tonight?" he asks, sliding into the sleeping bag beside mine.

I blink at him. "Didn't Leah ask you to share her tent?" I sound embarrassingly bitter rather than nonchalant.

There's a glimmer of something in his eyes—a smile he is trying to hide. "Yes, she asked. I told her I was happy with the tentmate I have. I guess you told her the same thing."

"I don't know that I said I was *happy* necessarily," I mutter.

He grins, and that dimple of his makes my stomach spin and swirl in the most delicious way. "Well, we're both here," he says, "so I'll ask you again: what are we watching?"

I smile back at him, weirdly grateful that he has chosen me over her when I shouldn't be. It feels as if I've spent a great deal of my life waiting for Miller to choose me, and tonight, he finally has.

FOR SOME REASON, the camp is entirely deserted. The tents are ruffled by the wind, which whispers through the brush. It's just me and Miller, standing ten feet apart. His dimple tucks into his cheek, and he looks both cocky and shy at once, such an unexpected combination in a man like him. When the smile fades out, I miss it.

I close the distance between us and press my thumb to the place where that dimple will exist when he smiles for me again. All his emotion now rests in his eyes, entirely focused on mine. He grabs my hand before I can pull it back, and then his mouth lowers.

There is nothing tentative about the kiss on my end or his. It is hungry and certain, something I know has existed inside me all along. It's waited feverishly for a decade, and it's not about to stop now.

He makes this sound low in his chest—a growl, a grumble —and then he is pulling me closer, and I need more and more of all of this. I need to feel his skin beneath this mountain of clothing that separates us. I want to be spread around him, glued to him, until I can't tell where he ends and I begin.

*The clothes, though. All these fucking clothes.* I am twisted and tangled and kissing him, and he is kissing me and—

"Fuck," I gasp.

I'm in the tent, still in my sleeping bag, but half on top of Miller, who I have apparently molested, though with the way his hand is wrapped around the back of my neck and tangled in my hair, he seems to have participated fairly willingly himself. His eyes open, and he looks as astonished as I feel.

"Sorry," he says. "Fuck, sorry."

I roll off of him as if I am on fire.

"Don't," I say, winded with shock...and other things. "I'm clearly the one responsible for that. I was just having this dream and...God. Never mind. I'm incredibly sorry. Can we forget that happened?"

He exhales heavily, running a hand through his hair. Even through two sleeping bags and our thermals, I definitely felt how badly *he* wanted it.

"That must've been quite a dream," he finally says.

Not if my life depended upon it would I admit that the dream was about him. "Yeah. I'm not even sure what it was about. Something from college. What were you dreaming?"

"I wasn't asleep, Kitten," he says. "I just didn't realize you *were.*"

It punches all the air from my chest.

Neither of us utters another word.

# 13

## KIT

DAY 8: MWEKA CAMP TO MWEKA GATE

**10,000 feet to 5500 feet**

"Good morning," calls Joseph for the final time, tapping on a tent pole.

I blink my eyes open and find myself facing Miller.

"Good morning," Miller calls back, watching my face.

*I wasn't asleep, Kitten.*

The memory of those words alone is enough to make my stomach clench with want. I have no idea if what I remember of last night was a dream or reality. Did we actually kiss, and if we did, was it as good as I remember? Did he actually groan?

I'll go to my grave without those answers because there's absolutely no way to ask.

"Maren still likes you," I blurt out.

His brow furrows, and then he releases a confused laugh. "*What?*"

It's so incredibly disloyal that I'm telling him this, and she'd be horrified, but I need to know that he will never, ever allude to what happened—or nearly happened—between us last night. In fact, I need to know that he won't go back and mention *anything* about me—that we spoke, that we were friendly, and most of all, that we shared a tent.

"It's just her personality. She's a romantic, and she's got it in her head that you're the one who got away." I sigh. "I know that sounds crazy, but her marriage sucks. Harvey is a dick, and I think she clings to this idea of you because she needs to feel hopeful about something."

His eyes are wide. He sits up, running his hands through his hair. I wish he'd put on a shirt—I can see about a million rippling muscles right now. "What's there to be hopeful *about*?" he demands. "Kit, I broke up with her ten years ago and we only dated for a few months. How could she possibly think..."

I sit up, searching my side of the tent for a ponytail holder. "She thinks—well, everyone thinks—that you left because I was such a bitch to you all the time. That I drove you off somehow, because, to be honest, I've done it to people before."

He climbs out of the sleeping bag...wearing only boxer briefs. For a moment, I'm remembering the press of him between my legs. The *substantial* press between my legs. My gaze jerks away.

"From what I've heard, you had every fucking reason to drive those people away," he says tightly, sliding on his hiking pants.

I finish twisting my hair up. "Yeah, but I was a bitch to you for no reason at all, so in their eyes, it was just Kit being Kit," I admit. "I didn't even tell her you were on this trip because I was worried it would get her daydreaming about ways this could lead you guys back together."

He stares at me, that brow still furrowed, something dark in his eyes. "Why are you telling me this?"

My cheeks heat. His gaze travels over the path of that blood rushing to my face with something that looks a lot like affection.

I glance away. "Because when we get back, it's really important that no one hears we shared a tent. Or, you know, the thing last night."

*I wasn't asleep, Kitten.*

God. That will never stop being hot to me.

He pulls on a T-shirt at last. "I kind of figured the fact that you've got a boyfriend would be the bigger issue."

It's almost laughable, how little I care about Blake's reaction —maybe that's because I already know I'm ending it when I get home—but it would matter far less than Maren's even if I weren't.

"Maren is my best friend, and she'd do anything for me. If I'm going to slap someone in the face, it will never be her."

His tongue darts between his lips as if he's about to argue, and then his jaw locks. "I wasn't going to say anything."

"Thanks."

"But that's fucking crazy," he adds, climbing out of the tent.

THE EXCITEMENT IS at fever pitch over breakfast. We dine on eggs and sausages and fried bread—three foods I will never willingly eat again—and talk about our firsts again with the ravenous awe of people coming off a month-long fast.

What's the first thing you'll drink? Most of us want Coke. Alex wants beer.

What's the first thing you'll do? Everyone says *shower.*

What's the second thing you'll do? Half of us claim we will shower a second time.

"I want a bed," Maddie says. "And a real pillow."

"And clothes that don't have any silt on them," I add, because the dust that got all over everything at Shira One never fully left.

"What about you, Miller?" asks Stacy. "You're very quiet this morning."

He looks up from his plate, slightly blank, as if he wasn't listening. His smile is forced. "Coke, then beer, two showers, a real pillow."

I wonder if I'm the only one who notices the unhappiness in his voice beneath it all.

We begin the final trek to the Mweka Gate after breakfast, descending five thousand feet over the course of three hours. My energy is endless this morning...aside from the incident with Miller, it was the best night's sleep I've had since I left New York, and the downhill climb is so easy it's hard to believe it's still considered exercise.

The path turns muddy as we enter the rainforest, and my feet begin to slip, but it's hard to slow down when the hike is easy for the first time the entire trip.

Miller is close to my back, clearly worried that I am going to wipe out if he's not there to catch me. A week ago, I'd have told him to fuck off. Now I just love that he's watching out for me, which he's done this entire trip, even when I was being a bitch to him.

"Slow down, Kit," he warns.

"I'm fine." I look back over my shoulder at him. "Worry about your—"

My feet fly out from under me. Miller lunges and grabs me before I go face-first into the jagged rocks below and suddenly I'm pressed tight to his chest, which is rising and falling fast.

"Jesus," he whispers. "You scared the shit out of me."

We are too close, and I don't want it to end, but it has to. I step backward quickly. "Thanks for—"

The words are barely out of my mouth when he has snatched me back to him and turned me so that my spine is pressed to the wall of boulders behind me. His mouth is a millimeter from mine.

I'm not sure what we're doing, but my breathing seems to have stopped. It's a half second at most, but I'm strung so tight that I can't think, can't move, can't breathe. The force of how badly I want Miller is like a virus, coursing through my blood.

I can hear last night's groan in my head as if it's happening in real time. I would give up decades just to have Miller's mouth on mine once more.

A porter is humming as he approaches from above. Miller releases me.

"Thanks," I say again, still breathless. As if the moment he spun me against that rock never happened. As if he just kept me from falling and set me politely on my feet.

I turn and continue to walk toward the gate, more careful than I was.

I need to be a lot more careful on many fronts.

After another hour, the buzz of the forest grows louder, and the trail flattens out. Everyone's pace quickens, as if we can sense our proximity to civilization somehow. The porters sing, Leah belts out a few more show tunes, and everyone continues to talk about showering until we reach the bustling Mweka Gate, where porters are already stashing the bags on top of our bus.

I'm too thrilled by the sight of a real shop to be sad that it's over. We go inside and buy Cokes, then sit around an outdoor table to drink them.

"God, I've missed carbonation," says Maddie. "Carbonation, I'll never leave you again."

Stacy laughs. "Not so fast," she says. "You haven't heard about the trip I'm planning for next year."

Maddie glances at Alex. "I don't know if I can go," she says. "I, uh, was going to wait until we got home to tell you, but I got into grad school. I'm gonna get my MSW."

Everyone looks at Adam. Even *my* breath holds.

"Honey, that's fantastic," he says, eyes shining with pride. "You'll make an amazing therapist."

Her smile is relieved. "Thanks, Dad." She glances at Alex again, and he shakes his head. Maybe he's not ready to tell his dad or perhaps he thinks it will be too many defections at once.

I hope he makes the break eventually. I hope I make the break, too. It's easy to think you'll change course when it's still a week and thousands of miles away. It's harder when all the forces that put you there are once again front and center.

We tip the porters and thank them before we climb on the bus and Miller takes the row behind mine as we collapse into incredibly plush seats. Did I notice how soft these were on the way in? Not for a minute. They're *amazing*.

"I think I'm starting to understand your six-month rule," I tell him.

He grins. "Wanna come to Everest with me next summer?"

He's joking, but there's a pang in my chest anyway. Because...yes, I would like that. A lot.

I force a smile. "You saw how I floundered on the *easy* climb, Miller."

We fall silent after that. We were both joking...but also not joking. This is really coming to an end and neither of us will be able to make it last.

On the drive back, we pass through Arusha. After a week in the mountains, it looks almost *too* busy, too crowded, when it's just a tiny fraction of New York City. It's also wildly different. Barefoot children stir up dust as they run past a gas station, kicking a can to each other. A stooped old man, the skin hanging from his bones, walks down a road that has no end in sight. A line of people—men, women, and children—stretches down a block, looking absolutely miserable in the bright sun. They're waiting to enter a tiny medical clinic, so small I doubt that half the people here can be served in a week, much less a day.

Miller looks at me. "Don't say it," I warn him.

"I don't have to say it," he replies. "You're already thinking it."

He's right. I am. I always wanted to be a doctor, and if I'd gotten my degree...I could help. Even if I messed up, wouldn't that be better than situations like the one we're witnessing here? Because there are children in that line suffering, children who will probably wait all day and never be seen, people who will give up on the line when they desperately need care.

How dare I claim that it's too much responsibility when the result is unnecessary suffering? I told myself at the time that I was recognizing my own limitations, but really I was just scared and selfish.

God. How could I have been wrong about so many things? Work, Blake...if my father hadn't sent me on this trip, I would've fucked it all up.

"What?" asks Miller as I shake my head.

I laugh. "I just realized I'm going to have to tell my dad he was right. Which absolutely sucks."

Our bus slows as we enter the gates of the resort. As we climb off, a staff member hands us flutes of rum punch and cool towels. We have definitely put hardship behind us.

I've just finished wiping my face when Miller stiffens beside me, staring at the couple moving our way—who are beaming at him as if he's their favorite person.

"*Fuck*," Miller hisses quietly.

"We just had to thank you again for switching," the woman says, setting her bag down on a marble bench behind her. "The Machame route was amazing, and the money is letting us stay to do a safari instead of rushing home."

"It was nothing," Miller says, with a tense smile. "Glad it worked out."

"It wasn't nothing," she insists. "We saved for years to come on this trip, and our plan was to start saving again...now we get to do all of it."

I wait until they've walked away and we've each grabbed a second flute of rum punch before I raise a brow at Miller. "Care to explain that?"

He sighs, looking so woefully embarrassed that I almost feel sorry for him. "I was worried about you going up alone," he admits. "I offered to pay for their trip if they'd switch with me."

He wanted to make sure someone had my back. He wanted to be the person who had it. And he was. It says more than a thousand of Blake's proclamations. Because Blake would never have done what Miller did. And I wouldn't have wanted him to.

I should totally give him shit for saying that I was stalking *him*, but tears spring to my eyes instead. "You paid them to switch, and you came on a longer, much easier route. For me."

"I enjoyed it, Kit," he says. "I wouldn't give up the past eight days for anything."

I smile at him through my tears. "Yeah, me neither."

Maddie and Stacy walk toward us. "We're going into town for dinner tonight. You guys in?"

I should say no. My flight leaves at the crack of dawn, but I don't want to leave these people yet. Mostly, I don't want to leave one person.

I look up at Miller, who shrugs as he glances down at me...the ball's in my court. "Yeah, we're in," I tell them.

I'm stunned by what I see in the mirror when I finally enter my tent. I'd sort of expected to look the same, but...Jesus. My hair is greasy and wild. My face is tan despite all that careful SPF usage. I have a bruise on my forehead—I'm not even sure what *that's* from—and a smear of mud going into my hairline that I hope has only been there today. Despite all the candy, I've definitely lost weight. My mother will applaud this, but she's psychotic. I look skeletal.

My appearance makes it seem even less likely that Miller was about to kiss me today. Was he just stopping me to confirm I was okay? Did I stand there like an idiot, dazed by lust? How humiliating.

I step into the shower. Despite all those wet wipes I used, the water runs brown at my feet, and I can *feel* it as the dirt caked on my skin begins to erode away.

I shampoo once, and then a second time. I shave every last millimeter of hair off my body, aside from the mess atop my head. I soap everything thoroughly and repeat that as well.

When I look at the mirror again as I step out, I'm slightly more myself. I don a plush hotel robe, dry my hair, then go to the bed with the phone I'd left charging, where a mountain of texts await— my friends Mallory and Lo sending memes; Blake sending me a couple of incredibly dumb videos of toddlers falling in the snow; Maren giving me the blow-by-blow of potty training her new puppy and sending designs for my condo, which she's dying to decorate; my mother demanding I tell a contractor she wants her deposit back, and asking if I want her to make a hair appointment for me because I'll "probably need one" before her birthday party, scheduled a few days after I return.

None of it makes me miss home. It just leaves me overwhelmed and empty at the same time. I set the phone on the nightstand, and then turn face down on the pillow and cry myself to sleep.

WHEN I WAKE, I open the suitcase that they kept here for me and go through my things.

I pull on jeans and a nice tank and have just added some mascara when there's a knock on the pillar supporting my tent.

"Come in," I call, emerging from the bathroom just as Miller ducks through the tent flaps.

"You've shaved," I say at the same time he says, "*Your hair.*"

We both laugh. I cross the room and let my palm slide over his jaw. My skin tingles everywhere we connect. "You look so much younger without it."

He holds still, watching me do it, not stopping me. The tension between us is so thick I can barely breathe.

"It felt so good to get rid of it." His voice is a low rumble in his chest.

I pull my hand back, though I don't want to.

"I was just going to put on some gloss," I say, walking to the bathroom.

"You don't need it," he replies, but he watches me smooth it over my mouth with my index finger as if I'm the pivotal scene of his favorite movie.

We shared a tent for a week, but right now there's a big, soft bed separating us, and he's watching me that way, and...

There's only one thing I want right now, and it isn't dinner in town.

"I'm ready," I tell him. I sound like I'm once again in need of oxygen.

We meet the Arnaults at the gate, and a car takes us into Arusha. We all agree that we probably should try the local cuisine, but when we spy a Chinese restaurant, we groaningly agree we can try the local cuisine later.

It's not the best Chinese food I've ever had, but I eat with relish as more and more platters are brought to the table while Maddie demands everyone name the most awkward moment of the trip.

"I learned some things about you around the campfire that I'd rather not know," Alex offers. "That's mine."

Maddie raises a brow. "You made some startling revelations of your own, but my vote for the most awkward moment was when you learned that Kit had a boyfriend."

Alex laughs. "Thanks, Maddie. I suppose this is now the second most awkward moment." He raises a beer in my direction. "Can't blame a guy for trying."

"I'm not sure that's true," grumbles Miller.

When the meal concludes, we crack open our fortune cookies.

"Your high-minded principles spell success," reads Alex, "in bed."

"A dream you have will come true," reads Adam, "in bed. Uh-oh." He grins at his wife.

"Gross, Dad," says Maddie. "Please stop."

"From small beginnings come great things...in bed," I say aloud. I hand it to Miller. "Here you go, buddy. Give yourself a little pep talk with that when you're home."

Everyone laughs, but his eyes catch mine, and there's a smirk on his face confirming something I was already pretty sure of: there'd be nothing small about it.

After dinner, Maddie and Alex convince us to walk to a bar across the street, where we all clink our bottles together and toast the end of the trip. The Arnaults still have another day in Tanzania. Miller leaves for his safari tomorrow, and I leave for New York at the crack of dawn. I'm suddenly wishing I'd planned it differently.

I wish I could stay.

The dance floor is crowded, the music varying wildly— country, pop, rap. They put on something salsa-ish, and when Alex demands that I dance with him as he refuses to dance with his mother and sister, I follow him onto the floor. He shows me the basic three steps to the dance and insists that I stop watching my feet. Eventually, I comply.

"So if things fall through with him," Alex says nodding toward Miller, "give me a call."

"As I have said many times, I am not *with* Miller," I reply, raising a brow.

"Oh really, *Kitten?*" he asks with a sly smile. "Look, I know you have a boyfriend or whatever, but you cannot expect me to believe that there is nothing going on there. If not on your end, there definitely is on his."

"I assure you there is not. When I leave here, I won't see him again for ages." The thought brings a lump to my throat.

He spins me. "Let's put this to a little test then."

"A test?"

"Hang on." He walks to the DJ booth and returns a moment later. "I asked him to play a slow song after this. A hundred bucks says that Miller is over here the *second* it starts because he's not about to let you slow dance with anyone else. He barely wanted to let you dance with me to *this,* and we're a foot apart."

I roll my eyes. "This is the easiest hundred bucks I'll ever make."

"We'll see," he replies.

But when the final notes of the song fade away and "A Thousand Years" by Christina Perri begins, Miller appears back beside us.

"I'm reclaiming Kit," he says firmly—not a request. A demand. Alex releases me, winking behind Miller's back and mouthing the words *one hundred bucks.*

"What's all the smiling about?" Miller asks.

I shake my head. "Alex being dumb."

I should probably tell Miller I'm done, but when his hand slides to the small of my back and jerks me against him, I go willingly. His hold is exactly as possessive as I knew it would be.

"I'm shocked you're out here," I tell him. "It runs contrary to the whole 'I'm ruggedly masculine' thing."

"I didn't realize you found me ruggedly masculine."

"That was *you* saying you were ruggedly masculine—not me. It was pretty arrogant of you, actually."

He pulls me closer. My cheek is pressed to his sternum and his chin rests against the top of my head. I breathe him in—soap and fabric softener—and count the beats of his heart beneath my ear. Maybe, in some parallel world, there's a version of me that doesn't have to walk away, and that version will smile at him when the song ends, grateful that he's hers, eager to strip him out of that T-shirt and fall asleep against his bare chest.

Among other things.

We don't say another word during the three-minute duration of the song, but I know even as it's happening that I will replay these three minutes in my head for the rest of my natural life.

The song's dying notes echo across the floor. Miller is slow to release me, and I'm slower to move away. When I glance up at him, neither of us is smiling. This is, obviously, all we're going to get. This dance—this trip. It should have been more, but my primary regret is that I didn't relish every second. That from the moment I first saw him at the airport, I ever willingly left his side, that I slept at all when I could have been staring at his sleeping profile instead.

"Well," I whisper, "I guess we should head out."

His finger slides into the waistband of my jeans to keep me in place.

"Kit," he says, his gaze burning straight through me, "tell me you're not marrying that guy."

My shoulders sag. In some ways, this moment makes me think that I *should* marry Blake. That when I fall for someone, it's always *this*...It's always intensely painful. It always leads to this thing inside me that aches and can't seem to stop, and now instead of aching for Rob, I get to ache for him and Miller both.

"No," I reply. "I'm going to end it when I get home."

His mouth opens and then shuts as if there were words there, words he'd be better off not saying. It's for the best. "Good."

I walk off the dance floor, him in my wake. The Arnaults want to stay for another beer, so we hug them goodbye and exchange contact info, and then Miller and I walk out, him close to my side as he hails a cab, his arm around me as if to warn the world that I'm not fair game.

He's been here, at this exact place, for the entire trip.

He was right, when he said that even if I didn't need someone to have my back, I might want to be with a man who'd have it anyway.

I do. God, I really, really do.

We are silent on the ride to the resort. The cab drops us off at the gated entrance and we walk toward the tents.

"How much are you looking forward to that bed?" he asks.

I know it's entirely in my head, but even hearing him utter the word *bed* sounds dirty to me. I am not thinking about the quality of the sheets or the softness of the mattress. I'm thinking about the way it would feel to be pressed into it beneath his weight.

"You know what's funny?" I ask. "The night we got here, I was bitching about that room to my dad. I was furious."

He laughs quietly. "Knowing your father, he did not feel nearly as guilty as you'd have hoped."

I shake my head. "He didn't feel guilty at all. I told him if I was murdered, I was going to hold him responsible, and he said that technically if I were murdered, I couldn't hold anyone responsible. Completely unrepentant."

Miller laughs. "Yep, that sounds like Henry. I was pretty pissed at him that night myself. I still can't believe he sent you. Things could have gone really wrong."

We've reached my tent. I stop and turn toward him. "I was fine. I had you looking after me, right?"

He gives me a half smile that fades too quickly. "I've got to tell you something. I mean, it's not really a bad thing, so I *don't* have to tell you, but I don't feel right lying about it anymore."

My stomach begins a long, slow dive. I have faith in very few men, but he was one of them, and I don't want to be disappointed. "What is it?"

He bites his lip. "There was nothing wrong with my tent."

I laugh, half relieved and half confused. "*What?*"

"There was nothing wrong with my tent. I was just worried about you sleeping alone, and I was undoubtedly being paranoid, but...my tent was fine. I collapsed it myself and told the porters that you and I decided to share."

I stare at him for a second, dumbfounded, and then I start to laugh. "You asshole. That's so sweet, but *oh my God.*"

He grins. "I'd tell you I'm sorry, but I'm not."

Tears spring to my eyes. "I'm not sorry either."

Somehow, in eight days' time, I'm leaving here feeling as if he's my best friend, the person I'm closest to. I have no regrets.

Well, I have one regret. It's that he can't remain my best friend, my everything, when we go home. After tonight, he is always going to be a stranger to me.

"Well," I say, glancing toward my tent, trying to subtly dry my eyes, "I should—"

"Kit," he says, pulling me toward him.

His hands cradle my jaw, and he pulls my mouth to his. It's soft and it's hard; it's kind and it's also relentless. His kiss is everything I knew it would be, and if I have ever been kissed like this, I certainly don't remember it. Not even with Rob.

It's the kind of kiss you could lose yourself in for a very long time. I have to force myself to stop.

I take a step backward, my breath coming too fast. My mouth opens, but he shakes his head. "I know," he says. "It's just something I had to do."

I nod and turn for my tent. I'm not sure how long he remains outside, but I never hear him walk away.

ONLY A FEW HOURS LATER, the sun is rising, and it's time for me to leave for the airport.

There's a pang in my chest as I walk toward the waiting car. I turn at the last minute, surveying the tents around me. I sort of love the people who still sleep in each of them. I know we've said our goodbyes, but I want to say them again.

Or better, I want to say, *"You know what? Why don't I stay? What if we all go on a safari together? Miller and I can share a room."*

Miller and I would go get some coffee. We'd wander through Arusha and try a local breakfast that didn't involve any foods we ate during the climb. We could even go to that clinic with the line that went down the street, just to understand if the issue is staffing or infrastructure. Between Miller's family and mine, we'd have the money to solve it. And then we'd go back to his room and watch *30 Rock* and—

"Miss?" asks the bellman.

I blink, turning away from the tents and facing the car door held open for me.

"Sorry," I whisper, climbing in. "Thanks."

All I wanted when I arrived was to get the hell out, and now I don't ever want to leave.

The driver begins to move down the road. I don't look backward. It hurts enough as it is.

At the airport, I begin to see that Miller was right when he said I'd be different after the trip. I no longer feel the punch of anxiety as I go through security or when people start lining up to get on the plane. When I'm jostled from behind, my first thought isn't that someone's trying to steal my bag; I'm not in a manic rush to disembark when we land in Doha; I don't panic that someone's not going to let me out into the aisle, that my next gate might be seventeen miles away.

I doubt it will last long, but just being able to see the world through new eyes for a few hours is enough. Even if it stops working, I'll always be aware that there's another way to perceive these things. That they don't *have* to stress me out the way they do.

I watch three movies in a row and only get out of my seat twice over the final fourteen-hour flight to New York. The lie-flat seats on the plane are the most comfortable thing I've experienced in ten days. The steak and potato are bliss.

What's Miller doing right now? The thought creeps up unbidden.

Regardless of what it is, regardless of how nice this plane is, I'd still rather be with him.

# 14

## KIT

MANHATTAN

I land at midnight—seven AM back in Tanzania—wide awake. New York is freezing, the cab line is twenty people deep, and my apartment feels very empty when I arrive.

I video-call Blake because I said I would. He's in Vegas until Monday, and though I was worried about having to pretend things were fine until then, it doesn't appear to be an issue.

He asks about Kilimanjaro but is only half-listening to the answer as he walks down a neon-lit street. I mention Miller and his brow furrows, as if he has no idea what I'm talking about. When I remind him, he says, "*Oh, right,*" and for a half second, he's focused, trying to make up for the fact that he wasn't before. All too soon, though, he is only half-listening. He tells me the London marathon is full and suggests we just run New York again. Just like I knew he would.

*How insane this entire relationship was.*

I was fine with calls where he didn't listen because I didn't especially want to listen to him either. His lack of attention was a fair exchange for the corresponding lack of care and affection on my part. I was fine with all the ways he kept me stuck in a

Tuesday because I sort of suspected I wasn't going to get to Thursday anyhow.

"I love you," he says, preparing to hang up as he enters a restaurant. "I'll see you Monday?"

I don't want to say *I love you* back, but he ends the call before I get the chance. I'm not sure he'd have listened if I said it anyway.

Thank God I'm getting out.

I WAKE the next morning to a ringing cell phone on my nightstand.

"I'm coming over," Maren announces. "Mom's upset that you haven't replied to her texts."

I groan. "For God's sake. I just landed at midnight. I've been up for twenty seconds."

"She pulled strings to get you in with Geoffrey for highlights and a cut, and now she's panicked you're going to blow it off and put her on his bad side."

"I won't," I promise. "You don't need to come up."

"I'm nearly there," she says. "I'm bringing you coffee if that helps."

I force myself out of bed. I know ending things with Blake is the correct choice, but in the cold light of day I also wonder what I'll have left in his absence. I'm about to be single and potentially unemployed, and home is no longer this apartment or even NYC but instead, a dusty sleeping bag inside a dirty tent I share with Miller...and I can't buy it back.

Since Maren is already on the doorman's list and has a key, she lets herself in while I'm in the shower and is curled up in one of my leather chairs when I emerge, with the New York City skyline framed behind her by the floor-to-ceiling windows.

The sun is barely peeking out beyond the skyscrapers in the distance.

My apartment is everything I once wanted...but I no longer want it.

"What's your passcode?" she demands, unabashedly trying to unlock my phone. "I want to see your pictures."

"We need some boundaries," I reply, tying my robe and snatching the phone from her hand as I take the chair across from her.

She pushes a cup in my direction across the glass coffee table. "Tell me everything."

I take a sip, stalling. Somehow, I just assumed I could skip the part where I admit that the love of her life was on my expedition, but that's ridiculous—Dad knows. Miller knows. One of them will say something to someone, and it will look *really* bad that I omitted the information. "Yeah, so did you hear who was on my trip?" I ask. I hope that the fact that I cannot meet her eye just looks casual and not nerve-ridden.

She frowns. "To Kilimanjaro? Who on earth would be on the same trip *there*? Someone *I* know?"

My laugh is tinged with misery. "Someone you know all too well. Miller. Miller West."

Her mouth falls open. "You're kidding."

I'm about to say *I wish I were*, as if he's still my nemesis, but I can't bring myself to do it. "Nope. I had no idea he'd be there."

She leans in, eyes wide, but also gleaming with excitement —and that's what I was worried about. She's already growing hopeful about the fact that he was there at all. "So, did you see much of him on the way up?"

She's picturing us just randomly on a mountain at the same time. She can't begin to understand how intimate it all was. "It was hard not to. There were only eight of us."

"Eight," she says, shaking her head. "Was he there with that girl he's seeing?"

Now it's my turn to be surprised, and holy shit, what an unpleasant surprise it is. If my stomach could literally drop from my body, I'd be picking it up off the carpet right now.

It shouldn't matter to me if he's with someone—hell, I'm still almost engaged—but if he was taken...he shouldn't have done a lot of the things he did. I suppose that's hypocritical, but at least I was open about my relationship status.

"No, he was there alone," I say, struggling to ignore the pit in my center. "He never mentioned anyone else."

She rests back in the seat, pulling a designer blanket over her lap. "The last I heard, he was dating Cecilia Love."

I like that even less. I know who Cecilia Love is, and she's exactly the kind of girl he might want to end up with—beautiful, but also smart and ambitious. If I were a better person, I'd want that for him.

"I don't know," I say quietly, "but like I said, we were climbing for eight days, and he never mentioned anyone."

"Did he ask about me?"

I sigh. I knew that this was coming. No matter what I said, she was going to find a way to turn this into something she could pin her hopes on. Maren would never in a million years cheat, but Harvey is a dick, and I think she just enjoys daydreaming about a different life—one she won't actually pursue.

"He asked about everyone," I say with a shrug. "Apparently, he's been having lunch with Dad every month for ages. I couldn't believe it."

"With *Dad*?" she asks. "What on earth would they need to meet about?"

"I don't think they're meeting about anything," I say. "I think they just legitimately enjoy each other's company. I was as surprised as you."

Now, of course, I am no longer surprised. My father is brilliant and entertaining and so is Miller. I honestly can't think of two people I would rather share a meal with than them, so it makes complete sense that they'd have sought each other out.

Maren does that fidgety thing with her fingers—tapping, tapping along the side of her disposable cup—which is what she does when she's excited and trying to be cool. She wants to hear more about Miller but knows her obsession is getting weird.

"So, how was it?" she asks.

"People were nice enough," I tell her. "There was an annoying chick and her boyfriend, who was older than Dad and obnoxious as hell, but otherwise everyone was great."

Better than great. So much better than great.

"What did you do the whole time?" she asks. "I mean, I know you were climbing, but you must've had downtime. I would die without Internet for that long."

My eyes fall closed for a minute as I picture myself curled up in a sleeping bag next to Miller, watching *30 Rock* and eating his chocolate. Lying in the dark, listening to him breathe. God, I was in so far over my head, and I didn't even know it.

I shrug. "You're pretty tired after the climbing. For the most part you just want to sleep."

"Let me see your pics," she says.

She'll only be scrolling through, looking for Miller. I hope I didn't focus on him too much. I open the phone, quickly hide the photos I took just of him, and hand it over.

"Jesus," she says, fanning herself. "He's just as hot with that full beard as he is without one."

*Please let this go, Mare. Please. It killed me to let you have him the first time.*

*I wouldn't survive it a second.*

I pull the phone away from her with my stomach in knots. "What time is this appointment Mom made?"

She glances at her diamond-encrusted Cartier watch.

"Argh. We better get going. Put on some clothes Ulrika won't have a tantrum about."

I laugh as I walk to the bedroom. "She'll have a tantrum about *something*. I'd rather it be my clothes than my weight."

Maren laughs. "Are you kidding? You look emaciated. Your weight is the one thing she *won't* have a tantrum about."

Thirty minutes later, we arrive at the salon to find my mother fuming, though we're not late. "You could have replied to my texts," she snaps.

"Mom," Maren argues. "It was after one when she got home."

My mother ignores this. "Your nails are a disaster," she says to me as she examines one of my hands. "Get that taken care of before my birthday party, please. I've got someone coming over to do our spray tans tomorrow night, and someone else will be there Saturday afternoon to blow us out."

I simply nod. It has been like this with her for most of my life—no matter what goal I set or what I accomplish, her primary concern has always been my appearance. Her beauty was what got her ahead in life, and she can't picture another way forward for her offspring.

I sometimes think that's why Maren wound up with Harvey...because my mother worked so hard to convince us both that our looks were all we had to sell.

"Well," she says, looking me over, "at least you came back skinny."

I laugh to myself. "Kilimanjaro was amazing. Thanks for asking."

My mother dismisses this with a roll of her eyes. "I refuse to dignify the whole experience by asking questions about it. I still can't believe your father made you go."

In a way, I can't either. My dad loves me—that is indisputable. And maybe Miller made it sound like a relatively easy climb and Dad figured, just like I did, that anyone who can run a marathon can climb to 18,000 feet. But having done it, I don't think I'd suggest anyone attempt the climb with as little preparation as I had. Unless they've got a Miller of their own there to help them along, anyway.

"It was one of the coolest things I've ever done, Mom. I don't regret it."

I think it's true. I just wish I hadn't returned quite so unhappy with the life I had before.

# 15

## KIT

I'm spray-tanned, my nails are done, and my hair is blown out. My mother's had a strapless red satin dress delivered to the apartment for me and it fits like a glove.

If this was anything but her birthday party, though, I'd tell them I was under the weather and stay curled up in bed.

I don't want to put on the dress. I don't want to do my makeup. I don't want to sit around with all Mom's friends while they grill me about a future that's now entirely uncertain.

I can't tell them it's over with Blake before I've passed on that information to him. And I'm not going to announce my intention to return to medical school when I've got no idea if I can get back in.

Blake calls while I'm getting ready. He's in a car, and I'm on speaker. As usual, I've got half his attention, if that. He's cursing at another driver, asking me to hang on for a second while he puts someone else on hold. I hate when he does this normally because it makes me feel like I've got to rush. Tonight, I'm just grateful.

"Hey, I've got us reservations Monday night, after my flight gets in," he says when he comes back to the call.

I'd hoped to just end things, but I can't think of a reason to tell him I won't be available, which is exactly how Tuesday girls are made—by agreeing to go to the dinner you don't want to be at, by letting your mother turn you into her personal American Girl doll, by politely saying things you don't mean to all of her friends.

Maybe my life has been a succession of Tuesdays simply because I didn't want to tell anyone *no*.

The heels are already pinching my feet as I go downstairs to hail a cab. The dress is too cold for the weather, even with a wool coat draped over my shoulders.

Once I'm finally inside the car, I open my phone and look over the pictures from Kilimanjaro, the ones I hid.

Miller, grinning at Uhuru Peak. Miller, smiling at me with a sea of clouds behind him at one of the lower camps. Miller in our tent, holding candy out of my grasp. Miller, walking ahead of me while he talks to Gideon.

I swallow hard. Those days with him felt like Saturdays. I'm not sure I'm ever getting them back.

The cab deposits me at the club, and I hand my coat to an attendee before I head to the reception desk. "Hi," I say. "There's supposed to be a room reserved for my mother's birthday? It should be under the name Dalton?"

"Kit," says a man's voice, and a shiver runs up my spine.

It sounds like Miller. Miller, walking up behind me as we ascend to the next camp, Miller, cutting in so that I can't slow dance with Adam.

I turn...

And find Miller standing there, all serious hazel eyes, and perfect mouth, and tall enough to make me feel small by contrast.

He's got a day's beard and isn't at all dressed for this occasion or any other that might be hosted here. He's wearing worn jeans and a T-shirt, with a down jacket over the top.

He looks exhausted and unshowered, and I've never seen anything as lovely. He grabs my hand and pulls me into an oak-paneled hallway to the left, then turns me to face him.

"What are you doing here?" I ask, glancing around us to make sure no one's exiting the surrounding rooms. "You're supposed to be on a safari."

He exhales, pushing a hand through his hair. "I thought you said you were going to end it with Blake."

"*What?*" It's bizarre that he's here, bizarre that he hasn't answered a simple question. "I am, but he's out of town, and unlike *you*, I don't dump people by text."

He smiles. "Ah, there's the acid tongue I've missed so much." His gaze moves over my face and pauses, briefly, on my cleavage before darting back up. "You look a little different than you did a few days ago."

"Well, I looked horrible a few days ago," I reply. "It's harder to get away with it here."

"You looked beautiful," he says, holding my gaze. "You looked beautiful there, and you look beautiful here."

I lean back against the wall, breathless. It packs exactly the hit I expected it would, having Miller West tell you you're beautiful and staring at you as if he's never meant anything more.

And somewhere upstairs, my sister is waiting. He probably said it to her too, once upon a time. She probably daydreams about this very moment and still feels the way it made her heart twist with want, the way it does mine.

"Why are you here?" I ask again. "My whole family is upstairs."

He swallows. "That's *why* I'm here. I don't know if I should even be telling you this, but Blake is going to propose tonight."

I stare at him. "*What?* No, this is just a thing for my mom's birthday."

"According to your dad, it's all a ruse. And the press is here to capture the moment along with your family and Blake's."

I shake my head. "That's...no. My dad must've been pulling your leg. My mother would never give up that much attention, not on her birthday, and I just talked to Blake like an hour ago. He was still in Vegas."

"Kit," he says, "come on. Do you have any actual proof that he's still there? I'm telling you right now...your father is upstairs, texting me one dire warning after another about this."

My stomach drops.

All the primping. Even for my mom it was over the top...the spray tan, the nails, the highlights. She wasn't preparing me for her birthday. She was preparing me for *engagement photos*.

"Fuck," I whisper, holding a hand to my throat, where my pulse gallops. "I don't know what to do."

Miller's jaw flexes. "You get the hell out of here. That's what you do."

I shake my head, torn between fleeing and accepting my fate. "If Blake organized this whole thing to propose, I can't just...not show. He'd be so embarrassed."

Miller reaches out, placing a hand on my bicep. I shiver at the contact. "Exactly. And then he proposes, and you won't want to embarrass him there either, and it'll get harder and harder to dial it back. You said your mother already has this wedding half planned, which means she's going to make it impossible for you to extricate yourself."

He's right. That's how it's always been with both of my parents when they want something. The cost of ending the relationship will only grow greater and greater, more and more excruciating. And my mom probably knows that Blake and I aren't a good fit, and that I was not completely sold. She's trying to get my signature on the dotted line before I come to my senses and walk out of the negotiation.

I could leave, but my mom, Maren, and Blake all have access to my apartment. I don't think there's anywhere in the city I could hide for as long as I'd need to while the dust settled.

"You didn't have to blow off your safari. You could've just... called me."

Something shifts in his eyes, a shutter closing, as if he's scared I'll see what is roaming around in his brain if I look too closely. "I was worried a call wouldn't be enough. That your mom or someone else would guilt you and guilt you again until you found yourself engaged."

I am not someone who gets bullied, but my mother would've tried to convince me I was being crazy, or that it was cold feet, or told me that this had been planned for weeks, and not showing up at the party would be atrocious. There are a million ways she could manipulate me successfully, and I guarantee she'd attempt every one of them if she had to, while the man in front of me just gave up a safari he'd always wanted to go on—after giving up the excursion he'd planned—all for me. Even Rob, as wonderful as he was, wouldn't have done that.

"Jesus," I say, rubbing my temples. "I don't know how to get out of this. They knew I was on the way here. There's no way to now tell them I can't make it."

"I have a house," he says. "Starfish Cay. In Turks and Caicos."

I blink. "That's a weird flex in the middle of this conversation."

He gives me a halfhearted smile "It wasn't a flex," he says. "It was an offer. We can leave straight for the airport right now. Text your mom; tell her you got sick. Say whatever you have to before they suck you in for good."

"So I'd be going there...with you?"

"If you want me along, yes."

Our gazes meet. I picture a few days alone with him in Starfish Cay. White sand. Clear water.

"As friends?" I ask, though in my head I'm already picturing a big, soft bed. His weight above mine.

"If that's how you want it," he says.

I glance away. That's not how I want it, but that's how it will have to be, for Maren's sake. "Yes, as friends."

"Fine," he agrees. "Nothing more than friends, no matter how hard you beg."

I laugh. "Let's be realistic. If I begged, you'd give in."

"Fair enough," he says, his grin brighter than the chandelier overhead. "I'd like to point out that you are taking this conversation back into the territory of one we'd have if we *were* going to have sex."

"We aren't," I insist.

He lifts his shoulders. "Don't even want to."

"Yeah, you do."

"Kit, you're doing it again."

"Okay," I whisper, looking around me. "Do I go pack?"

He hesitates for only a second and then shakes his head. "I think the important thing is that you get the hell out right now. We can go straight to the airport, get on a flight, and figure it out when we arrive."

I look down at my strapless, red satin dress and four-inch heels. "I'm gonna look pretty weird on the beach in this."

He bites down on a grin. "We can buy clothes there, and I'm guessing your father would pay a top designer to personally come outfit you if it meant you weren't going to be marrying Blake."

He's right once again. All that matters at the moment is getting out of New York City before my mother can guilt me into changing my mind. And now that it's decided, it almost feels as if I was being held captive. As if I'll be chained to Blake's side if anyone sees me here.

I was a willing participant two weeks ago. Now marrying him seems like a fate worse than death.

"I need my passport," I say frantically, looking around us. "It's still in my bag from the trip."

"I've got a car waiting outside. We'll swing by your apartment on the way, but I'm giving you five minutes or I'm coming in after you."

I smile at him. It's the exact sort of bullshit misogyny I'd have lashed out at a week ago. Now I'm simply glad that someone else has my back.

We get my coat—there are no familiar faces in the lobby, thank God—and rush out to the car. Even inside it, I still don't feel as if this is behind me—as if a SWAT team might descend from helicopters at any moment—and I have no idea how we'll pull this off regardless since most flights to the Caribbean leave New York earlier in the day. "Can we even get to Turks and Caicos this late?"

He grins. "We've got a flight. You might not love it, however."

"Oh God, you're not making me fly coach?"

He tugs a lock of my hair. "No, Kitten. I wouldn't dream of making you fly coach, and we were too likely to be seen at the airport if we flew commercial. We're taking your dad's plane."

I sigh, though I'm smiling. "He is *such* a meddler. And right now, he's probably back at the party, acting just as shocked and surprised as everyone else that I'm not there."

"I'm sure he's criticizing your tardiness the most of anyone," says Miller with a laugh. "And blaming your mother."

We pull in front of my apartment and I race upstairs to grab the purse I flew home with. I contemplate grabbing the ashes from my luggage but for some reason it feels wrong, bringing Rob along for this. I'm not sure why.

I lock the door and rush back to the car.

He glances at his watch. "Under three minutes. I'm impressed."

I raise a four-inch Louboutin in the air. "I wonder how these will fare in the sand."

He grins. "You'll be the sexiest girl on the beach."

"That went without saying," I reply, just as my phone starts buzzing in my lap—multiple texts landing at once.

> MOM
>
> Where the hell are you?
>
> MAREN
>
> You'd better not be in bed.
>
> CHARLIE
>
> Your sister and your mother are hyperventilating. It's fascinating to watch.
>
> DAD
>
> Your mother is making a scene, Kit. Please reply.

I reply to the entire family at once, telling them I got sick in the cab and had to return home. I guess they'll tell Blake. I wince at the idea of him in that room, excited for this big night. I remind myself that he'd probably start scrolling on his phone two seconds after I said *yes*.

My mother calls, and I turn the phone face down in my lap and blow out a breath.

Should I be doing this? Should I be leaving? It's shitty. It's *so* shitty. My mother will be upset, and she'll need someone to fix this. Normally that person would be me, but I'm not there. And Blake isn't a saint, but I guess he did plan this thing, and...

"I know you're feeling guilty," Miller says softly, "but if Blake knew the first thing about you, he wouldn't have done it like this. Or even worse, he *does* know you well enough and realized this would force your hand because you wouldn't want to embarrass him."

He squeezes my hand and I squeeze his back, examining his angular jaw, his lovely mouth. Miller would know better than to subject me to a public spectacle with the press there to capture it. When he proposes to his future wife, it will be a special moment, intimate, and even if a hundred other people are watching, he'll make sure it's something that belongs just to the two of them. My heart squeezes tight in my chest.

"Maren says you're dating Cecilia Love," I say, removing my hand.

He laughs, running his fingers through his hair. "And you thought your sister, who I haven't spoken to in ten years, would have more up to date info than *you*, who just shared a tent with me for five nights?"

A smile starts to move my mouth upward. "Just because we're sharing a tent doesn't mean you're telling me everything."

His gaze falls to my lips. "True, but I'd have told you that one. I dated Cece for a month, tops, and it was over a year ago."

I glance away so he won't see how relieved I am. I have no business being relieved. We're only going away as friends. Former tentmates. He's sharing his tent and I'll share my snacks. Nothing more.

My phone begins buzzing again. I reluctantly turn it over.

MOM

You can't possibly be THAT sick, and if you miss my birthday, I'll never forgive you.

MAREN

Mom's really pissed. You might want to come by for a few minutes.

CHARLIE

If a human head could explode, your mother's would be exploding right now.

DAD

Get well soon, Kitty Cat.

BLAKE

Hey, I came to dinner to surprise you, but your mom is saying you're sick. Just come out for a while. If you can climb Kilimanjaro, you can come to dinner for an hour.

I sigh and let my head fall back against the headrest. A part of me dreads ending things with him so greatly that I'm tempted to just...agree. Agree to marry him, have a big wedding, wait until he grows bored, and politely call it a day. "I really don't know how to reply."

"Kit," Miller says, waiting for me to open my eyes and look at him. "If Maren was in your shoes, you'd snatch the phone out of her hand and type up a polite but firm response. Have your own back the way you've had everyone else's for most of your life. Just do it."

I guess he's right. I pick up the phone, take a deep breath and begin to type.

> Hey, look, I'm so sorry, but I don't think this is working for me. It isn't fair to you or me to keep pursuing something that doesn't make either of us especially happy.

I hit *send* before I can take it back. Holy shit. I *already* can't believe I went through with it.

"Done," I whisper.

"How do you feel?" he asks, his gaze gentle on my face.

I shake my head. There are so many emotions inside me right now I can't begin to tease them apart. "A little relieved. A lot terrified. I think he's going to be mad. He's going to be really mad, and hurt, and probably lash out and say a lot of mean shit."

He briefly squeezes my knee. "Take a minute to consider the fact that you were about to marry a man who lashes out at a person he theoretically loves when his feelings get hurt."

My phone pings, and my stomach ties into a knot.

BLAKE:

Are you fucking kidding me? I came here to PROPOSE and you're breaking up with me? JFC, you are such a waste of fucking time. Fuck you. Good luck finding anyone who will treat you half as well as me, Kit.

Good luck finding anyone who will put up with your bullshit.

You know my entire family is here, and so is yours? I assume you just met someone else on your fucking climb. Apple doesn't fall far from the whore tree, does it? You're even worse than your mom.

"What's he saying?" asks Miller.

"A bunch of bullshit," I whisper. "Some of it true."

"How would you reply if he was saying it to Maren?" he asks.

"The difference is that if he was saying it to Maren, it wouldn't be true."

"I guarantee it's not true here either," he says, grabbing the phone, and then an animal noise rumbles in his chest. I can hear it from a foot away.

"I'm going to beat his ass when we get back to New York," growls Miller, his nostrils flaring.

I exhale. "He's just mad."

"No one speaks to you like this and gets away with it," he hisses, typing.

"What are you doing?" I demand, reaching for the phone.

"Replying. Send it."

Miller has typed, "The way you are handling this certainly convinces me I've made a mistake."

I laugh. "You're just making a bad situation worse."

"It's what you'd have said if you weren't upset. Believe me, it would be a lot worse if it was coming from me, and it's going to be a lot worse if I ever run into him. Send it. You'd do it for Maren."

I would. I'd type it for Mare, just like he typed it for me. And before that, I'd have snatched the phone out of her hand just as he snatched away mine.

I hit *send*. Blake replies, calling me a fucking cunt, Miller demands to see the phone and this time I don't hand it over because I'm worried Miller's going to have them turn the car around. I just delete it and block Blake's number.

The way I'd do for Maren. The way Miller would do for me.

"Done," I say, and this time, when my eyes fall closed and my head rests against the back of the seat, all I feel is relief.

"I would like to point out that you just dumped someone by text," he says, and we both start to laugh.

We are greeted on the tarmac by a young, nervous kid who hands us two small suitcases. "Just some clothes and toiletries," he says, "courtesy of *Elite*."

One of my dad's magazines. I imagine he asked an editor for help, and that editor pulled some low-level employee out of a wedding or her own baby shower to rush around, gathering clothes for us.

"I had nothing to do with this," says Miller, his brow furrowed.

I shake my head. "Believe me, I know. My guess is when you see the skintight vinyl pants and vest combo they packed for you, you'll wish they hadn't gone to the trouble."

"I happen to love vinyl pants on the beach," he says, plucking my suitcase out of my hand before we climb the steps to the plane. "One of many fun facts you'll soon learn about me."

We each take a plush leather seat and when I glance over at him, a couple feet too far away, my heart pounds in my throat.

I love his cheekbones. I always have. I love the sharpness of his jaw. I remember learning about the gonion—the exact point where the vertical and horizontal ramus of the mandible converge—and even then, it made me think of him. I love his dimple. I love his laugh. I love the way his hair starts to curl when it gets a little too long, the way it is right now, and how much darker his facial hair is than the hair on his head.

I love everything, and now we're going to be alone together, in a house and...I'm too warm, and my pulse is too fast, and there's a tight knot in my stomach because...

Holy shit. What am I doing here? I can't go away to the Caribbean with Miller West.

I can't. This is fucking insane and...

He narrows one eye. "What's going on over there, Fischer?"

As always, he's picked up on my change of mood before I've entirely figured out how and why it's changed.

"I don't know," I say, swallowing. I look around us frantically. The engine is on, the flight attendant is buckling herself in...we'll be taking off any second now, and I think maybe I've made a terrible mistake.

He crosses over to the seat beside me.

"It's gonna be okay, Kit," he says. "Deep breaths."

"Maren would never forgive me if she found out," I whisper.

That muscle in his jaw flickers. "She won't find out, and you're not doing anything wrong."

"That would be more convincing if you didn't keep looking at my rack."

He cracks a smile. His dimple is all the reassurance I could ever seek. "Resolving to take this trip as friends doesn't magically erase my interest in breasts."

I laugh. "I guess that's fair."

"And you're sure not trying to hide them in that dress."

I elbow him. "Now you've gone too far, tentmate."

He buckles himself in and pulls out his phone. We watch *30 Rock* for most of the four-hour flight and while I'm all too aware of my own phone, currently turned off and tucked in my purse, I don't pull it out. No doubt it's now full of irate messages from multiple family members and if I read them now, I'll lose my nerve. I'll direct the plane straight back to NYC.

I'd be resigning myself to more than an argument with Blake and emotional blackmail from my mom.

I'd be agreeing that a lifetime of Tuesdays is okay....and it's really fucking not.

WE LAND on a private airstrip a little after one in the morning and climb down the stairs into a balmy, breezy night. Even if this was a terrible idea and winds up going drastically off the rails...there's no place I'd rather be, and no one I'd rather be here with.

A waiting car drives us less than a mile to an isolated white cottage that sits right on the sand, surrounded by nothing but a few squat palm trees. Somewhere nearby, waves are lapping gently against the shore.

Miller thanks the driver, grabs the bags, and leads me to the front door, where he quickly presses a key code to let us in.

The door opens directly into the kitchen and living area, which are clean and white, with a soaring, exposed-beam cathedral ceiling, and doors that look out toward a deck, a small pool, and the moonlit ocean. On either side are what I assume are the bedrooms.

"This is amazing," I tell him, my voice hushed.

His teeth sink into his lower lip. "I was worried you wouldn't be all that impressed, given how much money your father has. He could probably buy the entire island."

I shake my head. "I don't like big places. This...is perfect. It's the perfect size."

His eyes catch mine and hold there for a moment too long, thinking something I know he won't share. "I'm glad you like it. Just wait 'til you see the view in the morning."

For all of my initial nerves and all the moments since we left New York when I've thought this might be a horrific mistake, I am one hundred percent certain now that this is where I'm meant to be.

"Let me show you to your room," he says, walking toward the doors to the right and sliding them open. It's nearly as large as the living room, with another exposed-beam cathedral ceiling and wood accents. A ceiling fan hangs over a massive canopy bed, and the entire ocean-facing wall is made of glass. The water is illuminated by a huge full moon. The view tomorrow will be incredible.

"You can lock the doors if you like," he says, showing me how the glass panels on the ocean-facing wall slide open, "but it's pretty safe here." He points toward the bathroom. "I had some basic toiletries delivered, and we can get whatever else you need tomorrow."

I sink onto the bed. "Miller...I don't know how to thank you. For everything. No one else would've done all this."

"I hate that it's so shocking to you that someone finally has," he says quietly before he walks out.

Once he's closed the door behind him, I step out of my heels and open the suitcase. My father has had stylists pull clothes for me in the past, and it generally hasn't worked out all that well. The outfits are either too high fashion, too uncomfortable, or way too skimpy.

This time, though, they've done okay. There's a pair of flip-flops, some shorts, and a few sundresses and T-shirts.

And sure, the clothes are more revealing than anything I'd

choose on my own, and there are enough negligees and silk thongs to last me a lifetime, but I can live with it.

I unzip the dress and hang it over a chair, remove my strapless bra, and slip on a negligée before I traipse barefoot to the blue-tiled bathroom, where a toothbrush, toothpaste, makeup remover, and face wash await.

I brush my teeth, wash my face, and climb into the big, soft bed, listening to the quiet roar of the waves and the buzz of insects.

This is the happiest I've felt since I left Tanzania.

I'm not going to think too hard about the common denominator in both.

# 16

## KIT

The ocean is the first thing I see, such a perfect blue that it looks as if it was Photoshopped. The sand is powder white—no weeds and no grass—so the view is nothing but shore and sea and a cloudless sky.

On the other side of the door, there are quiet sounds—Miller, I assume. My heart begins to skitter, thrilled to have him back to myself when I'd thought I might never spend time with him again.

I brush my teeth and wrap the robe *Elite* sent around me before I walk into the main room. He's in baby blue swim trunks and nothing else, his back to me while he does something at the kitchen counter. My mouth waters.

"Good morning," I say quietly, newly re-aware of the fact that it's just the two of us here alone.

He turns, with a coffee scoop in hand, and his eyes immediately drop to the tiny robe covering a tinier negligée. He blows out a breath.

"Wow," he says. "Telling me we're just here as friends and walking out here dressed like that seems more than a little unfair."

"Obviously, I didn't choose the outfit. I'm not sure who was giving them direction, but about half of the suitcase was lingerie. How was yours?"

He takes another glance over me and turns away to hit a button on the coffee maker. "Fine, actually," he says. "Not a single pair of leather pants in sight, though there was a pair of pink swim trunks."

I cross to the kitchen and jump onto the counter. "What's wrong with pink swim trunks?"

He glances at my legs, and a muscle tenses in his jaw. "The Kit of ten years ago would've been able to tell you exactly what was wrong with pink swim trunks. In fact, she would have told me in great detail what was wrong, and I guarantee the phrases *little rich boy* and *douche prince* would've come into play."

I laugh. "That does sound familiar actually. God, I was such a bitch."

He pulls two mugs out of the cabinet and looks over his shoulder at me. "You were, but I kind of liked it."

He pours us each a cup of coffee, and we walk out to the covered wooden porch just outside the open wall.

The breeze is warm already, but the porch roof provides enough shade to keep it comfortable. "This is the most beautiful beach I've ever seen in my life," I tell him. I want to know if he brings a lot of women here but that probably isn't something you ask a friend. "Do you come here a lot?"

He shakes his head. "No. I bought it a few years ago, but I travel so much for work that there hasn't been a lot of time to get out here, and I don't necessarily want to be here alone."

"You say that as if you don't date."

"I haven't dated anyone that I've wanted to bring here," he says.

I wonder if he'd have been willing to bring me here under less dramatic circumstances. Probably not.

"Well, I appreciate you breaking the rule on my behalf," I

tell him. "If you hadn't shown up last night, I'm pretty sure I'd be engaged right now."

I'm still stunned by how close I came to making a terrible mistake, and slightly unnerved by the extent to which my mother—and perhaps Maren—were willing to help me make it. They had to have known, just like my dad did, that Blake and I weren't right for each other. Maybe their willingness to over-look it is just a sign of their loyalty to me—that they took me at my word when I implied Blake made me happy—but it sort of feels like it's one more way that they've just left me out to dry, the same way they do anytime I have to intervene on their behalf.

"*Kit went a little nuts,*" I once heard my mother telling a friend, without ever mentioning that it happened because I'd just watched a guy swing her onto the floor by her hair.

I close my eyes and breathe out, releasing the memory. Things haven't always been great, but look where I've ended up: I'm in one of the most beautiful places in the world, with one of my favorite people—a man who has my back in a way my mother never did.

"It's so peaceful here. Like...I don't hear anyone. I don't see any other houses, either."

"There are thirty miles on this island, a tiny twelve-room hotel and only thirty-eight homeowners—who aren't here often. Speaking of which, if you're hungry, there's a restaurant at the hotel. I also had them stock the fridge before we got here."

I grin. "I hope you have the stuff for a good stew."

He takes a sip of his coffee. "That's one way to send you running back to Manhattan. And let me make it clear that I don't *want* you to go running back. My office still thinks I'm in Africa, so I'm here as long as you want to stay."

"You're lucky I'm joining the finance team a week from

tomorrow, or I'd make you regret how open-ended that offer is. Let's go to the beach."

He nods, biting his lip as he takes in the robe one last time. "Okay, although I'm a little scared to see what they sent along for swimwear."

I'm a little scared too, but also...regrettably excited. I shouldn't be excited to prance around in front of Miller in some barely-there bikini, to watch his gaze stutter in response. Knowing I shouldn't feel this way, however, doesn't change the fact that I do.

And indeed, when I return to the suitcase, I discover the two bikinis they've sent are basically pieces of floss up top and more floss below. I can't imagine that my father was behind this, because he *is* still my father, the same man who once forbade crop tops, but it sure looks as if somebody was trying really hard to get me laid.

I twist my hair up on my head, grab a towel and flip-flops, and find him in the family room.

"Jesus Christ," he mutters, wincing as he looks away. "If your dad could see what they packed for you, he'd be shutting that entire magazine down."

I grin and turn toward the open doors, with him in my wake. We step off the back porch and steer around the pool to reach the long white beach. Ahead, the crystal blue water stretches out toward a sandbar about two hundred yards away, as sparkling white as the sand we're on now. How is a beach like this so empty? There isn't a single person, a single chair, a single trash can, or other sign of life.

We could strip out of our suits, wander out to that sandbar and have sex repeatedly in the middle of an endless blue sea, and as long as a plane didn't fly over, no one would be the wiser.

I point toward it. "I want to go out there. I have no idea why."

He steps forward and grabs my hand. "Come on then," he says.

I don't normally hold hands with my *friends*, but this time I'll allow it. We wade in and the water's so clear I can see the chipped polish on my middle toe.

"Unbelievable," I whisper.

"Yeah," he says, but he's only looking at me. As if I'm the thing that's wondrous to him here and not the view, as if I matter more than everything else combined.

*You deserve someone who has your back. And you belong with someone who wants to have it for you.*

I'd never thought he was suggesting that *he* might want to be that person when he said it. The way he's looking at me now, though? It makes me wonder.

"I think if I owned this place," I say as the water reaches my waist, "I could never be persuaded to go do something like Kilimanjaro instead of coming here."

"But how much more amazing does this trip seem to you, having just suffered through the climb we did? How much more do you appreciate the ease of our lives?"

He's right. Maybe we need to suffer a little. Maybe we need to spend some time in the dark so we can spy the tiny bits of light we couldn't distinguish, so we can marvel at the sun when it finally arrives.

I think I've been in the dark for a very, very long time. Since the day Rob's mother called to tell me he was gone.

And here, with Miller, I'm finally coming back into the light.

# 17

## MILLER

**K**it used to be addicted to cherry popsicles. That summer in the Hamptons she wrote a note on the box with a Sharpie—*Eat cherry at your own peril.* In turn, I made a point of pretending to pull a cherry popsicle out of the freezer every time she was in the room.

I texted the island's concierge to get us some last night. If that's not a sign that I'm fucking whipped, I don't know what is.

Leaving Tanzania was the easiest decision I've ever made in my life because I want to step in and protect her from all the shit that gets thrown her way. I want to be the one who tells Ulrika *no* when she calls asking Kit to intercede on her behalf, the way I know she *still* fucking is because if she used Kit as a crutch ten years ago, there's not a chance she stopped.

I want to be the one who shields her from a photographer when she doesn't want to be seen.

I want to be the one who gets to kick Blake's ass for that text he sent last night, and I'm *going* to be the one who does it, whether she approves or not.

I'm in so far over my head, and I always have been...for a woman who was my girlfriend's sister. For a woman who is just getting out of one relationship and still carries another man's ashes with her because she can't let him go.

A woman convinced her sister would never forgive her if anything happened with me.

She smiles at me over her shoulder, in a bikini that covers none of her. The wind is blowing that mess of gold hair across her face, and her nose has three tiny new freckles I haven't seen before. There's something in her eyes, something very, very adult.

I promised her nothing would happen and therefore nothing will, but Jesus Christ, she's not making it easy on me.

# 18

## KIT

*You'll never be this happy again.*

It's a thought I've had several times this morning. And maybe it's not true—I *hope* it's not true—but I'm a realist. I'm between jobs, in the most beautiful place in the world, and I get to share it with the only guy I've ever adored, aside from Rob.

What are the odds that this is ever going to repeat itself? I'm pretty sure it can't. I know Maren and Mom are blowing up my phone and guilt would gnaw at me if I allowed it to. I'm trying to ignore that. I really want to enjoy this while it lasts.

After a morning in the water, we head back to the house and make avocado toast and smoothies, which we carry out to the patio, him on the wide lounger and me in the big, comfy chair a few feet away. The smoothies are okay...the avocado toast is appalling.

"It troubles me that we managed to fuck up avocado toast," I say. "Your mom should have taught you how to cook."

"*Your* mom should have taught *you* how to cook."

"I believe you've met my mom, have you not?" I ask.

He laughs. "Fair enough. She should have had one of her husbands teach you to cook."

When we're done eating, I persuade him to take the paddle boards out. There's a long inlet off to the right of the bay, the water so clear you can see to the bottom, running between miles of white sand beach, dotted with nothing but small, squat palms.

"This place is magic," I tell him, as we paddle side by side. We've yet to see another person here. There's no noise—no music, no cars, no construction. Aside from the occasional plane passing overhead, it's as if we've dropped back three hundred years.

"It was my first big purchase after my company took off," he says. "I came here as a teenager and it stayed in my head from then on."

"Maybe if I ever hit it big," I reply, "I'll buy here too. And by hitting it big, I refer to coming into my trust fund, obviously."

He shakes his head. "You're probably out of luck. Only a handful of us own the island, the land can't be subdivided, and no one's selling. You may just have to keep staying with me."

I smile and look away, suddenly bashful and swept with a longing for that precise thing: to keep coming back here with him, year after year. Of course, in this fantasy, he doesn't have a wife or children. It's still just the two of us, platonic besties, with lives that never move forward.

"I'll have to figure out a way to earn my keep," I reply.

His gaze sweeps over me, head to toe, and I shiver in response. "This conversation suddenly turned interesting."

I laugh. "I meant, you know, cooking or something domestic."

"From what I've seen of your domestic skills," he says, "we might need to consider other options."

We exchange another glance, and my throat is suddenly dry. There's something about having a devastatingly attractive man say those words that sends my brain to all the worst places. Or maybe it's just when that man happens to be Miller.

Back at the house, I strip out of my suit and step into the huge shower off of my bedroom. Under the spray, with the massive skylights overhead and the breeze from the open door, it's as if I'm still outside...and I'm perfectly at peace. I guess I've felt like this all day because I'm more *myself* here than I've felt anywhere in a long time. Kilimanjaro came close, but there I was exhausted, uncomfortable, struggling with the altitude and the food and Gerald's bullshit, secretly worried that I was going to fuck it up for everyone else.

Here, I'm just me, and when was the last time I felt this way? When was the last time that I just felt *good*, and relaxed? That I wasn't fatigued by my life or dreading the next thing? It's been years...probably on some trip with Rob, and that's a very long time to not feel good, isn't it?

I walk to the deck in cut-off shorts and a tank, with wet hair. Miller's stretched out on the wide lounge chair, shower-clean and shirtless, reading a book he lowers as I approach.

"Your father texted me," he says. "He's asking that you please check your messages."

I sigh. "I'd really rather not."

He sets his book on the table beside him. "Just get it over with. You know there's a pit in your stomach wondering what they've said."

I suppose that, as much as I'd like to continue pretending the situation doesn't exist, I can't pretend forever.

I go to my room and retrieve the phone. When I turn it on, I have two hundred texts and the battery's at twenty percent.

"The battery's really low," I say as I walk out, hoping he'll let me off the hook.

He scoots over and pats the space beside him. "Kit."

By which he means...*it's not that low. Stop making excuses.*

I slide into the space he's vacated and swallow as I pick up the phone again and open my messages. Some of the texts are just from my friend group, the regular slew of memes and articles.

But there are dozens from Maren and dozens from my mom and several from Blake's mom and his sister.

I open them in order of *least likely to be furious* to *most*, beginning with my dad.

DAD

You'd better write them. I'm worried Maren's going to contact the FBI.

I told them I heard from you. Maren did, in fact, call the police. She also told them your apartment appeared to have been ransacked, as if that isn't its normal state.

Now they're upset that I'VE heard from you but they haven't, btw.

I go to Maren's next.

MAREN

Kit, what's going on?

Look, I hate that I'm ruining this, but you've got to come back. Blake's here and so is his family. He's going to propose. Mom's been setting it all up for the past month.

I'm freaked out that you're not replying. Please let me know you're okay.

I'm coming over.

I'm at your apartment. Where the hell are you? I called the police but since it's only been a half hour and you texted earlier, they won't do anything.

I wrote Dad. He says you're fine. Why aren't you answering?

There are more after that. Her feelings are hurt that she had to learn everything from Dad, and why wouldn't they be? Since when do I confide more in him than her? I'd be hurt too.

> I'm with a friend and I'm fine. Sorry about the radio silence. My phone was off and it's nearly dead now, but I'm fine.

MAREN:

Prove you're my sister so I know you weren't murdered or taken hostage.

> You want to be peed on. It's your secret kink.

OMG. I guess you're alive. I hate you. Never do that to me again. Also, disloyal much? Why are you texting Dad but not me?

"Your sister wants to be peed on?" asks Miller, wide-eyed. "I...would not have guessed that."

I laugh. "No, she doesn't want to be peed on. I told her this story about it happening to a friend, and she literally started retching. So I bring it up when she's annoying me."

He grins. "Okay, now read the ones you *can't* get out of with urination humor."

"My family loves urination humor," I reply. "You'd be surprised."

I go to my mother's texts next. They follow the same path as Maren's, but are more outraged, especially when she discovers my dad was privy to information she was not.

MOM

I fully expected you'd humiliate me at some point, and now you have. I'm shocked by your behavior.

> If you fully expected it, you shouldn't be all that shocked.

Miller laughs. "I love seeing your thorniness directed at someone other than me."

And then I'm left with the texts from Blake's mom and sister. I hand him the phone because I can't stand to read them myself.

"Blake's mom says she's appalled by how selfish you are. I'm personally appalled that she's spelled selfish with two e's. Does she not have spell check? You're going to tell her that," he says as he starts to type.

I laugh. "Stop. I think she already hates me enough. What about his sister?"

"Krestley? Is that her? What an incredibly stupid name. Krestley says she always thought you were a stuck-up cunt and that Blake could do better. She also says you think you're so hot but that your mother was prettier at your age, and your looks will fade." He frowns. "Your mother definitely was not prettier, but she may have a point here. I've heard looks can fade, over time, in a small percentage of women. God, maybe you should have married her idiotic brother. You know, just in case that part's true."

I laugh and lean my head against his shoulder as that last bit of worry releases inside me. "Thank you."

"Anytime, Kitten," he says softly. "That's what I'm here for."

A light breeze blows and I close my eyes.

"Why am I so tired?" I ask. "I wanted to take the bikes out."

"It might be because you're treating this trip like some kind of athletic event and trying to squeeze it all in at once," he says. "Take a little nap here."

I shouldn't. This is all getting too convoluted, and if I want to take a nap I could just return to bed. Except it's incredibly pleasant leaning against his warm shoulder. And I don't want to be away from him.

He wraps an arm around me and I rest my head on his

chest. His skin is warm and smooth and smells like his soap. There's never been a more perfect pillow.

"You won't be able to turn the pages of your book," I whisper.

"I like this better than reading."

Me too. And I love to read.

*I will never be this happy again.*

I WAKE ALONE. I don't know why I'm disappointed that he didn't stay.

I find him inside, making a pitcher of margaritas. When I hop onto the counter, his gaze jerks toward me.

"Sorry. Bad habit," I say, preparing to jump down. "I shouldn't be doing this in someone else's kitchen. Stepmother number three hated it."

His hand shoots out to keep me in place and lands on my thigh. "Stay," he says with a quiet purr at the bottom of his throat. "I like it."

My gaze falls to that hand, hot and rough on my skin. I picture it sliding higher. I can't quite get a full breath.

He releases me, but it's as if I'm still at high altitude and thinking some crazy, high-altitude thoughts. Like...*we're already here. This is already a secret...so what harm would another secret or two do?*

I cough. "I never pictured you being so domestic."

He grins, pouring a frozen margarita in a glass and handing it to me. "You've seen me make coffee and margaritas. I'm not sure that makes me Martha Stewart. And I wasn't aware that you'd pictured me at all."

"Until recently," I agree, "it was mostly about what I'd say to you in hell."

"*Hell?*" he asks, raising a brow.

I nod. "It's where you go when you break up with someone by text."

He shrugs. "That's fair. So, will you be needing a tentmate there?"

I grin. This is the extent of my infatuation with Miller: he suggests sharing a tent in hell, and it sort of sounds like a good idea.

For dinner, we take the golf cart and bounce down the bumpy dirt road to a small hotel that sits right on the beach. Even here, there are very few people, and the staff knows Miller by name. He introduces me as his "friend," but it's clear they think the word is a euphemism, and it's a strange, delicious thrill, being thought of as more. Being thought of as someone who slept in his bed last night, someone he might have pulled close to kiss right before we walked in here together.

Except if that were true, we wouldn't be here at all. We'd be back in that big, soft bed. Or at his kitchen counter, enacting my favorite fantasy—him the aggressor, unwilling to listen to a single one of my objections.

I order a burger. He orders a steak. I groan as I bite into it, and he watches with a look on his face that I'm seeing from him more and more. A look that says the choice is mine, and he really wishes I'd make it.

"What are you going to do when you get home?" he asks.

"About Blake?"

He shakes his head. "Blake is done. I'm talking about work."

I hitch a shoulder. "I can't just jump ship the day I get back to the city. I'll go join the finance team and see if I like it. But I haven't ruled out med school."

"Look," Miller says after a moment, "even if it's not med school...get out of publishing. If it doesn't interest you now, it won't interest you in ten years either. I'm not sure why you ever thought it would."

"I'm not sure I *did* think it would," I reply. I was broken after

Rob died. I'd tried to create a new life away from Manhattan by going to med school, by falling for a guy from California who didn't give two fucks about money. It went disastrously, so I ran home to what I knew, as if it could shelter me from all the coming storms.

"My family and New York—they were like this island of safety. And when my own island sank...I rushed back to theirs."

"That makes sense," he says. "But it's been four years. Don't you think maybe it's time to start looking for your own island again?"

That was what I'd thought I was doing. But on Monday I'll return to all of it, and I think I'd rather just stay here, on his.

I will definitely never be this happy again.

# 19

## KIT

In the morning, we make a huge breakfast, then snorkel out to the sandbar, where we stretch out in the sand, side by side. "This is so perfect," I whisper. Behind us, an endless blue ocean; ahead of us, the crystal water we swam through to get here, an unblemished white beach, and the small green palms that separate his home from the shore.

He lifts up a strand of my hair, already bleaching to the palest blonde in the light.

"I've always loved your hair," he says. "I loved the way it got during the summer."

"It's just like Maren's," I say with a shrug.

"No," he says. "It's really not. Yours has this little wave to it and it gets lighter. It was almost white by the time I left the Hamptons."

A fist squeezes in my chest at the memory of that week— wandering around lost in our beach house, sick with how much I wanted him, desperate for him to stay and also desperate for him to leave to make the feeling stop.

I used to look at the calendar every single night, counting

the days until he left for law school. I couldn't wait and I knew it would break me at the same time.

Right now, with my hair in tangles, my skin turning gold, it's as if I am seventeen again. Seventeen and so infatuated with Miller I can't quite think straight. So infatuated I'd have sabotaged my lovely older sister's relationship in any way I could.

"So when you got back from Kili," he asks, "how did you avoid managing to break up with Blake?"

I sit up with a grin, brushing sand from my arms. "Are you trying to give me shit for dumping him by text again?"

His smile is slight. "No, I'm just thinking it must have been awkward to act as if everything was normal. I'm assuming you didn't live together?"

I shake my head. "His business is in Vegas. He claimed he was planning to sell it and relocate to New York, but I got the sense that it might never happen. He kept trying to get me to move out there instead. But anyway, I just hadn't seen him."

He looks relieved by this for reasons I can't understand. "So, no amazing reunion sex after you got back from Kilimanjaro? I'm struggling to imagine dating you and not being in Manhattan waiting the second you got off that plane."

I squeeze my thighs together to ward off the hard press of want there. It's all too easy to imagine Miller waiting for me, eager for that reunion. I'd be eager for it too. So fucking eager.

"I don't think I've seen him since New Year's actually."

His mouth falls open. "So you're saying that the two of you went without sex for nearly two months?"

I frown. I suppose that means he *has* had sex in the past two months, which shouldn't bother me but does. "It just kind of worked out that way. But yeah, I guess it's a long time to go without it."

His gaze lands on mine, saying *I could fix that for you.*

I can't agree. But if he just...went for it...I already know I wouldn't be willing to stop him.

I really wish he'd just go for it.

I shower when we get back to the house and don the second of the bikinis *Elite* sent: bright red and as skimpy as the first.

He's in the kitchen, unloading the dishwasher. I grab a popsicle from the freezer and hop on the counter to watch him.

"I'm being helpful by providing you with interesting conversation," I claim.

He glances over his shoulder, his gaze lingering for half a beat on the bikini, on the popsicle as I place it between my lips.

I wonder if he remembers the way he used to tease me, threatening to eat the cherry ones whenever I left the beach house. I loved it. And I loved that he *didn't* tease Maren. It made me feel as if he and I shared something he didn't have with her.

"Go ahead," he grunts, turning toward the dishwasher. "Provide the interesting conversation, then."

I lick the sides of the popsicle first. "What would you like me to discuss? Global warming? Celebrities I think are overrated?"

He slams the dishwasher door and leans against the opposite counter. His gaze is on my face. On my mouth.

"I want to talk about the dream you had in the tent," he says.

I pull the popsicle out of my mouth. "I had a lot of dreams in the tent."

A muscle ticks in his jaw. "You know what dream I'm referring to. You said it was about someone from college. Who?"

My eyes fall closed for a minute. I could lie. I could make someone up. I just don't want to. "You know it wasn't about someone from college," I whisper. "What was I supposed to say?"

"Jesus," he whispers, his hands clenching the counter behind him. "You're lucky I didn't know that at the time."

My body is so tightly strung that a single touch could make it shatter.

I lick a trickle of juice running down the popsicle's side, stalling. His pupils dilate; his nostrils flare. And suddenly I know what that favorite fantasy of mine was based upon, the one I told Maren about: it was him, during that talk in the kitchen.

The faceless man who grabs me on the kitchen counter, the one who doesn't take no for an answer, was Miller. I needed him to take it from me because I couldn't offer it, and he was only faceless because I couldn't stand to admit to myself whose face it was.

I didn't run him off because I didn't *trust* him. I ran him off because I couldn't stand not having him for myself, and I kept right on wanting him for years and years.

My gaze slowly returns to his. It's the point where I should make a joke but none come to mind. The only thing in my head is *Do it, Miller. Close the distance.*

"Fuck it," he whispers, and in a single stride, he's crossed the kitchen to where I sit. He pulls the popsicle from my hand and tosses it toward the sink before he grasps my face in his palms and kisses me.

His mouth is warm against my popsicle-cold lips. His tongue finds mine, and my thighs spread wide to bring him closer.

"Fuck," he hisses, his erection pressing between my legs. I could come just from the feel of him there, from the gentle friction of him pressing closer when we're still separated by multiple layers of clothing.

I could come at the idea of how *much* is there, hard as steel.

He cups one breast, groaning against my lips as the pad of his thumb slides over my nipple, pinched tight beneath the top.

He pulls back just enough to watch my face as his hand slides inside the cup of the bikini. His nostrils are flared, his mouth ajar.

As if he could come just by watching me fall apart.

"This fucking bikini is as bad as the other one," he whispers. "You torture me, Kit."

I want to argue that he's the one who's tortured me, that I've waited ten fucking years for this, but his mouth is moving now...down, down to that breast he revealed, to the nipple pinched so tight for him.

"I've thought about my mouth here for so long," he groans as his lips fasten around it and tug hard enough to make me gasp.

His mouth continues—sucking, biting, alternating between soft, sweet kisses and tugs so pleasurable they're almost painful while his hand trails between my legs, slipping under the elastic of my bikini bottom, air hissing between his teeth when he feels me—slippery and swollen for him. My head falls back against the cabinet as he slides one thick digit inside me.

There's an awkwardness to your first time with someone, normally...*Will he think my ass is too flat? Will he think my boobs are too small? Is that scar from my appendectomy ugly? What if he's not good? What if I'm not?*

None of that exists here.

He knows everything already. If my boobs are too small and my ass is too flat, that couldn't matter to him less. And he won't be bad, because he's him, and I won't be bad either, because he wants this so much.

"I want to fuck you," he says. "Right here on this counter. Just like this. I'm not normally this selfish. Judge me for it later."

I respond by sliding the bikini bottoms off and widening my legs.

I might need more foreplay, under normal circumstances, but I've been fantasizing about this for a decade, and wanting him so much that the thoughts infiltrated my sleep, and I'm already so worked up that I'm worried I'll come before he even gets going.

His trunks fall to the floor and he grasps himself, running

the tip of his cock over me once, twice, three times, until I'm gasping and digging my nails into his back, desperate to feel the press of him as he enters me.

"Do I need—"

"No," I say with a frantic shake of my head. "Please."

With a groan, he lines up to my entrance and begins pushing inside me. As wet as I am, it's a stretch.

"Oh God," he whispers as his head falls to my shoulder. "It's too good, Kit."

"More," I beg, digging my nails into his back again.

He gives it to me. First in slow thrusts and then harder ones, with one hand braced against the counter and the other wrapped around the back of my head so that it doesn't slam against the cabinet.

His mouth is on my neck, his sounds muffled.

*Jesus.*

*So long. Wanted. For years.*

*Just like this.*

His words hit in hissed fragments, and each provides a new thrill...tingling up my back, making me clench harder around him. My hair is clinging to my skin; a drop of sweat is streaking down his chest.

"Not yet, not yet," I cry, pleading more with myself than him.

My teeth dig into my lower lip. I no longer feel anything but the way he is filling me, no longer see anything but the orgasm hurtling toward me, whether I want it to come or not.

"Oh, God, yes, just like that," I beg, my back starting to give way as if my body can no longer hold me up.

I come with a muffled cry and his mouth presses to mine, inhaling it, groaning as he lets go.

It's exactly what I fantasized about, but better. He's still hard inside me, twitching. His hands are on my ass. Mine are on his back.

His head falls to my shoulder, his breathing still fast, and the kitchen grows impossibly silent.

Any moment now, one of us will apologize and then the other will apologize and it will be awkward as fuck.

I should go. I should get out of here as fast as possible because this was such a mistake.

But God, what a mistake. What an amazing, fucking miraculous mistake.

One I now have to set right. My father's plane is probably gone. I can still get a commercial flight out if I hurry.

I open my mouth to say all this, but his hand grips the back of my neck and pulls my face to his before a single word of it comes out. He is kissing me again, and it is no less desperate, no less raw than it was before.

Which is an odd way to preface the awkward apologizing we both are about to do.

He releases my neck, still kissing me, and tugs my bikini top off. Also a strange way to preface an apology, or the suggestion that we just got carried away. He steps back and looks me over, his eyes dark and hungry.

"Jesus Christ," he says. "I have fantasized about doing so many things to you that I don't even know where to go next."

This is a bad idea. My sister will never forgive me, and we really should stop while we're ahead, but the way that he is looking at me right now keeps me silent. I place my palm against his bare chest, and that seems to be all the agreement he requires. With his hands beneath my thighs, he scoops me off the counter and turns, moving us toward his bedroom, where he places me on the bed.

He climbs on the bed between my spread legs, looking me over with dark eyes. And then he descends to kiss a trail down my neck, brushing over my lips and my eyes. I gasp and his mouth curves into a pleased smile against my skin in response, before it begins to lower. He pulls one tight nipple into his mouth, soft and then hard, making me gasp and arch.

"Fuck," he groans. "I want to go slow, and you make it so difficult."

He continues working his way down my torso, his hand still on my breast as he spreads my legs wide and runs his tongue over me, from my entrance and up, circling my clit, using his shoulders to spread me wider as he does it. He places one finger inside me and then another.

"I love the way you taste," he hisses. "I want to do this for the rest of my natural life."

Some distant voice inside me argues that this is unrealistic. We can't stay here, we can't be together, we wouldn't even survive if I continued to just let him go down on me twenty-four hours a day, but I can't seem to form the words. I tug at his hair as if I'm drowning and he is all that can keep me afloat.

"I'm going to—" I cry out. I come before I can complete the sentence, and his tongue moves faster, his fingers plunge harder, prolonging wave after wave, not relenting until my back has settled against the bed and my body's gone entirely slack.

I stare at him, astonished. "I didn't even realize I *liked* that. I apparently like that a lot."

He laughs, but inside that laughter there's a rasp of pain, and when he leans over to kiss me, he is like steel against my abdomen. I reach for him and he groans. Already, it's as if I haven't just come twice but have never come in my entire life and really, really want to see what all the fuss is about.

I should return the favor, however. I'm nothing if not fair-minded.

"Get on your back," I tell him.

He shakes his head. "I want that. I am going to want that a million times. But right now, I really need to fuck you again."

This time my gasp is half surprise and half desire. No one

has ever been quite so open with me before, quite so filthy, and it turns out I really, really like that too.

We're both starting to doze off when I think of Maren, and my pulse triples as the guilt hits.

I throw off the sheets, suddenly in a profuse sweat and breathing too fast.

*Oh God, I've really fucked up.* I've really, really fucked up, and I can't begin to imagine how I let this happen.

I pad to his bathroom and turn on the shower jets, simply to get some distance from him so I can calm the fuck down. My head hangs as the spray hits my face.

What the hell am I doing? How could I have let it go this far? It was such a betrayal. And whether Maren knows about it or not—*I'll make sure she never knows*—it will remain such a betrayal.

I've got to get home. Immediately. I've got to undo this and I can't, so the next best thing is to get out before I make things worse.

His arms wrap around my waist as he steps in behind me, resting his chin atop my head.

"Don't do this," he says. "Don't disappear on me."

I turn and press my face to his chest as my hands wrap around his back.

"I can't help it," I whisper. "I don't think you realize how hurt Maren would be by this."

"You slept with someone she dated briefly ten years ago," he says, "and I am naïvely hoping that you also might *like* the guy she dated ten years ago. I just don't see how this can be as big a deal as you think it is. She's married. Her life has moved on, so why shouldn't mine? Why shouldn't yours?"

I glance up at him. "She and Harvey are having problems,

and I think maybe somewhere in the back of her mind, she's wondering if there is still a chance with you."

"That can't be true," he says with a quiet, shocked laugh, pushing my hair back from my face. "Seriously. It can't be. I've barely seen her over the past ten years, and I've never once given her the impression that I regret breaking up with her. To think otherwise would be...delusional."

"Haven't you ever idealized something or someone in the past? It happened so long ago that you can barely remember any of the details, yet you somehow convince yourself it was perfect? I think that with her marriage falling apart and feeling alone, she's looking back at that summer and seeing it all with rose-colored glasses."

He tips my chin up with a finger. "I am not willing to just give this up because your sister is struggling in her marriage. You shouldn't be either. Haven't you been through enough? Haven't you sufficiently taken care of her and your mother, and suffered in the process? Take something for your-fucking-self. *Please.*"

I let my head press to his chest, hoping that it conveys everything I cannot say—that I would give up almost anything to make that possible, that I want him every bit as badly as he wants me, if not more, but that I also don't see any way forward without hurting my sister, and that's something I will never be able to do.

He turns off the shower and wraps me in a towel before leading me back to bed. I'm still committed to ending this but the damage is done, I guess.

Until we return, I'm going to take enough of him to make up for the past decade.

And to sustain me through the next one. Because when we leave, this is definitely over.

## 20

### KIT

With Blake, I didn't object to sex. I enjoyed it, mostly, but didn't especially seek it out.

With Miller...I don't want to do anything else. I want him to cover me, destroy me, and do it all again. I want him to tell me his filthiest fantasies so I can make each of them come true.

I wake with him curled against my back and give a small, contented sigh. The sun is out. I have no idea how late I've slept. I didn't realize how many empty spaces I held until I came here with him, but they're slowly but surely getting filled in. I'm sleeping longer, I'm eating more, and I'm laughing more.

I'm definitely getting other spaces filled more too.

"Are you finally up?" he asks. "I've been waiting."

"You could have woken me," I say, reaching backward to pull him closer.

He nuzzles my neck. "I figured you needed the rest."

"I think I'm good," I say, pressing backward until his erection is resting against the cleft of my ass.

His groan grazes my ear. "We really need to get going," he

says, lifting my leg and pushing inside me. "But I'm incredibly weak where you're concerned."

"Get going where?" I ask. Other than eating at the hotel, we've entirely set our own schedule thus far.

"A boat tour," he grunts, his hand firm around my hip as he thrusts inside me. "I booked it our first day here—I was worried you might get bored."

His hand slides over my pubic bone to find my clit. The effect is so immediate it's as if I've touched a live wire.

I can't imagine how it's possible to be bored with him.

A little after ten we arrive at the dock near the hotel to meet the boat, which takes us to snorkel over the coral reef and then delivers us to a mangrove, where we glide in glass-bottom kayaks over tortoises and stingrays.

As much as I'd just wanted to remain in bed, being in public with him like this reminds me how much I just *enjoy* him, whether he's touching me or not. That I like the way he treats other people and the way he treats me too. His protectiveness on Kilimanjaro wasn't an isolated thing. His hand is ready to catch me as I walk down a dock, as I climb into a boat.

We talk about his sisters and his mom's family in Greece and his best friend, Gray, who sounds like a total asshole but the kind of asshole I'd enjoy. I tell him about Roger, my current and favorite stepfather, and my shock that he and my mother have made it as long as they have. "Your dad loves Roger," Miller says. "You don't really think your mom will leave him, do you?"

I shrug. "I think she might have, but she knows that Maren and I would go with Roger and Charlie in the divorce."

He grins. "It's kind of cute that you like them so much. I've only met Charlie a few times, but he seems like a good guy."

This is still so weird. That he's *buds* with my dad. That he knows Charlie.

"The Douchiest Man in Manhattan. That's our nickname for Charlie, because he's always sleeping with at least two women at the same time, but aside from that aspect of his personality, he's wonderful."

He raises a brow. "*Maren* calls him The Douchiest Man in Manhattan?"

I laugh. "She's surprisingly mean to him, for Maren, although I guess it's me and Roger who call him a douche. She calls him The Handsomest Man in Manhattan behind his back but never to his face."

"I wouldn't want my wife calling another guy the handsomest, even if it were true," he says, and my thighs clench. I know exactly how Miller would be as a spouse: equal parts loyal and possessive. He'd demand everything of you, but he'd give you everything in return.

I want that. And with every minute we spend together, I'm wondering how the hell I'm ever going to give it up.

I DON one of the two nice dresses *Elite* sent along, paired with flip-flops, to go out to dinner that night. I barely recognize the girl I see in the mirror, the one with bright eyes and wild hair and kiss-swollen lips.

I walk out of my room to find him waiting in a fitted polo and khaki shorts. "Damn," he says, rising, his eyes falling to the V of my dress. "Maybe continue letting *Elite* pick out clothes for you. This is way hotter than what you wore at the summit."

I laugh, tucking my index finger into the collar of his shirt. "I sort of like the way they're dressing you too."

"Kitten, you're looking at me in a way that will definitely result in you not getting fed," he says, running his thumb over my lower lip.

I grin. "We can't have that. I *definitely* want to be fed."

He groans and reaches down to adjust himself. "God, you're impossible. Get in the fucking golf cart before I bend you over that table."

Which sounds pretty good too, but if I'm famished, I *know* he is.

As hungry as I am, even after we're sitting at the restaurant with our plates before us, all I really want to do is stare across the table at him. He has the loveliest nose. I have a childish impulse to say it aloud, but it would sound too ridiculous, too infatuated, for something with such a limited shelf life, and something that is probably a lot more one-sided than I want to admit.

He reaches across the table and runs his thumb over my lower lip. "Have I ever told you how much I love your mouth? It's like this little rosebud when you're mad, and it's like a peony when you're thinking about something."

I smile as my cheeks heat. Maybe it's not so one-sided after all.

The water refills our wine. Miller feeds me a bite of his steak; I feed him several bites of my pasta. Somehow it's already as if we've been together forever.

I smile. "I sure didn't picture any of this while we were sharing a tent."

He gives me a filthy smile. "I did. Repeatedly."

I suck in a breath. "What did you imagine?"

His eyes are heavy-lidded. "A lot of things, although the one where I'm standing and you're on your knees would have been hard to pull off in a tent."

I raise a brow. "I've tried to offer that several times over the past two days and you turned me down. I sort of assumed you weren't into it."

His laughter is hoarse. "I'm into it. I just suspected it would, uh, be over too quickly."

I take a sip of my wine and sweep my tongue over my lips. "The next time we're alone," I say, my voice suddenly husky, "I'm not taking no for an answer."

He exhales, pressing his palms flat to the table. "I think we'd better get the check."

The bill is paid and then we're driving as fast as we can in a golf cart, his palm clenched tight around the steering wheel. I reach across the divide between our seats and run my hand over his erection. He huffs out a pained breath the second I make contact.

We stop in front of the house and he pulls my face to his, kissing me hard, biting my lower lip, then reaching into the bodice of my dress to run his rough palm over my nipple.

My breath skitters, and he removes the hand. "Out," he commands.

I climb out and fake a yawn. "I think I'll just read for a while then go to bed," I say, walking toward the door.

His hand wraps around my bicep as he pulls me back to him.

I laugh. "Did I worry you?"

"No, Kitten," he growls, "because you promised me something back at the restaurant and I'm going to make sure you keep your word."

"Oh?" I ask, biting down on a smile, feigning innocence. "What was it you wanted again?"

He leans in, pressing his lips close to my ear. "Get on your fucking knees, Kit."

God. There's a rush of heat between my legs at those words.

We're still outside, but it's isolated enough that no one will see us, and I'm beyond caring if someone does.

I drop, reaching for his belt and then his zipper while he watches me with dark, drugged eyes. I pull his pants down, and then the boxers beneath them, before I bring his cock to my lips, licking the tip.

"That's right, Kit," he groans. "Just like those popsicles you love so much."

I let my tongue run over his length, then circle the head. My hand slides over his base and he grows even harder than he was.

"Take all of it, Kit," he demands, running a hand through my hair. "Take the whole thing."

I open wide and take him as far as I can, until I'm gagging, before I pull back.

"*Again.*" As if he's no longer the Miller I adore but someone else, some fiercer version, desperate to watch me struggle.

I moan around his cock and press my hand between my legs as if I can dull the ache.

"Fuck," he says, thrusting into my mouth. "Yes, Kit, make yourself come. You have no idea how good you look right now with my cock sliding between those lips of yours."

My fingers circle faster and faster. I'm already close, just from his words, just from the desperate way his hips are jerking to get farther inside me.

He tugs at my hair. "Are you going to come for me, Kit?" he growls. "Will you come while I fuck that pretty little mouth?"

I cry out, half-strangled, as his cock hits the back of my throat.

"Swallow," he gasps. "Fuck."

He comes so hard I can't keep up with it, so hard that the overflow spills out of my mouth and down my chest, and he watches from under those heavy-lidded eyes, still moving my head with his hand against my scalp, thrusting in and out, wreaking the last moments of pleasure from his orgasm.

"Did I hurt you?" he asks, still breathing fast as he pulls out and helps me to my feet.

I shake my head. "I wouldn't have come that hard if you had."

He runs a thumb over my lower lip. "You are so perfect, you know that?"

I smile. "Have you forgotten about my sharp tongue?"

"Oh, right." He presses a kiss to the top of my head and then lifts me up, wrapping my legs around his waist as we turn toward the house. "But I seem to like that tongue a lot too."

# 21

---

# KIT

The following afternoon, I'm on the patio making him a shell necklace he'll never wear—he's told me outright he'll never wear it, and I'm bartering with sex acts to convince him.

He slaps my bare ass—the bartering led to sex on the chaise once already, with no concessions made on his part, which is why I'm currently naked and he's only in boxers. "There's nothing you can offer that's going to convince me to wear a shell necklace at a social event. There's also nothing you can offer that I can't persuade you to give up *willingly*, as I believe I just proved."

"There are a *few* things I haven't given up," I taunt, continuing to string shells onto the thread, raising a brow at him. "Doggy style was low-hanging fruit."

He laughs. "If I hadn't just come five minutes ago, I'd take that as a challenge. Ask me again in ten minutes."

He starts typing on his laptop again. I can always tell when he's working by the speed with which he types—there are no pauses; the keystrokes are hard and decisive. I can't tell if this is simply because he's a decisive boss or if it's because he resents having to email anyone when he's on vacation.

"Do you like your job?" I ask when he slams the laptop shut.

He startles, as if doesn't understand the question, and then shrugs. "I do. I mean...it's not fun the way it was at the start but I'm in Turks and Caicos with a naked woman at my disposal—"

"I'm not at your *disposal*, cocky bastard. I might say no at any moment."

He slides a finger between my legs. "I don't see you saying no, Kitten."

I huff an exasperated, needy exhale. "I still could."

He removes his hand with a grin. "As I was saying, I've got a naked woman at my disposal, willing to do every filthy, degrading thing I demand of her—"

"You're seriously pushing it."

He laughs. "So I can't complain. And the company's at a point where I can tell them 'my phone is off, only email if it's an emergency', as I have now, and they mostly manage without me. It's a good gig."

I roll over to face him. "It *is* a good gig. That doesn't mean you can't complain."

He sets the laptop on the ground beside him. "It was more fun at the start, I'll admit. Back when I was just getting it off the ground and there were a million things to do. I think the part I like is the development stage. And that's really over now."

My head tilts. "Then why haven't you started something new? You've got the money. You've got the time, *clearly*."

He glides a hand over my hip. "I think I prefer spending my time the way I have for the past few days."

I look up at him from beneath my lashes. "The swimming? Making avocado toast?"

He leans down, his breath grazing my skin as he pulls my nipple between his teeth. "Those are okay, too."

A breathy sigh eases out of me. We've talked enough, I think...

The purr of a golf cart jolts us both.

"What the fuck," groans Miller, sitting up and covering me with a towel. "I canceled everything this week."

"Mr. West?" calls a voice, and then one of the hotel employees appears.

"Hey," says Miller, his palm pressing the towel flat to my back. "I canceled all the regular services this week."

The man nods. "Yes. Your guest? Someone is asking that she check her cell."

Miller thanks him, and I scramble upright the second the guy is gone, rushing to my room for the phone I've left on silent since *last weekend.*

There are multiple missed calls and dozens of texts, which are telling me the same thing.

Miller walks up behind me, wrapping his arms around my waist. "Is everything okay?"

My legs wobble. "No. My mom is in the hospital. They think she's had a heart attack."

"Fuck," he whispers. He pulls me closer and presses his lips to the top of my head. "It's going to be okay. You get dressed and pack. I'll get us back to New York."

My hands shake as I pull on jeans and a T-shirt and throw my stuff into the suitcase. I shut my phone off because I knew my mom would keep texting and calling and there was some vindictive part of me that felt as if I deserved the break. Because a piece of me was and still *is* so outraged that I can't keep Miller, though none of that was her fault.

I pick up the phone and force myself to open her messages now, sick to my stomach. If this goes badly, these may be the last words I ever hear from her.

MOM

Do you know how much work I put into this party? I gave up MY birthday in order to make your special day a surprise. Maren gave up a trip to Aspen to be here for it.

I've tried to call and you're not answering. Call as soon as you get this.

Why are you not calling? I need you to talk to someone at the IRS on my behalf. They're saying I didn't file my taxes. There's something in this letter about taking the house.

I can't believe you haven't replied. I can't go to the accountant because then Roger will find out, and he'll be furious with me. You've got to fix it before it gets that far.

Call me this instant. Or is your father the only person good enough to be included in your life now?

If she dies, she'll leave the world thinking I just didn't care enough. She was in an unbelievably stressful situation, and I made it worse. My ambivalence didn't cause her heart attack, but it sure didn't help.

I text Maren to tell her I'm on the way and drag my suitcase into the family room. Miller's in the clothes he was wearing the night he arrived at the club—jeans and a long-sleeved T-shirt. His jacket sits beside his bag.

I've gotten accustomed to shirtless Starfish Cay Miller, but I love Winter New York Miller just as much. I'm pretty sure I'd love all the versions: On The Way to Work Miller, Off To The Gym Miller, Black Tie for a Wedding Miller.

I'd love all of them, but this is the last one I'm going to get.

"It's gonna be okay, Kit," he says, pushing my hair behind my ear.

"She was having some issue with the IRS she needed me to fix." My voice wavers. "I never even saw the texts."

"Your mother is a fifty-five-year-old woman who's been working since she was sixteen. She also has a husband and an accountant. She didn't need you to fix anything."

I shake my head. "She didn't want Roger to know, though."

His jaw clenches, then relaxes. He presses his mouth to the top of my head. "Kit, she was asking you to fix a problem she's just as capable of solving because she wanted to lie to her husband about the whole thing. You've gotten so accustomed to taking care of her stuff that you don't even see how insane that is."

Maybe he's right, but that doesn't change the fact that I played a role in what happened to her. I contributed to her stress and then wasn't there for her when it worsened.

Miller slides the back doors shut. I take one final look out at that white, white sand and the endless blue water.

He joked about me coming back as his guest, but there's no way. It could never be as a friend now, and to continue this behind Mare's back...it'd just be going too far. Even for me. Even with what I've already done.

Miller carries my bag and his and tucks them into the trunk of the waiting car. I spend the entire ride to the airport with my head against his chest. Because we're about to be in public, so it can't ever go there again.

HE'S BOOKED us beside each other in business class. I wouldn't have taken the risk, but I suppose the odds of being seen are slim. When he reaches over to squeeze my hand, I don't have the heart to pull mine away, because this day consists of so many lasts. The last time I'll sleep with him, the last time I'll shower with him, the last time we'll sit together over a meal, that he'll kiss me, that he'll carry my bag or hold my hand.

I couldn't have treasured them more than I did, but I still

wish I had. Maybe if I'd known it was going to end today, this goodbye wouldn't feel as hard as it does.

When we land at JFK, we walk toward the exit a few feet apart, just in case we're seen. I'm the daughter of one famous model, the sister of another, and the eventual heir to a fortune. It's enough to merit the occasional photo, and I need to make sure Miller isn't in the frame if it happens.

We climb into a waiting limo and head straight to the hospital. Occasionally, I get the sense that he's about to say something, but when I look over, his mouth closes.

And what is there really to say? We both know it's over.

The limo pulls into the hospital's circular drive and he squeezes my knee. "Do you want me to come up?" he asks. "I said that wrong. I *want* to come up, but I know that will lead to questions."

I want him to come up too. I would give anything to have him there with me, but of course I can't. I lean over and place a kiss to his cheek. "That's okay," I tell him, "but thank you. Thank you for all of it. I will never forget this." I turn, reaching for the door, but before I can open it, his hand is sliding around the back of my neck and pulling my mouth to his.

"This isn't done, Kit," he whispers as he releases me. "Get through whatever is going on up there and then come back to me because this isn't done. I can't fucking stand for it to end here."

His eyes are burning, pleading with me to agree, and my stomach sinks. I can't stand for it to end here either, but I'm not sure what option I have. I slide out of the car and take one last glance backward, committing him to memory, before I shut the door behind me.

Inside, they direct me to my mother's floor. I'm surprised to discover she's not in the ICU, and the nurse who leads me back to her room is cheerful and has no sense of urgency. I've spent enough time in hospitals to know the staff isn't normally super upbeat when a patient's life is on the line.

She opens a door and there my mother is, sitting up in bed, hooked to a blood pressure cuff but nothing else. I see no leads for an EKG, and she and Maren are both scrolling on their phones as if this is Starbucks and they're waiting on friends.

*What the fuck?*

I drop my bag on the ground. "What's...going on?" I demand of Maren. "The messages you sent made it sound like—"

Maren raises wounded eyes to mine. I guess my tone was abrasive, but she has no idea what I gave up to get here. "Mom thought she was having a heart attack," she says, "but now they think it was just a panic attack."

"Did they do an echocardiogram?"

My mother looks blankly at Maren, and Maren looks at her. "They did some tests?" my mom says. "But I was already feeling better by the time I got here."

I squeeze my eyes shut, praying for patience. If it was only a panic attack, she wouldn't still be in the hospital, and if it was something *worse* than that, she should damn well be monitored in more ways than she currently is.

Air whooshes out of me. "Did it not occur to anyone to tell me they thought it was a panic attack?"

My mom shrugs. "We assumed you were on a plane by then."

*Wow.* I'm not at the point where I think they set the whole thing up, but their decision to just not update me was *absolutely* punitive. "So you're saying it was a panic attack and that you felt better by the time you arrived this morning. Then why are you still here?"

"We don't really know," says Maren. "They haven't told us anything."

I look around me. "Where's Roger? Is he finding a doctor?"

My mother shakes her head. "The hospital dinner was awful, so he's getting us carry-out."

I walk to the wall and hit the button for a nurse, who comes in at the leisurely pace of someone who knows there's nothing wrong with my mother—not that I fault her because that certainly appears to be the case.

"I'd like to take a look at any tests my mother's had today," I tell her.

"Oh," she says, her mouth forming a cartoon-like circle. "I'll need to check with the doctor."

This irks me—my mother doesn't need a doctor's permission to see her own fucking test results—but I let it go because Roger and Charlie are entering the room, and Charlie will definitely ridicule me later for starting a fight with the staff.

"There's our little runaway bride," he says, loping over to wrap an arm around my shoulders.

I shrug him off. "Were you with your dad just now or were you off with a hot nurse in an empty room?"

"They have no empty rooms at the moment," he says. "Regrettably."

I roll my eyes. "That makes it even *more* confusing that Mom is staying overnight when it appears she shouldn't be."

"We knew you'd come in and clear it all up for us, Kitty Cat," he says with a grin. "Though I've got to say, for someone who's normally so on top of everything, you've certainly been a little messy of late, haven't you?"

I silence a twinge of guilt. He couldn't possibly know I was with Miller—my dad is a bit of a shit-stirrer, but he couldn't out us without admitting his own role.

Besides, *he* has no idea how far it went.

The doctor enters the room with the weariness of someone who's been dealing with my mother for several hours in a row and raises a brow at Mom's carry-out container.

"We don't normally suggest people who've entered the

hospital with a possible cardiac issue dine on red meat and potatoes," he says.

She bats her lashes at him. "I was starving. The dinner was so abysmal."

He smiles only because she's still hot, and this gambit continues to work on men of all ages. "That's how they make sure you don't want to stay."

I don't have time to watch my mother work on seducing a sixth husband in front of her fifth. "I'd like to see the tests performed when she was admitted, as well as her labs," I cut in. "I assume there was an echocardiogram?"

"Are you a doctor?"

My teeth grind. "No, I'm not, and as you're well aware, I don't *need* to be a doctor to demand to see the tests myself, with her permission, so I would like to see them."

My mother gasps. "Kit." She shoots an apologetic look at the doctor. "I'm so sorry. She's been traveling all day and was very worried. She's not normally like this."

"She's not?" Charlie asks drolly, and Maren covers her mouth with her palm.

The doctor hands me the file. "Knock yourself out, but it won't mean anything to you."

I ignore him and begin flipping through its contents. Her Troponin I and T were in the normal range—they'd be elevated for days afterward if she'd had a heart attack. "Your labs are fine," I tell her. "The echo shows a bit of atrial fibrillation, but that might be associated with your possible panic attack and is more likely related to your intake of diet pills."

"Diet pills?" the doctor asks, taking the chart back and flipping through it. "I don't recall seeing anything about that."

My mother shoots an angry gaze my way. "They're not *diet pills*. They're just homeopathic supplements."

"That she gets illegally from China," I add.

"We'll need to know what she took," he says, scowling.

"Regardless of what she took, nothing in these results warrants an overnight stay, so I'm confused why she's still here."

The doctor looks between us. "Mostly because your mother requested it."

"Unbelievable," I mutter. "Thank you."

Ulrika needed attention. Apparently the whole *maybe-I'm-having-a-heart-attack* thing wasn't enough. She needed all of us freaking *here*. She needed Roger rushing out to get her steak and me jumping on a plane and Maren sitting anxiously by her side for twelve hours straight.

The doctor backs out of the room, leaving us all facing each other. As usual, somehow, I'm the bad guy here and I don't especially care.

"Good work, Mom. Glad I flew for four hours, sick to my stomach, when there was nothing wrong with you and you *requested* to stay. Hope it was a sufficient amount of attention."

Maren's eyes are wide. I tend to turn my ire on the people who hurt her and my mom...it's very rarely directed at them. A frown settles upon her delicate brow.

"Kit," she scolds, "you took off minutes before a party that Mom spent *months* planning, so you can climb off your high horse a little here. Especially when you left us to clean up your mess so you could go off to get a tan." She waves a hand at me, as if my skin tone is enough to condemn me for pretty much everything.

Normally this might chasten me, but not today.

"I wonder if you can begin to *conceive* of how many of *your* messes I've cleaned up?" I ask. "Both of you. Mom, how many boyfriends of yours did I have to pull into line? Mare, do you not recall that it was me and not you who had to go break up with Ryan Nicoll because you were too scared to do it? Do you recall that it was me and not you who moved all of your stuff out of that apartment afterward? And you both know that's the tip of the iceberg. So I'm sorry that, for once in your lives, you were left to clean up a mess of mine. But it would certainly be refreshing if you could've done it without this level of resentment, because I'm pretty sure I didn't act resentful the one million times I did it for you." I pick up my bag. "I'm glad you're okay, Mom, but you don't need to be here. I'm going to bed."

I walk out and Charlie follows.

My eyes narrow. He's not escaping my wrath either. "You, of all people, should have known this was bullshit."

He holds up his hands. "I'm not going to be the person who denies Ulrika attention when she's in need. And you realize none of this would have happened if you'd just stop fighting her battles. Maren's, too, for that matter."

I snort. "You're either out of your mind or you've begun drinking again."

"I never stopped drinking," he says with a grin, "as I'm sure you're aware. It's my favorite pastime."

I raise a brow.

"Second favorite pastime," he amends. "But anyhow...let them fight their own battles for a while, Kit."

"Fight their own battles?" I ask. "Have you seen what just occurred here? No one in that room had a diagnosis or even knew what tests had been run!"

"I'm not saying they'll be *good* at it," he says, more gently. "And I'm not saying that you shouldn't step in at a time like this, where it's life or death, potentially, and you're the only one with medical knowledge. But you've made them soft."

"I haven't made them soft. They *are* soft. They came into the world that way. That's why I had to step up."

"Everyone comes into the world soft, little sis. Life makes them hard." He laughs. "That didn't come out quite right, but you know what I meant."

It's possible, but that doesn't change the fact that Maren and my mom are entirely unequipped to deal with the real world.

"I just don't want to see them get hurt."

He nods. "I know. And that's because in certain ways you, also, are too soft. It hurts *you* to see them get hurt."

I exhale, suddenly exhausted by the conversation and this day as a whole. "This is all pretty reflective for someone who just spent six figures getting an incriminating video scrubbed from the Internet."

He laughs. "I was reading some articles about helicopter parents in the lobby and thought of you. But anyway...take it under consideration. It's possible you could have stayed wherever you were if they didn't assume you'd come rushing back to take charge."

I walk downstairs and hail a cab. I'm certain that Miller is back at his apartment by now, probably in bed and *definitely* relieved to have this all behind him. But since he texted asking me to let him know as soon as I heard something, I tap out a quick message.

> Hey, there. My mom is fine. There was absolutely nothing wrong with her, and I'm heading home now. I'm sorry it had to end like that. Thank you so much for taking me. It meant the world.

He doesn't reply, which I guess is for the best. It ended as well as it could have—no long speeches, no false promises, no suggestion that we could somehow keep it going, even if I desperately wish we could. It was as clean a finish as we were going to get.

The driver pulls up in front of my building. I wave to the doorman and proceed to the condo I no longer want to be in.

I used to love this place. I loved the windows, and the way I could see the Empire State Building if I stood in the outermost corner. But it's not Starfish Cay. It's not a white-sand beach and the clearest water. It's not Miller, following me as I climb into the shower.

Even the shower is disappointing. I want warm breezes blowing in and a skylight. I want Miller grinning at me, his dimple tucking in as he opens the shower door.

And then I want to wake with him warm and sunburnished beside me, giving me a sleepy smile as his eyes flicker open, pulling me close, ignoring my objections about morning breath as his mouth moves to mine.

I've just turned off the water and reached for a towel when there's a knock at the door.

It's too late for a visitor. My father, Maren, and my mother are all on the doorman's list, but my dad is across the country and the other two are, I'm sure, still at the hospital.

Which only leaves one other option—Blake. *Shit.* I have no idea how he knows that I'm here, and while I'm incredibly tempted just to turn off the lights and wait for him to go away, it's probably best to get this over with.

I throw on a robe and, mentally bracing for Blake's fury, open the door...only to watch Miller walk in instead.

I blink rapidly. "I thought you were Blake."

His eyes fall to my robe, and his nostrils flare. "You were going to open the door for Blake dressed like *that*?"

I glance down. I guess the robe *is* barely tied. "You were banging on the door...I just didn't think. How did you even get up here? You're not on the list."

"I know a guy," he replies.

My dad, I suppose. Meddling again. "Okay...why are you here?"

His eyes hold mine. "You can't possibly think we're done just like that. I'm here because I don't want to be anywhere else."

I swallow hard, leaning against the wall. "Miller," I say softly, "this can't end well."

He closes the distance between us. "Who says it has to end

at all?" he asks, flicking my robe open with his index finger and sliding his hand over my bare hip.

This isn't how it was supposed to go, and it makes it all so messy. Now we won't have a clean break, and it will end in some ugly way. I just don't have the strength to send him back out the door when he's all I want right now.

But I can't imagine when I'm going to get any stronger.

# 22

## KIT

I'm dead asleep on Miller's chest and his arms are wrapped around me tight when my phone starts beeping. Reluctantly, I climb off him to reach toward the nightstand for it.

MAREN

I'm sorry about yesterday. You were totally right. I had no business being resentful. I'm on my way over—just dropping off the puppies at the groomer first. What do you want from Zuri?

Shit. I know my sister, and there will be no dissuading her. I could make something up. I could claim that I'm not here, but then she would just insist on meeting me wherever it is that she thinks I am, and it would turn into an escalating series of lies. Still, I've got to try.

ME

It's all good. You don't need to come over. I'm in bed.

MAREN

I'm not going to feel as if you've forgiven me
until I've fed you something with a lot of sugar.
What do you want?

"Dammit."

Miller raises his sleepy eyes to mine and raises a brow. "What's the matter?"

I swallow. "Maren's on her way over, and she's not taking no for an answer. I'm gonna have to meet her out."

Let's meet at that breakfast place near you
instead. Give me thirty.

His mouth presses to my neck. "How long do we have?"

"Ten minutes, tops."

He rolls me beneath him. "I can work with that."

I'm stretched and a bit bruised from last night, because if he wasn't waking me up to go again, I was waking him—but that only makes me crave it one more time.

"You're like a mosquito bite," I say, clenching as he pushes inside me.

"Not what a man loves to hear when he's just started fucking you," he grunts.

My laugh is slightly breathless. "I just meant that I've scratched it once and I want to keep scratching."

His generous mouth curves upward, just a hint of a smile. "Good. Because I want you to keep scratching for a long, long time."

I'M FIVE MINUTES LATE. Maren is sitting at the table with her chin in her palm, watching the people outside pass by with a wistfulness that makes my chest ache. I don't think I even realized how *deep* her unhappiness was until Miller came into my life...because I was so unhappy too.

Maren jumps to her feet and throws her arms around me when I approach the table. "I'm sorry, pumpkin," she whispers. "You were absolutely right yesterday."

"I'm sorry too." Even if she was in the wrong—and I'm not sure she was—I'm unable to hold a grudge against Maren for long. "I was mostly mad at Mom, not you, anyway."

The women beside us huff in irritation—apparently we're in their space. I ignore them, shrugging off my coat, while Maren returns to her seat with an apologetic smile.

"I should have given you more of an update," she says. "It's not like you to just...shut me out like that, and my feelings were hurt. I didn't put it together until Charlie gave me one of his lectures."

I grin. "Since when is Charlie the emotionally healthy member of this family?"

"Right?" she laughs, sliding a latte my way—oat milk and cinnamon. Maren, like my mom, has often asked insane things of me, but she also cares enough to remember exactly how I like my coffee, to worry that my nails aren't done just before I'm wearing an engagement ring for the first time. Even my mother's obsession with my weight is a bizarre form of care—she wants me to be *her* idea of my best self: extremely thin, extremely spray tanned, perfectly made up. She just wants me to get the attention and accolades she got at my age, and she's never been able to understand the fact that I don't especially want them.

I don't need accolades. I just need Miller saying '*You looked beautiful there, and you look beautiful here.*'

"Anyway, I wasn't trying to shut you out. I was trying to shut *everything* out. I had a million messages from Mom, and Blake's mom and sister, and Blake himself, who I blocked when he called me a whore and—"

Maren's brows shoot skyward. "He called you a *whore*? How *dare* he? I'm going to hand him his ass the next time I see him."

I laugh. Apparently, my sweet, gentle sister turns into *me* when the occasion requires.

"But anyway," I continue, "everyone was acting like I'd just bombed an orphanage, and I couldn't deal."

She sighs. "I'm so sorry. I asked you a million times if you were sure about Blake and you said you were so I just... respected your decision." She grins. "I promise never to respect your decisions again."

"That's probably wise." Wiser than she knows, since I seem to be making some bad ones lately.

A toddler walks past us and Maren stares at her longingly for a moment before returning to me. "So where did you go?" she asks. "Obviously someplace with better weather than we've got here."

Fuck. I'm not great at lying to people other than myself. I'm not going to mention Starfish Cay—with as much cyberstalking as she's done of Miller in the past, she might know he has a house there. Hell, she might remember him talking about wanting a house there when they were dating.

"I, uh, was with Mallory. Down in Mexico."

Maren laughs. "That's incredibly vague. It's a big country."

I blow out another lying breath. "Los Ventanas."

"Oh, wow, you know who was staying there last week? The Donovans. Their baby is only nine weeks old, too. I'm not sure what you do with a nine-week-old on the beach. Did you see them?"

Fuck. *Fuck.* This is why I don't lie. *Especially* to Maren. Because I could have told her I was trafficking minors in Antarctica and she'd have known someone *else* who was trafficking minors there and would then be astonished we hadn't run into each other.

The waitress delivers Maren's green juice. I order a muffin, and then my sister is looking at me, waiting for more lies about Mexico.

"I don't know the Donovans."

"Yes, you do. Eliza? She's the one who was sleeping with that hot coach in high school. But anyway, what's going on? Why do you seem sad?"

Jesus. For someone who so frequently seems clueless, Maren has certainly turned into fucking Scooby Doo.

I consider just blurting out the truth: *I think I may be falling in love with your ex-boyfriend. I think it's possible I've been in love with him since he was with you, and that I was so awful to him because I didn't want you to have him.* But what good would that accomplish? She'd feel betrayed, and it's not as if anything could move forward with Miller anyway. Is he somehow going to slide back into our family dinners with Maren across from him, openly pining? And who knows if he even wants that? Sure, it's all very intense right now, but maybe he's a Charlie...only in love until he's had a sufficient number of orgasms, then ready to move onto a newer model.

The only solution is to reveal a tiny bit of the truth—though not the important part of it.

"I don't think I want to take over the company," I tell her. "I thought about it a lot when I was on my climb, and someone pointed out that I talked about health stuff constantly but never mentioned my job once."

Her eyes widen. Fischer-Harris has been our family's business since the 1920s. My dad would have been happy to bring Maren into the company, but she never had a moment's interest. If I'm leaving too, it means it won't stay in the family when my dad retires.

Maren waits until my muffin has been placed in front of me to continue. "Have you told Dad?"

I shake my head as I dump sugar packets into my latte. "I'm meeting him for lunch Monday. Maybe then."

"I've never seen you put that much sugar in anything," she says. "Anyway, I can tell how worried you are, but honestly? He's going to be okay with it—he just wants you to be happy. Will you go back to medical school, then?"

I shrug. "I hope so. I don't even know if they'll let me in."

She rolls her eyes, smiling. "You are Henry Fischer's daughter. I'm pretty sure you could have burned the school to the ground and they would still let you in. But before you work on that, you need to deal with Mom."

I sigh heavily. "Is that why you got me here? So you could convince me to go make up?"

She squeezes my hand. "We're your family, whether you like us or not. And even if we make mistakes, you know me and Mom would never do anything to hurt you, which means you've got to forgive us when we do."

The guilt hits hard. I think a part of me enjoyed resenting them because it made what I was doing with Miller seem almost justified.

But it wasn't. And with Maren sitting across from me now, so worried and kind and unhappy, my disloyalty seems even worse than it already did.

I DUTIFULLY PUT on an outfit slinky enough that my mother won't criticize it and head to her home that afternoon, though I know how it will go: she'll be snippy; I'll be snippy back. I'll make several good points and she'll make several nonsensical ones, and in the end—questioning how I could share half my DNA with someone so illogical—I'll apologize just to make it stop.

A maid smiles as she lets me in. It's undoubtedly the last pleasant moment of this visit.

"I couldn't believe how you behaved at the hospital yesterday," my mother begins when I walk into the kitchen.

I go to the Keurig and open the cabinet for the coffee pods only I use. "You let me fly all the way home, panicking, knowing you were fine. It was shitty and selfish."

"Your coffee pods were moved to the drawer on your left," she says. "And I didn't know I was fine, or I wouldn't have stayed at the hospital. You act as if I just love drama."

I arch a brow at her.

"I *don't*," she insists.

"You should have told the hospital about the diet pills, Mom."

She shakes her head. "I couldn't. I'm pretty sure they're not legal."

I groan. "You weren't being interviewed by the FBI, Mom. No one was going to raid the house for your ephedra or whatever it is that you don't actually need."

"That's easy for you to say," she replies. "You're still thin."

Like I said...nonsensical. There is no point in arguing.

"Did you solve the IRS thing?"

My mother's shoulders sag. "No thanks to you. Roger is so mad at me."

It's Miller's voice I hear in my head. *"Your mother is a fifty-five-year-old woman who's been working since she was sixteen. She didn't need you to fix anything."*

I press my hands to the marble island between us. "Mom, don't you think we're both a little too old for me to be fighting your battles? That was crazy. I mean, I was hours and hours away, enjoying a much-needed vacation—"

"You'd just *returned* from a vacation!" she cries.

I frown at her as I go to the fridge for oat milk. "You go sleep in twenty-degree weather on the ground for a week with no showers and tell me how much of a vacation it feels like to you."

"I've done plenty of things like that and loved it. I went to that place in Italy where they made us hike every morning and—"

I shut the refrigerator door with a laugh. "Are you really going to tell me that your room with a private plunge pool and daily massage was the same as sleeping outdoors for a week with no shower?"

"We weren't allowed to drink the entire time. No coffee either." She nods at the oat milk in my hand as if it's proof of her personal fortitude. "It was incredibly hard. If you were going to go anywhere, that's where you should have gone. I lost ten pounds."

I fight a grin and take a sip of my coffee. "Everyone else told me I came back from Kili too thin, while you're trying to say I should run off to fat camp."

"It wasn't *fat camp*," she says. "It was a resort devoted to the fitness journey. And I'm not saying you need to lose ten pounds, but my God, think how thin you'd be if you did. I still don't understand why you're not modeling. You'd be just as successful as Maren, but the clock is ticking."

I shake my head, carrying my coffee over to the table. I've never wanted my entire life and income focused on something I won't be able to hold onto...because that turns you into my mother: diet pills from China and plastic surgery she will lie about when people ask. "I don't want to model."

"You don't want your father's job either," she says, which is perhaps the most insightful thing that's come out of her mouth in a long time, "but you're still pursuing that. Not that I'm complaining. You'll be the one who can afford to buy me a private plane when I'm retirement age."

*Possibly not, Mom.*

"That doctor sure was cute yesterday, wasn't he?" she asks changing the topic.

I sigh. I like Roger—he's kind to my mother and puts up

with her bullshit—but what my mother likes is excitement. She wants a man who will worship her, then treat her like shit, then apologize with jewelry. She confuses emotional upheaval with passion, and she's had just a little too much stability with husband number five.

"I thought he was a condescending dick, actually."

"Only because you baited him," she argues. "He was lovely. He stopped by to see me this morning before I left."

I don't know if I want to cry or laugh. But as I leave her house, I know the person I most want to discuss it with is Miller.

I shouldn't reach out to him. If this morning proved anything, it's the impossibility of this continuing. But my fingers twitch impatiently until I've written him.

> Hey, are you around?

MILLER
I can be. Want to come over? I'll cook.

> It's not avocado toast, right?

Keep it up. I'll definitely have something to put in that smart mouth.

> Is it soft and green?

I haven't looked in a few hours, but I certainly hope not.

I run a few errands and I arrive an hour later at the address he sent with a bottle of wine, which feels oddly formal and also insufficient. The man gave up his trip to Kilimanjaro for me, then gave up his safari, then took me to his cottage in paradise and shepherded me home.

That probably deserves more than a nice Malbec.

The doorman leads me to the elevator and pushes a button

for the twelfth floor. When I step out, Miller is opening his door —barefoot, shirtless and sweaty—and walking into the hallway, as if he was so excited to see me he couldn't wait until I reached him.

His abs gleam, tan from Starfish Cay. I picture him beneath me the way he often was there, looking up at me from under heavy-lidded eyes.

"I sort of thought you'd wait to look all sweaty until *after* I'd had my way with you."

His dimple flashes. "I just got back from the gym. And I intend to look exactly like this again in an hour or two but let me shower first."

He leans down as I reach him and gives me a chaste kiss. Only Miller could manage to sweat like that and still smell good.

"Don't shower for my sake," I reply, my voice a little raspy.

He glances at the outfit I wore to my mom's. "I don't feel worthy of defiling you in my current state."

He pulls me into his apartment, which reminds me a lot of his place in Starfish Cay—the same cathedral ceiling, the same modern wood. I would like to stay here and never leave. "Make yourself at home," he says. "I'll be right back."

I walk toward his bookcase and thumb through a massive book about management. "I'm going to go through all your things," I warn.

He laughs. "I assumed nothing less."

When he's gone, I go to the window, which looks out over Central Park.

That's the first place I took Rob after he came here to visit me. He was supposed to be in California, with his parents, and got a flight here instead. I'm not sure why, but those memories of him seem more distant now. I don't want them to feel distant because it's as if I'm giving him up, giving him back to the world, but, perhaps, they *should*.

Maybe I've been clinging to those memories because it's the last time I was truly happy and I didn't want to forget what it felt like—and that it was possible.

I go into Miller's bedroom, which is as spotless as the rest of his place. There's a wide dresser that isn't piled with clothes the way mine is. A closet holds only a few of everything—a couple suits, some shirts, some jeans. I'd like to think that I'd be similarly spartan were I a man, but I seriously doubt it. I take a seat on his bed and glance at the nightstand. And stare. There, next to a glass table lamp, sits a woman's ponytail holder. Tossed there casually by someone who forgot her hair was still up until she climbed into bed. My stomach sinks. I have no right to be bothered—I was, after all, about to get engaged. But that ponytail holder is a small wound, one that reopens a little when he walks out in nothing but a towel and gives me that dimpled smile.

I don't want anyone to see him like this but me, and very recently someone did. And probably will again.

# 23

## MILLER

You're getting ahead of yourself.

No matter how many times I say it, I still find myself planning for a future that might not exist, not when Kit still believes we can't be together and continues to carry another guy's ashes in her purse. It's crazy, as pointed out earlier in the day by my closest friend.

*"Let me get this straight,"* Gray said, quietly mocking, *"you've barely been sleeping with her for a week, she says you can never be together, and you're already thinking about transitioning the company over so you can move away with her when she goes to med school, which she might not even do."*

I couldn't even defend myself. He was right. And yet with her face down in bed beside me once again, after all the times she's told me this can't happen...maybe there's more hope than Gray thinks.

"So what are you going to do?" she asks, as if she's somehow read my thoughts. She folds her arms beneath her and turns to gaze at me.

I grin, letting my palm glide over her perfect, bare ass.

"When you ask me that question completely naked, it's very difficult for my mind not to go in one particular direction."

She laughs. "You've already come twice since I got here and you're incredibly old. Surely you've got nothing left."

I press a kiss to the center of her spine. "I'm only five years older than you, Kitten. And don't bait me or I'll show you exactly what's *left*."

I know this feeling of obsession will pass eventually, but at present I seem to have two modes—wanting to be inside Kit Fischer and recovering from it. I'm already shifting from one phase to the next as we speak.

I'd like to stay in this bed with her forever either way.

"Seriously, though," she continues. "What are you going to do? If you're not in love with running the company anymore, you need a project."

I flop back to the space beside her. The business has kept me just preoccupied enough that I didn't spend a lot of time ruminating about whether or not I was fulfilled, or happy. But I've been wondering about it a lot since she asked me that question in Turks and Caicos.

"I'm not sure. To be honest, it's felt as if we were still in lift off and wobbling for a while. It's only been in the past year that everything's stabilized. But I guess...maybe I'd like to develop something entirely different."

"Health related?"

I shake my head. "I like finding these holes in the universe and plugging them." She raises a brow and I laugh. Jesus, I just came five minutes ago and now I'm thinking about it again. "Not *that* kind of hole. Well, yes, that kind of hole, repeatedly, but also holes of the non-sexual variety."

She rolls onto her forearm and runs her free hand over my chest. "So, what holes do you see? And maybe we should use a word other than *holes* because this entire conversation sounds like a double entendre and that wasn't my intent. Let's call them...needs. Vacancies."

The damage is done. They all sound sexual to me now—I've fully shifted back into *wanting to be inside Kit* mode—but for her sake I'll attempt to have an adult conversation while she's naked. It might be possible.

"Ever since Kili, I've been thinking about adventure travel. I'm not the only person out there who's looking to challenge himself, and the problem is you have to do a lot of research to find unusual trips and when you find them, you still have no idea how to prepare. You want to kayak in Antarctica, for instance, but you don't have a fucking clue where you'd stay and who'd take you out there and what kind of gear that would require. So, picture a globe that's lit up with hundreds of unusual, difficult challenges, and then you click on one of those challenges and find out exactly what's required."

Her hand stills. "That's incredible. You came up with all that since we left *Kili*? And here I was, thinking you were just a pretty face."

I grin at her. "I think I started coming up with it on the bus from the airport, when I realized this ridiculous little princess in the seat across from me was about to ascend to eighteen thousand feet without a fucking clue what she was doing."

"How dare you?" she demands, pulling away with mock indignation. "I was completely fine, aside from being exhausted, and doing no training, and thinking I could turn it into a diet."

I yank her back to me and press my mouth to hers. I love the way she yields when I kiss her, how she goes from smart ass to soft and pliant in the space of a single gasp. "You were perfect."

"Because I had you," she says with a soft smile, and I light up inside like a kid on Christmas. I want this to work out with her in a way I can't even describe. I want to follow her across the world, and I'd give up every fucking thing I have to make it happen.

I'm getting ahead of myself, but in moments like this...I can't help but think it all might work out anyway.

## 24

---

## KIT

Miller and I spend nearly all of Saturday in his apartment. I keep offering to leave and then he suggests a movie, takeout, his bed... At some point, the ponytail holder disappears. If it had simply remained, it might indicate a lack of awareness—it had been there so long he'd stopped seeing it, or it mattered so little he'd thought nothing of it.

But no...it's gone, so it belonged to another female and probably someone relatively recent, and I'm not about to ask who it was but I wish I could.

"I'm really leaving," I tell him on Sunday morning. "I've been here since Friday. I still haven't unpacked from either trip, and tomorrow's my first day of work."

"I've been a little selfish," he says, burying his face in my hair.

"I like it," I tell him. "I desperately wish I could avoid being a grown-up for another week."

I leave him and return to my apartment. It's an absolute wreck. My bags from Kili are open on the floor, their contents filthy. My suitcase from Starfish Cay sits waiting in a corner.

But the worst part is that it's lonely. It's too quiet. I pick up my phone and call Miller. "You want to come over tonight?" I ask.

It certainly doesn't feel like I'm bringing this all to its necessary conclusion.

In the morning, I wake early and begin getting ready. A part of me still can't quite believe I'm sitting here in a bra and underwear, applying lipliner while Miller watches from the bed, covered only by a sheet.

"You're pulling out all the stops today. Are you nervous?" he asks.

I shrug. I don't know if it's nerves necessarily. "What I mostly feel is dread. Every time I enter a new part of the company, I know they're thinking that they're stuck with Henry Fischer's idiot daughter, which means I have to work my ass off to prove I'm not the worst nepo hire in the history of time. I usually wing it until I figure things out, but I'm not sure I can do that in finance."

"This entire enterprise weighs on you," he says. "Every time you even looked at that book on publishing in our tent, you seemed to shrink. Please just tell your dad the truth over lunch today and quit."

"What am I supposed to do with myself instead, though? It's March. Even if I *can* get back into med school, I can't just twiddle my thumbs for the next six months."

He pulls me down beside him. "We'll go to Starfish Cay. I can work anywhere. We'll lounge around naked and snorkel and brown ourselves until our skin turns to leather. You'll learn to cook. I'll throw out all the popsicles that aren't cherry."

My eyes fall closed. I can imagine nothing better, no way I could possibly be happier. I hate that I'll never be able to agree.

MUCH AS I EXPECTED, everyone in the finance department is polite but weary, as if already fatigued by the experience before I've even had a chance to fail. "So, what kind of accounting courses have you taken?" asks the section's manager.

"I, uh, didn't actually take any? I was pre-med."

Her polite smile holds, but barely. "You can use Quick-Books, at least, right?"

I wince. "I'm sure I can figure it out?"

She leaves me going through expense reports because I'm not competent enough to do anything else, and I dutifully play along for an hour before I sit back and look around me.

I graduated summa cum laude from Brown. I got halfway through medical school. I will soon come into a trust worth many millions. Why the fuck am I here, in a windowless office under these fluorescent lights, going through expense reports like a high school intern? And how many times have I found myself in this position over the last three years?

I could be in Starfish Cay right now. Or I could be doing the shit that rich kids everywhere do: "exploring my art," "developing my craft," or turning a hobby into a business and letting everyone think it's profitable when it's not.

Hell, I could help with one fundraiser a year and fuck around the rest of the time and just claim that I've devoted myself to philanthropy.

I've been telling myself that my father's philosophy made sense: that I should need to know what occurs in every department. I've been telling myself that it'll be worth it when I'm in senior management, simply so that no one can say, "*This idiot has no idea what we do here.*"

Now I wonder if it was also a form of self-flagellation. If I continued to accept one unrewarding situation after another because I thought I deserved to be punished.

I get through three more hours. When I leave for lunch, I take all of my belongings because I won't be coming back.

They'll remember me as *Kit Fischer, who couldn't even stomach working at a real job for half a day*, and they're welcome to think it. I've been trying to prove myself to people who don't matter, in fields I don't care about, for years.

The person who matters is me. And I'm done.

I MEET my dad inside his building's rooftop restaurant. "You're looking particularly *well rested*," he says. If he's trying to imply something about Miller, I'm not taking the bait. "How was Kilimanjaro?"

I frown at him. "Question—did you actually want me to write an article or was it all a ruse?"

He smiles as if I'm an especially clever child who's just performed a new trick. "Of course it was a ruse. If you'd like to submit the article you can, but obviously the staff writers will be furious that you got to take an all-expenses paid trip instead of them."

I sigh heavily and pour some of his wine into my glass. "As I recall, that's exactly what I said when you first brought Kilimanjaro up. So...how much of this was about me risking my life on a climb I wasn't ready for and how much of this was about you wanting to put me and Miller in the same place?"

He laughs. "How could I have known who he'd go up with and when?"

I roll my eyes. "Because you asked him some questions and knew he'd go with the best company. It's a little late in the day to play dumb here, Dad. There's no way that it was a coincidence."

My father leans back in his chair, his glass of wine held aloft. "I knew he was going to Kilimanjaro, yes, and I knew *when*, but I didn't have any idea which route he was taking. I thought you needed the experience. I thought you needed to challenge yourself and get out of the Upper West Side bubble."

The conversation pauses while the waiter takes our order and picks right back up once he leaves.

"You knew that he would change routes," I accuse, "because he's the type of person who'd worry excessively about me, enemy or not."

"I *did* know that," my father says with a brow raised. "And what father wouldn't want that exact sort of man for his daughter?"

My chest squeezes tight. Of course he'd want me to end up with someone like Miller. I want it too. But it's so much worse to know everything he is when he's not going to be mine.

"Have you forgotten that he dated Maren?" I ask, squeezing the wine glass so hard I'm surprised it doesn't shatter.

"Of course not. But Maren now has a spouse and is trying to get pregnant, so it's safe to say she's moved on."

She hasn't moved on. At all. And my father knows that even if she had, this would never be okay.

"Anyhow," he continues, "how's your first day in finance going? You were always proficient at math, so it seems like a good fit."

"A good fit?" I laugh. "You do realize finance requires some very specific expertise, right? I've never taken a single finance or accounting course in my life. I'm totally unqualified. I've spent the past four hours going through expense reports."

He holds his glass up to the light. "Are you asking me to say something? You've never once asked me to interfere before."

"I'm not asking you to interfere." I take a deep breath and push my wine glass away. "I'm not going back. I don't think I want to manage the company."

I wait for him to express disappointment or shock. Instead, he nods and takes a sip of his wine. "I never thought you did, but I'm glad you've finally realized it for yourself."

My jaw falls open. "Are you *serious*?"

"Of course I am. Why would you want it? You're interested in people, not management and, for better or worse, you don't care nearly enough about money...which is probably because you've always had it and know you always will." He sighs. "I should have raised you better. I guess it's too late."

I stare at him as the waiter deposits our meals in front of us and hustles away. "Then why have you had me jumping through all these hoops, year after year?"

My father lifts his fork and knife. "Because *you* thought you wanted it. You were looking for an entirely new life after you left Charlottesville, and you'd pinned your hopes on mine. If this was what I believed you wanted, I'd happily have handed over the reins eventually."

I huff out a miserable laugh. "So instead, you just kept giving me one boring job after another so I'd realize that I didn't want it on my own."

He finishes chewing before he replies. "You see, the fact that you just called all the jobs here boring proves you were never meant for it. All the jobs you did are part of my day at some point."

"Sorting mail? Climbing Kilimanjaro?"

He chuckles under his breath. "Okay, perhaps not those. But everything else. And if you don't enjoy the small pieces of the pie, you're not going to like it more when the entire pie is yours. The way to end up doing what you love isn't by taking on even more of what you hate."

I wish he'd shared this logic with me a few years earlier, not that I'd have listened. "Mom won't be happy."

"Being unhappy is what fuels your mother. Well, that and diet pills. She'll dine for weeks or perhaps months on what a disappointment you are, and in a few years, she'll make a point of letting every person she runs into know that *her* daughter is a doctor."

I still. "Did Maren tell you I was thinking about med school again?"

He laughs. "No, my love. She didn't have to. You never stopped thinking about medical school. Of course that's where you'll end up."

It's annoying, how well he knows me. It's annoying that he's let me spend *years* arriving at an answer he apparently had on day one.

And it's heartbreaking that with all his knowledge and money and power, he won't be able to give me the thing I still want most.

# 25

# KIT

"I have a thing tonight," I tell Miller the next morning. He's wearing nothing but suit pants at the moment and pulling on a dress shirt.

I could die happy, watching Miller get ready for work.

He tugs at the shirt cuffs. "Will I see you after?"

"Yes, but it'll be late. Expect me to be in a bad mood."

He grins. "I always expect that, Kitten."

I throw a pillow at him and climb from the bed to pull on yesterday's clothes. "If you always expect that, it's a wonder you want to see me at all."

He crosses the room and tugs me against him. "Your mood mysteriously improves around me."

I go on my toes and kiss him. "Arrogant. But probably true."

When I get back to my apartment, I research returning to medical school while lacking the courage to actually call and discuss it with anyone, and then get dressed for tonight's family dinner.

I wish I wasn't spending the evening away from Miller, but the bright side of these get-togethers is that Harvey doesn't normally come while Charlie and my dad usually do. Charlie will bring some model or heiress who can't keep her hands off him and pouts when he ignores her to go talk to Maren. My dad will refer to Roger as "the longest suffering man in Manhattan" at some point, and my mother will be furious for a solid ten minutes before she forgets why she was mad. Maren will be there with her badly behaved puppies, who will destroy something or shit on the floor, only to be disciplined by Maren with cuddles and baby talk, which will provide a strong indication of how my future nieces and nephews will turn out. All in all, it's pretty entertaining. I wish Miller could see it. I wish he could become a permanent part.

I arrive at the club and head to the room my mother has reserved—The Skyline Suite, her favorite, because it has a lovely view of the city through the floor-to-ceiling windows that line one wall and an endless mahogany table big enough to seat all of us, along with any surprise guests we bring along.

My stomach sinks the second I enter: Harvey has shown up tonight. Worse, he's brought his idiotic brother, Buck, who has long "joked" about how we should have had a double wedding with Maren and Harvey.

"Let me know when you cut Blake loose" is how he's ended every conversation I've had with him over the past year, so it's no surprise when he immediately sidelines me and starts bragging about today's gains on the market. I excuse myself to get a gin and tonic, but picking up on no social cues, he follows me to the bar, and he's still following me when the door opens... and Miller walks in, his brow furrowed for a moment before his gaze lands on me.

I stare at him. Maren stares at him. My mother stares too. Only my father is unsurprised, reaching out to shake Miller's hand. "The intrepid explorer! Glad you made it." He turns to face me, my mom, and my sister—all of us incredulous. "I invited him to tell us how many times our Kitty Cat fell climbing that mountain."

"Henry," Miller says to my dad, "I was trying to give you the benefit of the doubt about sending Kit to Kilimanjaro, but you make it difficult by openly admitting you knew about her coordination issues."

Everyone laughs aside from me. Why the fuck didn't Miller tell me he'd be here?

Granted, I didn't specifically say I'd be at the family dinner, but I told him I'd be in a bad mood and surely he could have connected the dots. We should have discussed it, at least. I'd have dissuaded him from coming at all, but even if he disagreed, there are a thousand questions that could be asked that might prove awkward, answers we should have worked out in advance.

*Did you spend much time together?*

*Did anyone hook up on the trip?*

*Miller, where's your place again? The Caribbean? Been there recently? Oh, you were gone the same days Kit was! How incredibly curious!*

Miller circles the room, greeting everyone, and Maren is unable to take her eyes off him. He thought I was making too big a deal of the situation, but I know my sister: Miller has only gotten more handsome. He's also charming and intelligent and funny and kind, whereas Harvey could basically only pretend to be those things for a minute or two and no longer pretends at all anymore.

And while I'd welcome her realization that Harvey is a bag of dicks, I don't want her focused on Miller instead. So, in other words, nothing has changed in the last ten years: Maren and I both want Miller, and because of that, I'm going to insist that neither of us have him.

Miller finishes talking to my mother—I'm not sure why I resent how traitorously pleasant she's being to him after he dumped Maren when I just had him going down on me over coffee this morning—before he moves on to me.

"Hello there, little Kitty Cat," he says, giving me a hug.

"What the fuck, dude?" I whisper.

"I'll explain later," he replies before he draws away. "You look fucking amazing, by the way."

He gives me a glance that says he would like to take me around the corner and repeat everything we did this morning, and as furious as I am about being blindsided, my core is clenching.

My mother is traitorous. My vagina is just as bad.

We're all seated eventually—somehow I've wound up across from Miller and beside Buck, who is trying to look down my dress while telling me about the boat he's just bought in a way that indicates I'm meant to be impressed. I murmur appropriately timed *hmmm*s and *ohhh*s while typing out a text to Miller.

> WTF? How could you not tell me you were coming?

MILLER

> Your father invited me to dinner. I didn't realize YOUR WHOLE FAMILY WOULD BE HERE.

> But why would he do that?

> I suspect it's so you'll see how easily I fit in and that this isn't a big deal.

Except it hasn't shown me how well Miller fits in at all—Maren has practically gone into a fugue state as she stares at him, as if she's looking at both her past and her future at once. My dad might think he's solved something but really, he's just shown me how intractable the issue is: Maren thinks she loves Miller, and she thinks I'm the reason he left a decade ago, and the one outcome that will *never* be okay is if I get him instead of her.

I pick up my phone to reply but don't get far.

"Kit," snaps my mother. "No phones while we eat."

Like I'm seventeen again. I'm surprised she hasn't consigned me to a children's table in a different corner of the room.

As dinner is served, Buck tells everyone about his boat, and they all manage to sound more impressed than I did. He's the type of guy who loves holding court—the second someone asks Miller about his app, Buck's trying to draw me into a secondary conversation, which I ignore.

I have no right to feel this, but I'm flooded with pride as Miller describes how he came up with the idea and how he was able to monetize it to an extent while making it free of charge in less developed areas. He's even added a way to connect people without resources to surgeons who might be willing to treat them pro bono.

Maren is listening to him as if he's hung the moon. Her eyes sparkle. Her cheeks and lips are flushed—signs of arousal.

I press a hand to my cheek—it's warm, so I'm probably flushed too.

This is the effect Miller has on women. All women. Including, I'm sure, the woman who left her hair tie on his nightstand.

More questions are asked, and he sounds so fucking adult, and hot, as he answers, but every time he pauses, his eyes rest on me. Is it obvious to everyone at this table that we are not merely people who climbed a mountain together once?

"So," says Charlie, turning to me and Miller, "I want to hear about Kit's disastrous falls in Tanzania."

"Screw you, Charlie," I say. "I'm not *that* uncoordinated."

"Remember that time Kit stepped in a bucket before we knew she needed glasses?" my mom asks Maren.

I'm the only one at the table who isn't laughing. "As I recall, Mom, we *did* know that I needed glasses. You said the prescription was low enough that I could get by without them and that I didn't want to be *that girl*."

"Anyway, you were telling us about Kit's biggest falls," says Charlie, turning back to Miller like the utter dick he is.

Miller's smile is gentle. "I don't recall her falling. But I do remember her saving a guy with a broken leg."

"You saved someone?" Maren gasps. "How could you not have told us this?"

I frown. "Because I *didn't* save anyone. I wrapped up a guy's leg. That's it."

"She also monitored everyone's oxygenation and made sure that someone was directly behind one of the girls she was worried about." Pride gleams from Miller's eyes. It's sweet but far too obvious.

"There isn't a chance Kit didn't fall over the course of an eight-day climb," Charlie says, as a waiter refills his wine.

"I did," I reply, "and Miller is being too much of a gentleman to allude to it. You should take notes, Charles."

Which begs the question: why didn't he just address the hair tie rather than hiding it? He's a good guy...it seems really unlike him to be hiding proof of the woman who came before me rather than just confessing. All he had to do was admit he'd been sleeping with someone before he left for Africa. Hell, he's slept with at least two women at this table...I was well aware he wasn't a saint. It's the *deception* that bothers me. The sleight of hand, as if I'm too dumb to have noticed it there or put it all together.

My phone vibrates.

MILLER

Put on your sweater. Buck keeps looking down your dress.

I smile at Miller and tug my dress a little lower, leaning over slightly in Buck's direction. "Could you pass me the salt?"

Buck makes sure to take a lingering look. I've slept with

men who've spent less cumulative time looking at my rack than he has now.

"Which leads to another important topic," says my dad, though I have no idea what was said prior to this. "Have you told them, Kit?"

I freeze, and my mouth goes dry. Is he about to out me and Miller? Was the previous topic of conversation *disloyal sisters* or *backstabbers* or *inappropriate sexual relationships*?

He doesn't know for sure that anything happened between us, unless my doorman informed him about my recent overnight guest. Which, I suppose, is very possible.

"Told them what?" I whisper.

"Kit's leaving Fischer-Harris," he announces. "In fact, she's already left."

There's a cry from my mother's end of the table, which is the sound one makes upon discovering you've lost your last bit of access to your ex's billion-dollar company.

"That's good," says Harvey. "No guy wants to marry a woman at a job like that. It would be so emasculating."

"It sounds to me as if you might be easily emasculated, then," Charlie replies.

"What's *emasculating* about being married to a CEO?" asks Miller.

"A man wants to feel like he's the top dog in his marriage," Harvey says. "You know it's true, whether you'll admit it or not."

Charlie tips back in his chair with a brow raised. "Then I guess for your sake we should hope Maren never chooses to monetize any of her other talents."

"Talents?" scoffs Harvey. "Since when is spending my money a talent?"

"I'm sure there are a million men in the city who'd kill to take her off your hands if that's all you see," Charlie replies with an icy smile as he swallows the remainder of the wine in his glass. The animosity between them slices through the room, rendering all of us silent as the plates are cleared.

"I'll take an available Fischer girl if any are on the market," Buck says, grinning at me.

Miller's nostrils flare. "Back to the topic of conversation," he says, looking my way, "what are you going to do instead, Kit?"

As if he doesn't already know.

I hitch a shoulder. "Hopefully med school. I don't know— my family hasn't built a library for anyone lately, so it might be a little hard to get in."

His mouth tips up at the corner.

MILLER

Oh you want to play, Kitten?

It was just an innocent comment about the ease with which YOU got into an Ivy League school. Maybe it wouldn't bother you if you'd achieved more on your own.

I'm going to bend you over the kitchen counter as soon as we get home. Once for every time Buck has stared at your rack.

I glance up. He was watching me read the message, and there's intent in his eyes as if he's already planning his steps, first to last.

Of all times, this should be the one where I say *absolutely not*, and I already know I'm not going to.

"I need to head out," I announce, rising. "Thanks for dinner."

"I'll help you get a cab," says Buck, and Miller stands.

"I'll help her," he says. "I've got to run too." He's so smooth. The kind of smooth that means he could juggle multiple women easily if he wanted to. I don't think he would. But why did he hide the hair tie?

Buck says something about texting me—*ugh*—and I make a beeline for the front door.

Miller follows me out. We take different cabs but arrive at my building at the same time.

"That was ridiculous," I say as we step onto the elevator.

He pushes my back to the wall and kisses me hard, as if we were apart for a very long time.

The elevator arrives on my floor, and he ushers me off. "Buck looked down your dress the whole fucking night, and you never tried to stop him."

"I didn't realize you and I were at the stage where I stopped letting other men get a good look at my tits," I reply as I open the door.

He doesn't even give me time to turn on the lights. His hand fists my hair as he leads me to the counter, guided by moonlight.

"Bend over, Kitten," he growls.

I do as I'm told, now slippery and swollen with want. He could demand anything of me and I'd agree to it.

"Whose ponytail holder was on your nightstand?" I demand.

He stiffens for a millisecond. "You're bothered by a fucking ponytail holder? You're carrying a guy's ashes in your *purse*."

His hand slides between my thighs, pushing my panties to the side so he can play there for a moment, sliding down my center—torturously slow—before he presses two fingers inside me, and then does it again.

"Please," I whisper. "Please. *Fuck*." He's using both hands now. My palms press flat to the counter, needing to hold onto something.

"You look so good like this, Kitten," he hisses. "With that perfect ass in the air and your legs shaking."

"Fuck me," I plead.

He laughs. "Oh no—you ran your smart little mouth once

too often tonight. I'm going to take my time with this. You're going to drench my hand before I finally give you what you want."

My knees wobble. "Miller," I beg. And then it hits me and all I can do is whimper, biting my lower lip to keep my sounds in as I come.

I'm still coming when the sound of a zipper lowering hits my ears. "Spread," he demands, forcing me to widen my legs, and then he slams into me. There's nothing gentle about it—nothing considerate. He's barely begun and I already feel as if I'm going to come again.

I gasp and he bends low, his mouth against my ear, his left hand covering mine, his right hand between my legs. "You love baiting me, don't you, Kit?"

"You love it too," I gasp. "Don't act like it's all me."

"Yeah," he grunts. "I always have."

I'VE COME three times before we're finally at the cuddling-in-bed stage of the evening. I sort of feel like we just had our first fight, but I'm not even sure what it was about. The ponytail holder? The ashes? Buck looking down my shirt? I really have no idea. But I was mad, and I think he was mad, and now neither of us are.

"So, how much does my dad know?" I ask.

Miller's arms tighten, as if he suspects the answer will make me bolt. "He hasn't heard anything from me," Miller says. "But Kit...you did go away with me for four days. He's a smart guy. I imagine he's made some assumptions."

"Well, I don't know what he thought that dinner would accomplish, but it definitely didn't—"

I'm interrupted by my ringing phone. I don't know why I jump out of bed to grab it. Perhaps because this whole situation feels like a grenade is in our hands, and Miller's appearance at dinner was the slow slide of the pin.

Or perhaps it's because there's a fifty percent chance that at least one member of my family watched me and Miller tonight and figured us out.

"Kit, I'm coming up," sobs Maren. I hear the *ding* of an elevator.

"You're coming up *here*? In *my* building?" I shout, looking toward Miller.

His eyes widen and he jumps from the bed, pulling on his khakis.

"I'm going to ask Harvey for a divorce," she sobs.

"Okay," I whisper. "I'll be here."

I hang up and turn to him. "Maren is on the elevator," I gasp. He grabs his shirt and shoes and looks around him frantically.

"I'll go down the stairs?" he asks.

When I nod, he presses a quick kiss to the top of my head and runs out the door with his shirt and shoes in hand while I race to my room for a robe, snatching up the boxers and socks Miller left on my floor and shoving them under the bed just as I hear Maren letting herself in.

Her eyes are swollen from crying, but she comes to a dead stop when she enters. "Is someone else here?" she asks.

"What?" I reply, my voice weak. "No. So what happened?"

"This apartment *reeks* of sex," she says, wiping her eyes. She steps forward, past the kitchen, and points at my room off to the left. "That is a sex bed, and you have sex hair."

"I have no idea what you are referring to."

"Was it Blake?" she asks, swallowing and forcing a smile. "He was so pissed last week. You must be incredibly good in bed if you were able to win him back that fast."

I lead her to the couch. "It wasn't anyone. Tell me what happened."

Her shoulders sag. "I just...Harvey was such a dick over dinner and such a dick on the way home, and all I could think was about how nice Miller was when I dated him. I mean, I know he bickers with you, but he was never like that with me, and then he kind of put Harvey in his place with that whole thing Harvey said, about how it would be emasculating to have a wife who works, and—"

My heart is in my throat. "That was Charlie, Mare."

She shakes her head. "No, it was Miller. And he also said the thing about how millions of men would be happy to take me off Harvey's hands, which I thought was—"

"That also was Charlie."

She shakes her head. "I don't think so. But anyway...I finally saw Harvey through everyone else's eyes, and I mean, yeah, I knew he was kind of a pompous dick, but I didn't realize how bad it had gotten until tonight. It just suddenly hit me that I could be so much happier with someone else."

And the *someone else* she has in mind is Miller. He represents, for her, all the things in the world that could make her happy.

"I don't blame you, you know," she says, "for him leaving? I mean, if we'd kept dating back then, it would have ended. We were both so young that maybe you did us a favor."

It hits harder than it should. I suspected for a very long time that she thought I was at fault, but this confirms it. And...I no longer think I was.

Miller liked sparring with me. And in my seventeen-year-old mind, it seemed entirely possible that I'd just pushed him too far. As an adult, one who knows him fairly well, I'm certain nothing I ever said would have driven Miller off had he wanted to stay.

"Did you a favor?" I ask weakly.

"He left then, but now, you know, we're adults. Our lives are in different places, and we've both grown up."

She thinks this is their second-chance romance. This is *Atonement* and I'm the bratty little sister who drove them apart, all so they could find each other again. It's incredibly far off the mark, but the wrongness of what I've been doing is absolutely suffocating.

If she finds out—and she will if this continues—it's going to look as if I drove the love of her life away only so I could claim him for myself. She's going to think I stole something from her twice, something that would have made her perfectly happy.

And I knew this. That's why I was panicked to even let Maren know he was on my trip, why I swore him to secrecy about meaningless things. And now here I am, sleeping with him every night, sexting him at a family dinner.

I've been slowly boiling myself to death, falling deeper and deeper into something that I shouldn't even have had a toe in.

And now I've got to force myself out.

She cries for a while about how hard it's going to be to leave Harvey. Not because she loves him, so much, but because she wants children the way I want my next breath, and they've been doing *in vitro*, and now she's going to have to start over.

*I'm* worried because Harvey is the type to take it all very, very poorly.

"Do you want to sleep here tonight?" I ask.

She smiles, wiping away her tears. "In your sex bed? No thank you. I'm gonna go to Mom's. There's nothing like several veiled suggestions about weight loss to cheer you up during a marital dispute, I always say."

I hug her. "She'll probably suggest ways you could be livelier in bed too."

She laughs. "She will. Thank God I have you, so I know there's some hope for normalcy, despite our gene pool."

I see her out, and then slide down the wall with my phone clutched to my chest. It has to end. It unequivocally has to end.

"Hey there," he says, answering on the first ring. "Is Maren okay?"

"I can't do this anymore," I whisper, the words choked. "I've loved every minute, but it's got to stop."

"Kit, don't do this," he says. "Look, let's talk this out. I'll come over and—"

"No," I whisper. "That will just make it harder for me to do what I should have done a long time ago. Miller, Maren is getting a divorce and half the reason for that is you. Because she remembers how nice you were, and she's even giving you credit for things you didn't say tonight. I know you and my dad think it's crazy, and maybe it is, but I know my sister. She convinces herself of shit, and she's convinced that I broke you up the first time and that maybe now things are going to get sorted out."

"Except I don't want Maren," he says. "There's nothing anyone can say that will change that."

I swallow. "It doesn't matter. Because she believes these things are true, and I can't be the one to crush her when she learns they're not."

"I'm crazy about you, Kit," he says. "I don't think you have a clue. Please don't do this."

"I love you, Miller," I reply. "But don't call me again."

I hang up, so heartsick it's hard to breathe.

I've said those words to people before, but it never hurt the way it just did.

Because this was both the first and the last time I'll say them to him. And I'd like to keep saying them forever.

# 26

## KIT

Overnight, I've gone from a life that was perhaps too full to one that's entirely empty.

I'm unemployed. I'm no longer Blake's girl-friend, nor am I Miller's dirty secret. Although I guess, techni-cally, *he* was the dirty secret, not me.

I spend a lot of time with Maren—Harvey is out of town for work right now, and she's going to need to figure things out before she tells him. My mother is also around—surprising no one, she is rooting for Maren to *find her soul mate* and *take life by the horns*. This is one of the phases my mother loves: that moment in the story when all is lost. She enjoys being the plucky victim and having everyone tell her she deserves more. She's enjoying it vicariously through Maren now, and while Maren isn't entirely buying into my mother's *I am woman, hear me roar* glee, she's definitely in her optimistic phase: the quiet smile, the dreamy, infatuated thing in her eyes.

"Miller looked really good, didn't he?" my mom asks us. "If I were ten years younger, let me tell you..."

"Let's be honest, Mom," I say with a sigh. "His age isn't what's stopping you."

She laughs. "It sure wouldn't in his case. At least for one thing."

"Mom," Maren and I say in unison. "*Ewww.*"

And then Maren turns wistful while my entire heart seems to sink into my stomach like a dead weight. I miss him so much that I'm sick with it, and she's convincing herself a little more every day that they were meant to be.

When I'm not with Maren, I'm talking to various people in the administration at UVA. I've had two very long conversations with advisors, establishing again and again the chain of events. If I can convince them I didn't simply melt down from academic stress, I'll then have to retake the exams. I unearth my old notes and try to study to take my mind off things, but it doesn't quite work.

I miss Miller so much that it's all I can do at night not to text him, that when I wake up in the darkness, there's always a moment when I assume breaking up with him was a bad dream, and if I scoot backward an inch I'll find him there, warm and solid and entirely mine.

The weirdest thing is that during all these nights...I don't dream about Rob once.

"You sound sad," my father says when we talk. "What's this about?"

"Nothing," I reply. "You know I hate New York in the winter. It's just depressing here."

"Your mother says you look too thin."

"*My* mother said I look too thin?"

He sighs. "No, actually she said she was jealous of how thin you'd gotten, which tells me you're too thin. Why aren't you eating? You're not working for me anymore...hasn't this made all your wildest dreams come true?"

I want to weep. I'm going to weep. *Fuck.*

"I'm really not in the mood for sarcasm, Dad." I hang up before he hears me cry.

DAD

Kitty Cat, that wasn't sarcasm. You're not happy and it's obvious, and I just want to know why.

I don't answer him because what good could it do? Telling him the truth is guaranteed to only make things worse.

I go to Maren's house the next day. She tries to make me a green juice and asks what's wrong. My mother comes around and asks what diet I'm doing because she wants to do it too.

I don't know how much longer I can keep pretending.

I'm pretending that I'm not miserable when I am, I'm pretending that I want to be in New York when I don't, I'm pretending I don't know what I want from life when I know *exactly* what I want from life—it's just off-limits.

I spend a lot of time thinking about that fucking hair tie. She feels like a threat, the girl who left it behind. Was she the fallback he's already returned to? Every time I picture it on his nightstand, then picture it missing...panic seizes my chest, as if it represents a ticking clock, the limited time I've got to tell Miller I was wrong when I *can't* tell him I was wrong. Ever.

I meet Maren for lunch at the week's end. Something has changed in her: she's no longer fretting but she's no longer hopeful either. "What's up?" I ask.

"Nothing," she says with a forced smile. "I just think it's going to be harder to leave than I thought. He's going to be such an asshole."

She's not wrong, but... "You knew that from the start. What changed?"

She runs a finger over her lower lip. "I know it will sound ridiculous because I shouldn't be letting my crush on someone be the determining factor in deciding whether I leave my husband, and it really isn't, but *hoping* something might work out with Miller was like...the teaspoon of sugar I was taking with my medicine. A life raft. Something to feel optimistic about."

I swallow. "Yeah, it's probably best not to conflate the two things."

"You know me. I start daydreaming and half the time I convince myself the thing has actually happened. It was nuts."

Does that mean she realizes she's not in love with him? Does that mean it would ever be okay for him to move on with me? "So you're letting that whole thing go?" I ask.

She sighs. "I'm not sure I had a choice anyway. Miller's seeing someone."

My breath holds. "Cecelia Love?" I ask, and my breath is *still* holding while I wait, praying the ax isn't about to fall.

She shakes her head. "Some astronomy professor who was in Germany for a few months but has been flying back and forth. I guess she's coming home at the end of April."

My eyes fall closed as I picture him saying he'd just arrived from a meeting in Germany. Pointing out constellations that no longer exist. Obviously she was the source.

Maybe it was all in my head, how good it seemed with us. The way it was so easy to picture our lives continuing on together and how certain I was that he was thinking the same things. Maybe I've been just as good at fooling myself as Maren is. But hearing this now confirms one thing: I was only surviving this because I wasn't allowing myself to picture him with someone else.

And now I can't picture him any other way.

After lunch, I walk. It's technically spring now, but the wind is blowing, and the sky is a deep charcoal gray, warning of the snowfall expected tonight.

Is she here this weekend? Is she being pleasant and nonargumentative and making him realize what a bullet he dodged with me?

I am not the easiest person to love under even the best of circumstances. Eventually, he would have realized he'd be better off with someone sweet like Maren, someone less prickly, but I hope there's some part of her he wishes was slightly more Kit-like.

It's the exact sort of selfishness that makes him well rid of me.

The snow starts to fall and I stare upward, letting the flakes wash over my face. I wish it could've all been different. I wish I could figure out how to be happy without him.

I don't think I can.

## 27

## KIT

For two days the snow falls, and I'm stuck in my apartment.

I'm not actually stuck. Outside, people are in boots and ski pants and hats, walking through unplowed streets, marveling at this version of the city that's only existed a handful of times in the past hundred years: no cars, no honking, no traffic. Just ice-laden trees hanging heavy, the pavement a carpet of unbroken white, people who actually notice each other again as if they've woken from a long trance.

If Miller were here, I'd be out there with him.

I'd lose a mitten, and he'd try to give me his. If I refused, he'd remove his, too, and put my hand in his pocket.

When the phone rings, for a half-second I think it's him. That maybe he's thinking about this as well and wondering if I'd like to share his pocket once more.

"Let me up, Kit," says Charlie. "I'm downstairs."

"Why?" I ask.

"I've heard a rumor that you're languishing."

"I'm not even sure what that word means so I can neither confirm nor deny."

He laughs. "Fucking let me up."

He arrives a minute later, handsome and smiling like a guy who just got blown by three models on the way here, which is entirely possible where Charlie's concerned. He shrugs off his coat and takes a seat without being invited.

"Ah, languishing it is," he says.

My hair is unwashed and I'm wearing torn leggings, so I guess *languishing* is not a compliment. "I still don't know what that word means."

"I don't want to define it for you in case I'm wrong because I'm now questioning my own definition, but it seems like something people did when they were dying of consumption. *She languished away*, that sort of thing."

"So you're saying that I've got tuberculosis?" I ask. "If so, it's an odd thing for the family to be gossiping about behind my back."

He lays his phone on the table and smiles at me. "I'm saying that you're clearly brokenhearted and pining, and given the way Miller was eye-fucking you all through that dinner I assume it's about him."

My eyes widen. I knew someone would notice. "That's crazy. He's Maren's ex and she thinks she's in love with him."

He sighs. "Mare was just looking for a mast to cling to in the storm. Harvey's going to be awful when she tells him, and she wanted to believe that some big strong man would be there to stand up to him since you've trained her not to stand up for herself."

My eyes narrow. "This is fun. Anything else you want to blame me for?"

"Loads, but am I right?" he asks. "You and Miller?"

I stare out the window, at the streets I should be walking along without a glove. "I have no idea what you're referring to."

"It's funny the way you both got so tan while climbing a mountain in subzero temps."

I turn back toward him, jaw locked defiantly. "Have you never skied before?"

"I have, and it doesn't normally lead to arms as tan as yours or his," he says with a smug smile, nodding at where my sweatshirt is pushed up around my elbows.

I pick up a magazine. "Charles, I'm extremely busy right now. What is it you want?"

He kicks my foot. "Don't worry about Maren, Kit. She can take care of herself."

"I'm not sure what you're basing that upon."

He bites his lip. "You know what Maren's issue is? It's that she's smart, and strong—just as smart and strong as you—but she doesn't know it. You know why she doesn't know it? Because every time you fight her battles for her, it's the opposite of a vote of confidence. It's like you've just said, 'Sit back and look pretty while the adults take care of this issue, dummy.'"

I frown. "I know she's smart. But she's a people pleaser, and she never wants to make anyone mad, and she ends up getting taken advantage of a lot."

"What she cares about—more than people pleasing and far more than Miller—is her baby sister. And if she thought she was the reason your hair looks that bad, she'd never forgive herself."

I laugh, unwillingly. Maren is incredibly vain about her hair and therefore mine, I'll grant him that much. But that doesn't mean she'd forgive what I did...especially if I let it continue.

"Take a shower and get out of here," Charlie says, rising. "It's supposed to be in the sixties tomorrow. Spring is here, summer is coming, and you Fischer girls always like to have a boyfriend when the weather's good. I'm pretty sure we both know who yours should be."

~

WHEN I WAKE the next day, the sun is out and the gutters are dripping, so I guess Charlie was right. I force myself into the shower not because I think Charlie was right about anything *else*, but simply because I promised my dad I'd meet him for lunch.

I blow out my hair, apply careful makeup, and put on an outfit even Ulrika would approve of: camel wool wrap dress, red Louboutins—just so my dad won't agree that I'm languishing.

The restaurant is predictably swanky—floor-to-ceiling views of New York City's skyline, a hundred bucks in flowers on every linen-clad table. My father's favorite waiter rushes over as we're seated and my dad orders a 1955 Pinot Noir and steak for us both.

I'm not sure I have the appetite to eat, but whatever.

"You look thin, Kit," he says, as the waiter leaves. "And pale. You were glowing when I saw you at dinner."

I open my mouth to make excuses when I see Prescott Hughes heading toward us. People are constantly swinging by to kiss my father's ass—one of the least enviable parts of his job. Maybe if I were happier right now, I'd let him come and go unscathed, but I'm not happy so I flip him off, and Prescott turns the other way.

"What was that about?" my dad asks.

"He dated Mom," I say, meeting his gaze.

There's a hint of softness in his eyes. My mother is legendary for the sheer number of husbands and boyfriends she's brought through her home and what incredibly terrible taste she has. It's honestly hard to keep the misdeeds straight at this point.

Rich men, poor men. The one thing they have in common is that they think they can fucking get away with anything.

With a few notable exceptions. My dad, Roger, Charlie.

Miller and Rob.

Dad gives me a sad smile. "Then I guess we're lucky you didn't swing a golf club at his head. So you're thin and pale and sad, which I assume is about Miller, so what's your plan?"

I suck in a breath. "Miller?"

"Kit, I know your palpable distress is not about a career shift. And you don't run off to a private island in the Caribbean with a man who's just a friend."

*Dad knows. Fuck.*

While he and my mother don't get along, they do enjoy a good bit of gossip about their offspring. I wait until the waiter has set our steaks in front of us to ask the question on the tip of my tongue. "Have you told Mom?"

He shakes his head. "I figured I should let you work it out first."

"Work *what* out?" I ask. "There's nothing to be worked out. He's seeing someone anyway."

Dad raises a brow. "I'm not sure how you've come by that bit of information, but I know for a fact that it's not true."

My pulse races for a second. It shouldn't make a difference. It *doesn't* make a difference.

"Even if that's the case, I can't have him, Dad," I whisper, my voice shaking with unshed tears. "And you know good and well that I can't. He's Maren's ex. And she still thinks he's the guy she should have ended up with."

"At a certain point in your life, Kit, and I really hope that it's this one, you'll learn that sometimes you have to hurt other people to get the thing that will make you happy. Miller does not want her. He didn't want her ten years ago, and he doesn't want her now, which is why I brought him to that family dinner...so you'd see it for yourself."

"All I saw was that Mare still thinks he's the one that got away," I reply, while my dad adds wine to the glass I haven't even touched. "It was that dinner that made her decide to leave Harvey. And whether he wants her or not isn't really the point."

"Eventually Maren will realize that she's been glorifying a relationship she really didn't understand at all, and she will find the sort of man who *can* make her happy. And when she finds herself happily married, and probably producing loads of badly behaved children, and you've lost the man you should have been with, will it have been worth it then? Will it have been worth everything you gave up?"

He isn't wrong. And I think Maren already understands, to some extent, that she's been glorifying that relationship. But it doesn't mean she wouldn't be deeply hurt if she learned the truth.

I blow out a breath. "If she was your biological daughter, you'd be far less calculating about this."

"I love Maren as if she's my own," he argues. "I just don't entirely respect the decisions she's made."

My mouth opens to rush to her defense, and he holds up his hand, nearly upsetting his wineglass in the process. "To be fair, I don't entirely respect a lot of yours either. But Maren has always seen beauty where there's none and convinced herself it's real. She could probably do something amazing with that if she put it to use in the right way. Unfortunately, she's put it to use by seeing what's not there with the wrong men. And you shouldn't be the one who pays the price for that."

I almost believe him. The problem with my father, however, is that he's slightly too good at putting disparate facts together and making them look as if they're puzzle pieces that have fallen into place. It doesn't mean he's right. He's just good at selling a story.

"Did you ever wonder why I forgave him?" my dad asks.

I glance up from the steak I can't manage to eat. "Yes, I wondered it nonstop for the first three days of the trip. I finally assumed he'd just charmed you into it."

My dad tips back in his chair and smiles. "I'll admit that it was hard to stay angry at him, but no, that's not it. There's only one excuse for what he did to Maren that I'd have accepted, and it happened to be the excuse he gave me. He did it for you."

I stare at him. "For *me*? How did it benefit *me*?"

He swirls his wine in the glass. "Your sister is a lovely girl, but there are men in the world who prefer a woman with a little spine. Or in your case, a lot of spine. An unreasonable amount of spine, some might say—"

"You can stop now."

He smiles. "And Miller, to his credit, is among them. So the minute he realized he was in love with his girlfriend's seventeen-year-old sister, he did the most responsible thing he could, and left. Because he knew you were too young, and extricating himself as fast as possible was what would serve you best."

I think back to that moment in the kitchen in Starfish Cay. I'd thought it was simply *my* fantasy, a reenactment of that day in the Hamptons, taking the things I'd wanted for a decade.

But maybe it was his too.

That's what was going on, wasn't it, that whole summer? Bickering is foreplay for me and Miller. I was too young to realize it at the time...and maybe he was too young to realize it as quickly as he should have.

But when he did, he left, because what else could he possibly do?

As I put it together, none of it surprises me. Miller, above all else, is a good man. He wouldn't want to hurt Maren, and he wouldn't want to hurt me, and the way to minimize the damage was to let us both believe that he'd suddenly turned into a selfish dick, which he continued allowing us to believe for another decade. All while changing routes in Tanzania to protect me, and giving up his safari to keep me from getting sucked into a tragic mistake. He's been giving and giving in the ways that were available to him for years while I've been...flipping him off from across the room and accusing him of stalking me at the start of our climb. I press my face to my hands.

Oh, God. I don't want to cry here. In public. With my mother's society friends watching us from across the room, with at least a dozen people here who've got a gossip columnist on speed dial.

"It would always be weird, though," I say quietly, once I've pulled myself together. "I mean, if I dated him, it could never go anywhere. Think how awkward every family event would be. And people would gossip."

"Indeed," he says, nodding. "It would be very awkward for a very long time."

We both sit in silence for a moment. He eats, and I push my food around. Nothing he's said is wrong—I'm not taking something from Maren, and men like Miller are once in a lifetime. But it could mean fucking up so many other parts of my life to make it happen. And it would definitely mean hurting her.

"You know, when you were a toddler," he continues, "we bought this book for the nanny. *Controlling Your Strong-Willed Child*. You couldn't even read yet, but you got the gist of it, I guess because she'd open the book and then quote it to make you behave, so you attempted to flush it down the toilet. And for a long time, you remained that same kid. You entered every room and every conversation primed for battle, but it also turned you into someone who had to get everything right—and you fell apart when you didn't."

We exchange a look. He's talking about Rob.

"You haven't been happy for a long time, and you also stopped fighting to correct course until you got back from Africa. That's where you regained a little of that spark. You wouldn't have run off before the proposal if you hadn't. You wouldn't have told off your mother at the hospital, the way Charlie claims you did. So fight for the things you want. Be willing to hurt some people so that you don't hurt Miller or yourself. It's time to become the kid who flushed a book down the toilet again."

I look around the expensive restaurant, at all the people who don't seem happy—staring at their phones rather than listening to the person across from them. How many of them are like that because they gave something up, because they settled for an okay ending instead of a happy one? They are Tuesday people, just like I've been now for years.

Going for the things I want most isn't guaranteed to turn out well. Miller and I might not last; Maren might never forgive me.

But...I know I'd get a life that held more Fridays and Saturdays than mine does now, until it ends.

And even if it doesn't work—even if it's woefully brief—I'm willing to fight for a few more of them with him.

I WALK THROUGH CENTRAL PARK. It's one of those early spring days that tricks you into thinking winter might be over. The trees drip; the snow is turning to slush in the grass. Rob loved days like this. Rob loved a lot of things, and that's why being around him was such a joy: because he reminded me why I should love them too. He had so many wonderful qualities, but I think what initially drew me to him was the way he reminded me of Miller—that he had a lopsided smile and the same broad shoulders, that he was the type of guy who wouldn't leave a friend behind or even allow a girl who was terrible to him to risk her life hiking Kilimanjaro. I loved the way he embraced the world and tried new things and wasn't scared to walk away from all the privilege he was raised with.

But I loved Miller first. I know that now. I loved him from the moment he entered my mother's dining room, and it never fully went away. I just pushed it down, as far as it could go.

I think maybe all my grief these past few years was less about Rob than it was what he represented. He was the last time I felt hopeful about the future, the last time I truly felt happy, and I didn't want to let myself forget that had existed.

But I remember it now.

I cut across to the Central Park boathouse. Maybe it's not the perfect place to say goodbye and maybe Uhuru Peak would have been better, but he'd have liked it, I think. He'd have liked to leave a small imprint in the place where he took my hand and said I was the person he wanted to end up with.

I'm not entirely sure about the legality of spreading these ashes here, but if I'm going to return to being someone who takes risks, I guess this is a good place to start.

I clutch the cup to my heart and I hold it there, tight.

"I'm so sorry," I whisper. "I'm so sorry I fucked it up. I wish you'd gotten to live every last day between then and now, and I know you'd have made the most of them. I can't take it back, but I can't keep being broken by it either. I love you, Rob. I hope you knew that. I hope you still know it. I love you, but I really want to live again."

I'm crying as I empty the cup over the lake's melting ice.

When my eyes open, the ashes are mostly gone, and that makes me cry harder, but Rob's the last person who'd want me standing here, wondering if I'd made a mistake. Just like Miller, he'd want me to go ahead and live a big life for us both.

I plan to try.

When the last of the ashes is gone, I pull out my phone to embark on the next step of that big life I really want.

"Hey, Mare?" I ask when she picks up. "Can I come over?"

## 28

## KIT

Maren's condo on 57th Street is a thing of beauty. It's been featured in magazines. A very famous Oscar nominee once made a ridiculous offer to buy it on the spot. Sure, she hired decorators, but the riotous vision was hers. The bold palm wallpaper on one wall, paired with hot pink velvet chairs. Another wall painted glossy charcoal gray, with pale gray hardwood. Of course, the floor is covered in dog toys and what appears to be excrement, which detracts a little from the chic vibe.

"Sorry," Maren says, picking up dog poop off the floor, walking toward the kitchen. "Echo was a bad little girl today."

I take a seat on the couch while she washes her hands, not quite ready to say the things I need to. "What have you been up to today?" I ask, stalling, when she returns.

She gives me a confused smile, as if she's not sure of the answer. "Harvey wants to buy a beach place," she says, kneeling on the floor to start collecting dog toys. "I was thinking about how I'd decorate it."

I arch a brow, glancing around me. I'm not going to discuss the divorce here. I've seen too many movies where someone learns something they shouldn't from a hidden camera. "So things are good?"

Her smile fades. "I don't know. I wouldn't say they're good, but I guess they could be worse."

I really wish she'd provided a happier answer, but I'm not sure, ultimately, that it would make the discussion we're about to have any easier.

"I lied to you," I blurt out. "When I went away? I wasn't in Mexico with Mallory. I was in Turks and Caicos. With Miller."

Maren carefully places the dog toys she's collected on the table beside her. Her eyes are wide and confused. "Miller? Miller West?"

We don't know any other guys named Miller. It's just a reflection of her disbelief. It's a reflection of the fact that she can't imagine I, of all people, would stab her in the back like this. My stomach knots so tight that it hurts.

I nod. "He knew I was going to end things with Blake, and then Dad told him about the proposal and he flew back to...to sort of rescue me from it. He knew if I got in there with all those people watching, I'd just cave, and I'd keep right on caving."

Maren sits up straighter, sucking in her cheeks. "He flew *back* to rescue you? From where?"

I sigh. In retrospect, it's so crazy that I didn't see it. A man doesn't rush onto the first plane from Tanzania for someone he just sees as a friend. "Tanzania. He'd stayed for a safari."

She grips the edge of the coffee table, her eyes already tear-filled before she closes them. "Wow."

"We weren't together," I tell her. "We weren't together there, and that wasn't meant to change when he came here, but then..."

"It did," she says flatly, climbing to her feet. "You and him. I guess that means you're together? Is that why you're here?"

She's angry and hurt and I don't blame her. I let her sit across from me for weeks talking about Miller, knowing how wrong she was. Knowing I'd taken what she thought was hers. I lied by omission. I also lied to her face.

"Jesus, Kit," she says quietly, walking out of the room.

I sit, with no idea what I should do next. Do I leave and let her process it? Do I follow her wherever she went and beg her to forgive me? Because it was so shitty. I'm sort of the reason she lost him a decade ago and now, not only am I trying to claim him, but I also made her look like a fool.

Am I really going to do this if it divides me and Maren forever? I don't even know what Miller *wants*. But...yes, I am. Because I'm tired of being miserable. But it's really going to hurt if I lose my sister in the process.

Soft steps come down the hall. Her jaw is set, her face is pale, and she's cuddling Echo as if her life depends on it.

"You should have told me," Maren says. "It's absolute bullshit that you've been with him this whole time and let me sit there like an asshole saying he was my soulmate."

I shake my head. "I ended it. I ended it the second you said you were leaving Harvey and started talking about Miller as if you were interested. But I'm here because I'm miserable without him." My voice breaks. "I love him, Mare. I am so head over heels in love with him that I'm sick with it. And I know how you must have felt when you broke up because...that's where I am now. It's as if nothing else matters anymore."

I swallow, trying to pull myself together—those words were harder to admit than I'd expected. Because they're true and they're going to remain a little true forever. I might recover, mostly, but there's always going to be a piece of me missing without him. "He makes me happy," I finally continue, "in a way no one since Rob has. But I don't want to lose you in the process."

She places her fingertips against her closed eyelids, as if divining the future or easing away a headache. "You can't lose me, idiot. I'm your sister."

My throat aches, and I bury my head in my hands as I start to cry. I had no idea until this moment how scared I was to tell her, how scared I was that it would ruin everything. And I should have known better. Because when has Maren ever held anything against me? She's put me before herself again and again, and she's doing it even now.

A second later the couch sinks as she takes a seat beside me. "Kit, what I felt versus what you're feeling is apples and oranges," she says, clasping her hands together tight. "I was infatuated with him, sure, at least half because he was the first guy I'd dated who wanted me less than I wanted him. But I never felt like nothing else mattered. Loads of things still mattered to me when Miller and I broke up, and I was dating someone else five days later. Miller was like...my crush on Henry Cavill. I can picture Henry Cavill being the perfect husband because I'm not married to him. And because I don't really know him. Miller was around all the time that summer, but I still didn't know who he was. Even back then, I remember wondering why the fuck he seemed happier talking to my kid sister than me."

This makes me cry harder. In part because it does make me feel as if I took something away from her, in part because she's so wonderful and yet I'm here planning to screw her over regardless.

She wraps an arm around me. "I can't believe you just stole my boyfriend and I'm the one comforting *you*. Being the oldest absolutely sucks."

I laugh and cry at the same time. She's smiling but there are tears running down her face too. It's not going to be easy on her, this transition, and I wish I wasn't adding to her pain, because I know she's not happy with Harvey, and I don't think she's going to stay with him, but I really do need to take this one thing for myself.

"I'm so sorry, Mare. I'm so, so sorry."

"Little Kitty Cat," she coos. "You've had a really shitty couple of years. If you've found someone who makes you happy, I'm not going to ask you to give it up. Though it's going to be really weird if it lasts. I mean, think about it. At Thanksgiving dinner, Mom will be the only female in the room who hasn't slept with him."

I hiccup a laugh. "She went through that wild period after husband number four. I wouldn't rule it out."

She releases me at last and curls up on the other end of the couch. "What does Miller have to say about it? I assume you wouldn't be here telling me this if he didn't feel the same way."

"I haven't spoken to him about it since I ended things," I whisper, as my pulse speeds up. "It's been two weeks and I'm hoping his feelings haven't changed, but I wanted to talk to you first. And spread the ashes."

Her eyes widen and she sits up straight. "You did it? The ashes?"

I nod. "It was time."

"Wow," she whispers. "I thought you'd never get to that point. What made you decide?"

"I love Miller. I'm ready to move on."

She leans over and presses a kiss to the top of my head. "Then you must mean it. And as much as I'd like to make you stay and help me clean, I think I probably need a good cry, and it sounds like you need to go have a chat with Miller."

"I don't want you to cry."

She smiles. "You clearly have no idea how miserable it is being married to Harvey. I cry everyday anyhow."

I glance toward the mantel, which used to hold several pictures of her wedding day and now only features photos of her dogs. "We should work on that."

"Later," she says. "Right now, you've got someone to see. But Kit?"

I wait for her to tell me something meaningful...*don't hurt him*, perhaps, or *be sure this is what you want*.

But no, this is Maren.

"Borrow my lipstick. Umbrellas in Paris. It's on my vanity. It'll look amazing with those shoes."

I throw my arms around her. "That's my lipstick, you bitch."

She laughs. "You took my ex. Let's call it even."

# 29

## MILLER

I left the Hamptons a decade ago because I had to.

Maren and I had been...unhappy. On edge. Faking it. I had no idea how to explain that I couldn't see a future with her, but I also didn't want it to end.

I didn't understand it myself.

We were there for her birthday, and the only bright spot of the entire week was Kit.

She looked so much like Maren, but increasingly, I found no similarity between them. Maren was sweet, but Kit was challenging. Maren's eyes smiled and Kit's flashed. Maren was pleasant, while Kit had a sauciness to her, a thing that said, '*I dare you to try.*'

She sassed me at every turn. She made fun of my swim trunks, called me a freeloader, asked me if I planned to devote myself entirely to defending rich douchebags when I finished law school or if I might consider defending other types of rich people too. In turn, I made fun of her taste in music, her bad temper, her sweet tooth, her ambition.

I wanted to take care of her—not the way an adult wants to care for a child, but the way I'd want to step up for anyone I saw being taken advantage of. Because Ulrika had, at some point, decided she and Maren were too fragile to fight their own battles and that she'd needed a sword, so Kit had fashioned herself into one.

*Go tell those photographers to get off the property,* Ulrika would command, and Kit, all curves in her tiny black bikini, would go out to tell them off.

*Go tell the hostess we want our table. Tell that man to stop taking pictures of me.*

I fucking hated it a little more every day, and that final morning in the Hamptons, when Maren let her dumb friends hit on Kit as if she wasn't five years younger, it all came to a head. It was the only fight Maren and I ever had—she insisted Kit could defend herself just fine, and I insisted that she shouldn't have to.

But I still didn't put it together until that moment in the kitchen.

Kit had left the beach, and I knew why—because I'd been a dick to her. Because I'd wanted her gone, though not for the reasons she thought.

I went back to the house, presumably to refill the cooler, but mostly to check on her. She was sitting on the kitchen counter, still in that tiny black bikini, with one of her cherry popsicles.

I wanted to tease her. I wanted her to fight me a little, to let me know she was okay. "Is that why you left the beach? So you could sit up here and eat popsicles in peace? Maybe I'll have one too."

But she didn't fight back. She licked down the side of the popsicle and I turned toward the fridge, wincing.

"You guys didn't want me there," she said. Blunt, but that was Kit. Either she was fighting with you, or she was brutally admitting things other people would not.

I hated it. I hated that we hadn't wanted her. I hated that she knew.

"That's not true," I said, turning toward her.

Her mouth was around the popsicle. As she pulled it out of her mouth, it made this noise that seemed to suck all the air from the room. I couldn't stop staring at her cherry-stained lips, at her pretty pink tongue.

"Yes, it is. You should realize by now it takes more than that to hurt my feelings."

Her mouth on that popsicle, her tongue sliding over it...I was frozen, fighting a realization that was arriving far later than it should have. "That wasn't about you," I'd replied, trying to think of *anything* else. "It was about that kid she knows from Columbia who kept hitting on you."

Kit's tongue coasted over the popsicle. A trickle of juice ran down her chin, and I thought my knees were going to buckle. "Why would it matter?" she asked. She caught the dripping juice with her finger and sucked it between her lips. And then it was the popsicle again.

That motherfucking popsicle.

"Because he's five years older than you."

"But why does it *matter*, Miller?" she asked.

And that was when it finally hit me. That I'd spent the whole goddamn summer with Maren because I wanted her seventeen-year-old sister. Desperately. That it mattered because I was fucking sick with jealousy and couldn't admit it to myself. That the reason I hadn't been able to call the time of death on the thing with Maren, a thing I knew couldn't make me happy, wasn't because we had something.

It was because she was the only way I could stay near Kit.

And no matter who I've been with since then, she was still what I wanted.

The past two weeks have been hell, the worst of my fucking life. The one thing keeping me going is a single text from Kit's dad, saying, "*She'll come around. She's as miserable as you are.*"

But that was two weeks ago, and in the meantime, there's

been a blizzard, followed by a balmy spring day, and it's as if the seasons are changing and the whole world is moving forward, while I'm going to remain stuck in the same goddamn place I was a decade ago.

Dying for a girl I couldn't have. One I *still* can't have.

I leave my office at dusk. Spring is in the air, and New York has emptied itself into the streets to celebrate. I want to be out here with her, walking hand in hand. I want to be planning our night, our weekend, our summer, our entire fucking lives.

But she's still worried about her sister and mourning someone she lost years ago. I can't demand she stop. It'll take time, if she comes around at all.

I love her enough to wait. I love her enough to sit here like a jackass, hoping she comes around and to accept that a part of her still belongs to someone else.

But it really sucks to love her that much, that wholeheartedly, when she can't love me back the same way.

My sister calls. She's been my sounding board about all things Kit- and Maren-related for a very long time.

"Hey," I say.

"You're moping," she replies. "Walking and moping. I can hear it in your voice."

"I realize it's counterintuitive but calling me on my bad mood doesn't actually do a lot to *improve* my bad mood."

"Come over," she says. "I'll make you dinner."

"No offense, Ro, but that's unlikely to improve my mood either."

She laughs. "Jesus, you're an asshole when you're moping. I'd forgotten. I'll order in."

"I think I just need to be on my own tonight," I tell her, "but I appreciate it."

We end the call and not two seconds later, the phone buzzes. Which I assume means Rowan has told my mom or

Leila that I'm upset, and they'll hound me for the rest of the fucking night.

Sighing heavily, I retrieve the phone again. I swear to God, I'd just turn it off if I wasn't still hoping to hear from—

Kit. It's *Kit* who's texted.

> KIT
>
> Hey, are you around? Can we talk?

It doesn't sound like she's saying she's had a change of heart. It sounds like the text you send before you explain how final your decision is.

I want to ignore it, just to prolong the inevitable, but because I love Kit Fischer, because I want to be the one person who never leaves her uncertain, or scared, or gnawed with dread, I text her back.

> I'm nearly home. Do you want me to call?
>
> KIT
>
> I'll come over if that's okay.

I start to make a joke about dumping people by text, but it's all too raw. I can't bring myself to do it.

> Of course.

I'm already at my building. I get upstairs, take a quick shower, and change into sweats. I consider allowing her to see all the signs of my devastation: the pizza boxes I haven't recycled, the bottle of whiskey I emptied myself, the clothes I abandoned on the floor because I no longer fucking care about anything. But I'm not going to make her feel guilty. She gets enough of that from everyone else.

I've just shoved the last of the clothes in the closet when the doorman calls to ask if she can come up. I tell him it's fine, and two minutes later she knocks on the door. I spent my entire shower trying to read something into her texts, and as I turn the deadbolt, I'm trying to read into her knock. Was it reluctant? Was it nervous? Is she just here to retrieve something she left behind? Was it the knock of a woman about to deliver the final blow? She basically already did that, so doing it once more seems unnecessary.

I open the door and she stands there in all her glory: beige wrap dress under a matching coat. Bright red heels, bright red lips. All that glorious hair hanging around her shoulders. A small, nervous smile.

The nervous smile makes my heart sink. It's the smile of a woman delivering bad news.

I step aside, and she walks past me. Two weeks ago, she'd have buried her face in my chest the second she saw me, but not anymore. She walks into the kitchen, then turns, as if bracing herself, I can't keep waiting for the final blow.

I run a hand through my hair. "Kit, just—"

"I talked to my dad," she says at the same time.

"You go first," we say simultaneously.

Her eyes fill and there's a buzzing sound in my brain as I wait.

"My dad told me that the reason you left the Hamptons was because of me," she whispers.

My laugh is equal parts surprise and misery. Is this why she's here? To dig up shit from a decade ago? "I assumed you knew."

She shakes her head. "How could I possibly have known?"

It takes all my restraint not to pull her against me. "How *couldn't* you have known? I was two seconds from pouncing when I left you in the kitchen that day. It was the most sexually charged moment of my life until our *second* moment in the kitchen."

She blinks back tears. "You left because you were protecting me."

I hitch a shoulder. "What was I supposed to do? You were seventeen. A five-year age difference at that point in our lives... it was way too much. You were still in high school, for God's sake."

She brushes at her eyes. "I'm not quibbling with you about it. But I just never realized what a well-established pattern it is."

"What pattern?"

"You giving things up on my behalf," she whispers, leaning against the counter behind her. "You having my back when no one else does."

I can't stand being apart from her. I can't. Even if she's about to dump me again. I close the distance, letting my hand rest on her hip, and pressing my mouth to the top of her head. "I know you can't hurt Maren. I know you're still getting over Rob. But no matter how long that goes on and no matter who else comes into your life...I will always have your back."

"I spread the ashes."

I step back, stunned. "*What?*"

"In Central Park. Rob and I had a date there once. And it wasn't about me still being in love with Rob. It was just about me clinging to a time when I was happy. I don't need to cling. You make me happy. You make me happier than anyone ever has."

My hand tightens around her hip. "But Maren—"

"I told her," she says. "And it wasn't perfect, but it was okay."

I stare. I was so convinced she was coming here to deliver one final death blow...and I'm still waiting for her to deliver it.

"But?" I ask. "I still hear a *but* coming."

She exhales heavily. "But I need to know about the ponytail holder. I mean...I know you were seeing someone in Germany before and that's fine, but...is it over? I heard it wasn't over."

I blink. "*What?* You mean Tatiana? That ended over the holidays, and it wasn't a big deal even then."

"But you flew to Germany, and her hair tie was sitting right there—"

That was the hesitation I sensed, the uncertainty. She wasn't unsure about what *she* wanted. She was unsure about what *I* wanted.

"Wait," I demand. I go to my nightstand and withdraw a wooden box I bought in Tanzania, and then return to the kitchen to hand it to her. "I flew to Germany because I had a meeting there. I didn't even see her. And the hair tie?" I place the box in her hand. "It was yours."

"Mine? But I'd never been here before."

"Open it, Kit," I tell her softly, so she does.

Inside, she sees the hair tie—which I slipped off her head the day I was washing her hair and wore around my wrist for the rest of the trip. Alongside it, there's the fortune she gave me at the Chinese restaurant, and the shell necklace she made me at Starfish Cay, and her boarding pass from the flight home.

All these meaningless little things I held onto solely because I was trying to keep a tiny piece of her if I couldn't have them all.

Her eyes fill with tears. "I was worried you'd already moved on."

My palms cradle her face. "I've been in love with you for a decade. You really think I wouldn't wait two more weeks?"

I kiss her. Her soft lips open, and her tongue tastes like mint. I reach inside her coat to grab her hips tight, but she resists. "Miller...just so you have all the information up front, I'm pretty sure I want to go back to med school. I don't know where I'll be the next few years and—"

I lift her up and set her on the counter, my favorite place for her.

"I just want to grow old with you, Kit Fischer," I tell her. "And I'm going to follow you for as long as you let me."

She bites her lower lip. "You're moving awfully fast for a guy whose fear of commitment is legendary."

"I was never scared of committing. I just didn't want to commit to anyone but you," I reply. "Now I simply need to get our families and the press together for a big, public proposal."

She grins. "We only started officially dating thirty seconds ago."

I tug her skirt up enough that I can push her legs apart and step between them.

"Have I ever told you my grandfather built a library to get me into school? When the Wests do things, we don't go halfway."

She laughs and presses her lips to mine. "Thank you for finally admitting that."

# 30

## KIT

JUNE

Everest Base Camp sits at 17,600 feet...only four hundred feet below the highest point we reached in Africa.

It's where I've left Miller, after eight long days of climbing and acclimating to get there, and the real work—the *dangerous* work—lies entirely ahead of him.

I left to pursue a challenge of my own, and I'm sick to my stomach about his and mine both.

My program is letting me come back ...*if* I can pass the finals I took at the end of my second year. I tried hard to convince them to let me wait until Miller was done in Nepal, but beggars can't be choosers...if I want to prove I'm ready for year three, which will primarily be rotations, I've got to prove I still know what I did when I left. And I have to do it on their schedule, which means the timing couldn't be worse—the same tests I was taking when Rob died at high altitude are the ones I'll be taking while Miller endures far greater challenges.

"You look terrible," Maren says when I walk into the trendy little restaurant she's chosen in Battery Park.

I fan my face with a menu as I slide into the booth—it's a

million degrees today. "You try camping for eight days followed by nineteen-hour days of study."

I've been working like a dog, and I just want it behind me so I can get back to Miller.

"That's no excuse for that hair," she says. "And those nails. Lord."

"Okay, *Ulrika*," I say.

She laughs. "Maybe I do sound a little like Mom, but don't you want to look fucking fantastic when Miller sees you at base camp next weekend?"

Reluctantly, I smile. "Simply being the only person there who hasn't been camping for weeks on end will probably be fantastic enough."

"Nonetheless, Mom got you an appointment with Geoffrey after we're done here, and Elsa will be at your apartment on Friday night after you're home to give you a spray tan and do your nails."

They can't begin to imagine what rough shape everyone at base camp is in now, nor how ridiculous I'll look with a fresh spray tan and French tips. But I love Maren too much to complain. She's the only person alive who could have taken the cards I've dealt her and handled them with such grace.

Yes, there were a few awkward dinners at first, but it didn't take long for the weirdness of me dating Maren's ex to dissipate. There's nothing wistful in her face when she looks at Miller and half the time, she treats him like an annoying kid brother. There's *something* she isn't telling me, but I suspect it has nothing to do with Miller. She'll share it when she's ready, I suppose.

"Okay," I reply. "I guess I don't mind having a spray tan and fresh highlights before I sleep in a tent for seven more days."

We place our order and I reach for the sweating bottle of Perrier in front of me.

"How's it going?" Maren asks. "Have you talked to him?"

My hand tightens around the bottle. "Yesterday. Now he's climbing up to camp three to acclimate."

"Is any of that dangerous?"

I exhale heavily. "All of it is dangerous." There's the altitude, avalanches, blizzards. And they've got to go over the icefall—the divide between two glaciers, which Miller will cross using a *ladder*—anytime they ascend from or descend *to* base camp.

"Then you definitely need to reward him by looking like a million bucks when you arrive," says Maren. "I'll even loan you my red lipstick."

I laugh. "You're just baiting me at this point."

I FLY to Charlottesville with freshly cut and highlighted hair, which probably doesn't convince anyone that I'm going to make a very committed medical student, but does look good. The exams are surprisingly easy. Easier, even, than they were when I was in school. I've had months to study, first of all, but I think I also spent so many days replaying memories of what I was doing when I should have been saving Rob that half the information imprinted itself on my brain. Reviewing for the exam was a lot like encountering a friend you went to war with—it was painful, but I hadn't forgotten much.

When it's behind me, I board one flight after another until I arrive in Kathmandu, where I shower in the club lounge and then fly to Lukla. From there, I catch a helicopter to the base rather than climbing for eight days. The cost is insane, but my father was thrilled to cover it. He now refers to Miller as *the child I never had*—when I pointed out how insulting this is, he doubled down by explaining that Miller is kind like Maren and interesting like me, which didn't improve matters as it implied Maren and I were still found lacking.

As we take off, my heart speeds up. It's not nerves...I'm

simply desperate to lay eyes on him and press my face to what is, at this point, an undoubtedly filthy parka. Unfortunately, I won't see him right away as he's climbing down from Camp Two today, but at least once he's slept for a solid twelve hours, we'll have a very happy reunion.

We take off over the lower elevations, which are still several thousand feet above sea level. From the air, the ground looks like massive piles of dirt, with tiny blue marbles at their base. They are actually mountains, and the puddles are lakes, but it's all relative here. They're so much smaller than the summit and the peaks surrounding it that it's hard to believe they're anything at all.

Soon, we are approaching Everest. The mountains rise around us on three sides, snow-glazed and intimidatingly huge, and we bank right toward a long sweep of snow-covered slope. In the distance, there are tiny, colorful dots in yellow and blue and red: the tents of base camp.

I'm so excited that I'm sick with it.

Sherpas are waiting on the ground to direct the helicopter and help me carry my stuff in. But one of the men standing down there is a foot taller than the rest, wearing a familiar yellow jacket and the widest smile.

Miller. I have no idea how he could possibly be here already, but he is, and we've barely touched down before I'm jumping out the door and running to him.

He scoops me up, burying his face in my hair. "God, I'm so glad to see you."

I want to ask how he's here, why he's so clean-shaven, why he isn't resting in his tent if he got down the mountain early. As always, with Miller, there are too many goddamned things to say.

"Your face," is all I get out, tears running down my cheeks as I press a palm to his jaw.

His grin is bashful, dimpled. "I didn't want to rub you raw

the second you landed."

I go on my toes and kiss him. "My face would have survived."

"It wasn't just your *face* I was worried about, Kitten," he growls against my ear.

Ohhhhh. "There will be none of that," I tell him. "You need to rest."

"Don't you think I deserve a small reward for getting through stage two?"

I smile. It seems like more of a reward for *me*, but I'm not about to refuse twice.

We make the trek to base camp together while he tells me how he got here (by waking up at the crack of dawn, climbing down from camp two as fast as possible, dumping his backpack, and running to the helicopter landing pad.) When I ask how it's been, he says, "No one's died yet," which I don't find especially funny. I tell him how my exams went and he says he knew I'd ace them, which is why he's had a realtor sending him listings near campus for the past month.

At camp, the supplies and food I brought for Miller and his team are eagerly torn into, and when the team jokingly suggests we all sit down for a meal, Miller tells them to fuck off and takes me to our tent.

He's got a solar heater going to keep us toasty. "Undress, Kitten," he demands, leaning back. "It's been too long. I want to see all of you."

My layers are removed. He's down to boxer briefs, and the outline of him—hard and ready—makes my mouth water. I reach for his waistband, and he shakes his head. "Not yet," he says, his half smile predatory in the tent's dim light. "Spread your legs for me."

I recline on the sleeping bag, and he pushes my thighs as wide as they'll go before he takes one long lick from my entrance to my clit. His tongue circles and moves inside me, and I'm already so close that it would take absolutely nothing to push me over the edge.

"Use your fingers," I demand, arching upward.

His laughter huffs out over my sensitive flesh, and he sucks my clit against his tongue. "Yes, I know what you want," he says. "That's why I'm not giving it to you."

He continues to play, to lick and suck and bite, keeping me right near the edge but not letting me go over it. I manage to run my foot over the outside of his boxers, and he hisses. "God," he says. "Don't. I'm so hard right now you'll make me come in my pants."

I sort of like the idea of that, but he grasps my foot before it can approach him again.

"Kit," he growls, and then he returns to torturing me, except it's all too much, suddenly, the idea of him that desperate to come, the idea of how hard he'll fuck me once I finally do.

"Please," I beg, thrashing, and with a groan, he shoves his boxers to mid-thigh and slams inside me.

"Oh God," I whimper, clenching, and when he pulls out, biting his lip not to finish too fast, and pushes back in, I can't hold out a minute longer. My head arches backward as I come and he gasps as I tighten around him, cursing as he joins me.

"That was embarrassing," he laughs. "I was only inside you for five seconds."

"At least now I know you missed me," I say as he rolls to the side and pulls me onto his chest.

"You already knew I missed you," he whispers.

"Let's not be apart that long again, okay?" I ask.

He pushes my hair back from my face. There's something secretive in his smile. "I'm not planning to," he replies.

～

THREE DAYS LATER, he leaves me at base camp at dawn to begin his ascent; he'll reach camp two today, remain there to acclimate and rest, and then progress to camp three and camp four over the following days. At midnight, after reaching camp four, he'll leave to attempt the summit.

I get up to see him off, with my jaw locked not to burst into tears.

Which does not work.

"Don't cry, Kit," he whispers, pulling me close. "I'm coming back. You know I'm not letting you grow old with anyone else. It would make your father so sad."

I laugh and cry at the same time. "Don't do anything stupid," I whisper. "Check your oxygen tanks. Wear a hat. I'm sorry. I'm treating you like a child. But still...don't do anything stupid."

He presses a kiss to the top of my head. "You're not treating me like a child. You're treating me like someone you don't want to live without. Believe me, I've been in your shoes."

I remain outside, watching him and the rest of the guys until they are tiny spots of color against the snow-covered slope in the distance, and then there's nothing left to do but wait.

## 31

### MILLER

Summiting Everest makes Uhuru Peak look like a walk in the park. This comes as no surprise, since we essentially *began* this journey at the equivalent of Kilimanjaro's highest point. But I had no idea how the lack of oxygen would fuck with me and how passing frozen corpses would *really* fuck with me.

I'm worried for myself, yes. I want to live a long life with Kit. I want children and grandchildren. I want to spend months at a time in Starfish Cay, snorkeling, and I want her beside me, wearing nothing but my ring on her finger.

But mostly, I'm worried for Kit. When I picture her waiting at base camp and getting the call that I didn't make it, I wish I hadn't attempted this at all.

For her sake and my own, I won't risk my life like this again.

I'll still do my six-month excursions going forward, but they won't be things that terrify her. Hopefully, they'll be things she'll do with me.

The sun rises during our final push but the wind is blowing so hard that the snow is blinding. I put on goggles and dream of Kit. If all goes as I hope, we'll be leaving for

Starfish Cay just after we land in New York, though she's unaware of this—Maren has already packed her bags. It'll be our last vacation for a while. Work on the new app is already underway and she'll be back in school...so I'm hoping to make it a good one.

The image of Kit grinning at me in waist-deep water becomes so real that I actually think she's here. I turn on the regulator to take in some oxygen, and that becomes my rule for the next two hours: when I start thinking I see Kit standing in the water or sitting on a kitchen counter, I know I need air.

We reach the summit around seven in the morning. The sky is a cloudless blue and the white-capped peaks—illuminated by the bright morning sun—stretch so far in every direction that it would be easy to believe they go on forever if you didn't know better. It's magical, an unforgettable moment, but I'd give it all up to be looking at her face instead.

We take some pictures and then Magnus, the expedition's leader, grins at me. "We doing this?" he asks.

I nod as I pull out my phone and the SatSleeve that will allow it to connect. "Wish me luck."

The guys line up. We take the picture, and I hit *send* just before I call her. It'll take a few minutes for the photo to arrive.

*I hope this works.*

She answers immediately, breathless. I'm guessing she didn't sleep all night, which makes two of us. "Did you make it?" she asks, her voice tight with panic.

"I'm here right now."

"Thank God." She exhales in relief. "You're okay? You've got enough oxygen?"

"I'm great," I reply. "But I had a question. Can you check to see if the text I sent arrived?"

"You *texted* me?" she asks. "Hang on, wait, oh, yeah, something's here. It's—"

She sucks in a breath. Behind me, the guys are still holding the sign asking her to marry me, one I've had rolled up in my backpack now for forty days straight.

They're holding it in the photo.

I'm holding a ring box.

"Oh my God," she whispers, all the breath leaving with the words.

"Will you marry me, Kit?"

She sniffles and laughs. "I guess I know why Mare was so insistent on getting me a manicure. Did you get my dad's permission?"

"I asked him months ago. And he said I was welcome to try but that you'd probably make me work for it. Was this good enough?"

"It was good enough," she says, crying. "Yes. I'll marry you. Now get down here so you can ask me in person."

TWO DAYS LATER, we finish the descent. She's waiting outside the tent, stamping her feet to stay warm. She runs when she sees me, and I drop my pack on the ground as I pull her close.

"I like that greeting, Mrs. West."

She wraps her legs around me and presses her mouth to mine. "I'm not taking your name. I'm proud to be a Fischer."

"Hyphenated then. Fischer-West?"

"We'll see," she says, and she kisses me again.

I start moving toward the tent. "What about when we have kids? You're not going to insist they take *your* name, right?"

"We've been engaged for two days. Don't you think you're getting a little ahead of yourself?"

"I've been ahead of myself since you were seventeen. You can't expect me to break the habit now that you're mine."

She smiles, placing her hands on my jaw. "Maybe I'll hyphenate if your grandfather builds me a library."

For over a decade now, she's been giving me shit about that. I suspect she'll be doing it for the rest of my life.

As long as she lets me grow old with her, she can say any damn thing she wants.

## THE END

Grab the bonus episode (a steamy peek at Miller and Kit's engagement party, along with a moment on that kitchen counter in the Hamptons) at www.elizabethoroark.com (the bonus tab). And for a hint of Charlie and Maren's story, turn the page.

# MY FAVORITE LOST CAUSE
## A SNEAK PEEK

**Charlie**

Female laughter wakes me. Never a good sign.

I peel my eyes open, but my bedroom offers few clues. It's a disaster, sure, but it's been a disaster for a while. I vaguely remember the girl in my lap at the bar, and a bottle of wine opening after we met a friend of hers in the lobby, but nothing afterward. It troubles me, this gap. Mostly because threesomes don't just fall in your lap. They're the sort of memories that will keep you warm in your old age, but you've got to actually remember them.

There's more laughter. Dammit. A hundred bucks says that Maren's making them a nutritious breakfast while she administers STD tests. And now these two nameless girls are happily settled into my apartment rather than tucked into a cab the way they should be.

I throw on sweats and trudge down to the kitchen, where they're all busy drinking from large mugs and eating...muffins. Where the fuck did they get muffins? *Or* the oversized mugs?

"Good morning," I say with a forced smile.

"I didn't know you wore glasses, Charlie!" one of them cries gleefully.

*Unsurprising, since we met ten hours ago and I still don't know your name.*

"I can't believe Maren Fischer is your stepsister!" squeals the other.

They're loud. And cheerful. Was I the only one who was drunk last night? Should I worry that I was taken advantage of?

"Yes, lucky me," I say, shooting daggers at Maren, who beams back at me with her clear blue eyes and pink-flushed cheeks. A living blonde Barbie doll as always, with a kind word for everyone she meets.

Except...I've got Maren's smiles memorized, and this is a new one. It's not the brave, false one she wears when her husband ridicules her or the patient one she wears whenever Ulrika, her insane mother and my tiresome stepmother, says something ridiculous. Nor is it the unfettered, happy one I spy sometimes when I've made her laugh.

This one has an edge. And might be vengeful. Did I intentionally make a lot of noise last night? It seems...possible. I'm not the best version of myself when blackout drunk.

One of the girls starts asking Maren why she's no longer modeling, and I can see that this hang-out is never going to end. "I'm sorry to cut this short, ladies, but I've got a—" I scan my brain for a lie Maren won't be able to refute. "Meeting."

"A meeting?" Maren asks. "Who would you need to meet with on a Sunday?"

Apparently she *can* refute it.

"Tokyo."

Her raised brow and that glimmer of a smirk on her mouth scare me, because behind Maren's Mother Teresa act lies an evil streak. I'd enjoy watching it unleashed. Just not at me. And not right now. She glances at her watch.

"It's eleven at night there."

*Dammit.* "Yes, they are finishing up dinner then calling me on Zoom."

The girls make pouting faces, but gather their things and say goodbye. They seem sadder about leaving Maren, but she's been far nicer to them than I've been, which is fairly typical.

Maren wants everyone to love her, but never seems to grasp that some people's love isn't worth earning. Like that of these girls she'll never see again. Or my own.

I wait until the door shuts behind them and turn. "What the fuck, Maren," I groan.

"You deserved it, after what I had to listen to last night." She throws her head back. "Oh, God, Charlie, yes, yes, yes!"

"You're good at faking an orgasm," I reply, turning toward the coffee maker before she realizes exactly how good she was at it. "Not surprising. I bet Harvey gives you a lot of practice."

"Would it kill you to have had breakfast with them?" she asks. "Would it kill you to get to know them beyond the moment you blew your load?"

Fuck. My favorite appendage was beginning to settle until she used the expression "blew your load". It was unusual phrasing from Manhattan's sweetheart. Is there porn involving Barbie or a Disney princess getting railed from behind?

Probably. I'll check later.

"Maren, my life is hard enough without your bullshit. And you've broken every single rule I set, so it's time for you to go impose on someone else."

"Charlie, we need to talk—"

"Not really a good time, since you're leaving and I'm about to host a fictitious Zoom meeting at 11 pm in Tokyo."

"I'll go if you tell me what's so hard about your life, and that wasn't an opening for you to talk about your dick. Tell me what's wrong." There's something genuine in her voice, but firm at the same time.

Knowing I'll regret it, knowing she's still not going to fucking leave, I cross the room and grab the letter.

Arriving August 28, 2025.
Available for preorder on Amazon

# ACKNOWLEDGMENTS

Thanks so much, first of all, to the people who made this a better book: my editor, Lauren Clarke; my copyeditor, Christine Estevez; Laura Hidalgo for the designs and my beloved beta readers: Michelle Chen, Katie Friend, Katie Meyer and Jen Owens.

Thanks next to everyone at Valentine PR—Nina, Kim, Kelly, Christine, Sarah, Josette, Meagan and Jill—where would I be without you? I don't want to know, so let's not find out.

Thanks finally to my amazing agent, Kimberly Brower and assistant, Christine Estevez; thanks to all bloggers and members of Elizabeth O'Roark Books/the Parallel Series Spoiler Room for their encouragement; my besties (Deanna, Katie and Sallye) for believing in me when I didn't believe in myself; Laura Pavlov for listening to my five-minute long rants about nonsense; and my children (Patrick, Lily and Jack) for mattering so much more than everything else that I don't lose perspective.

# ALSO BY ELIZABETH O'ROARK

**The Summer Series:**

1. The Summer We Fell (Luke & Juliet)

2. The Summer I Saved You (Caleb & Lucie)

3. The Summer You Found Me (Beck & Kate)

4. The Summer I Destroyed You (Liam & Emmy)

5. The Summer I First Saw You (Harrison & Daisy)

**The Devil Series**

4 funny, angsty, grumpy-sunshine, enemies-to-lovers romances

**The Langstrom Brothers**

Coach-student and best friend's girl romances.

**The Parallel Series**

She's been dreaming about him since she was small. And now, weeks before her wedding, he's appeared in real life.

# ABOUT THE AUTHOR

Elizabeth O'Roark spent many years as a medical writer before publishing her first novel in 2013. She holds two bachelor's degrees from the University of Texas and a master's degree from Notre Dame. She lives in Washington, D.C. with her three children. Join her on Facebook at Elizabeth O'Roark Books for updates, book talk and lots of complaints about her children.